BETRAYAL

BETRAYAL

KAREN FENECH

FIVE STAR

An imprint of Thomson Gale, a part of The Thomson Corporation

THOMSON

GALE

Detroit • New York • San Francisco • New Haven, Conn. • Waterville, Maine • London

THOMSON

GALE

LIBRARY OF CONGRESS CATALOGING-IN-PUBLICATION DATA

Fenech, Karen.
　　Betrayal / by Karen Fenech. — 1st ed.
　　　　p. cm.
　　ISBN 1-59414-523-7 (hardcover : alk. paper)
　　I. Title.
PS3606.E54B47 2006
813'.6—dc22

2006021216

U.S. Hardcover:
ISBN 13: 978-1-59414-523-0
ISBN 10: 1-59414-523-7

First Edition. First Printing: November 2006.

Published in 2006 in conjunction with Tekno Books.

Printed in the United States of America on permanent paper.
10 9 8 7 6 5 4 3 2 1

ACKNOWLEDGMENTS

With each book I have found helping hands when I needed them. My deepest thanks to:

My husband Andrew and our daughter Pamela for your love, faith, and humor in putting up with the day-to-day craziness of living with a writer.

Editor John Helfers, who championed the book, and didn't stop there.

Editor Brittiany Koren, a wonderful editor and a lovely person.

Editor Tiffany Schofield, who accepted the book for publication.

Fellow writers and good friends: Judith Gelberger, Kenneth Puddicombe, and g.b.reist for your comments that are always right-on.

For Andrew, always.

CHAPTER ONE

England, 1122

"Lord Ranulf is through the gate, my lady. Our men won't be able to hold him off much longer."

"Through the gate" meant Ranulf was minutes away from entering the keep. Her small force had put up a valiant fight, holding Ranulf and his knights off for almost two days, but Katherine knew the defeat was inevitable. Her force could not stand against the might of Ranulf's.

And once he was inside . . . Katherine closed her eyes.

"My lady?"

Katherine focused on Sir Guy, commander of her guard. He stood at the foot of her bed, where Katherine lay propped against pillows cuddling the boy she'd delivered three hours earlier. "Any word from de Lauren?" she asked softly.

Sir Guy shook his head slowly.

When Ranulf had first attacked, Katherine had sent a messenger to Nicholas de Lauren, asking for aid. De Lauren's keep was a half day's ride from her own. Her message had been urgent. De Lauren would have arrived here by now . . . if he were coming.

" 'Twas never certain de Lauren would heed your call, Lady Katherine. We can wait no longer."

Nay, she had not been certain Nicholas would come. But she'd hoped. She and Sir Guy had come up with a plan if de Lauren did not render aid. In keeping with it, Sir Guy now stood garbed as a peasant. He was right. They could wait no longer for de Lauren.

Katherine ran her fingertips over the blonde hair so like peach fuzz that covered her son's pink scalp. Tears blurred her vision of him. His very existence as heir to Stanfield would condemn him to death.

Marriage to Ranulf would end this siege. He'd made his terms plain. He wanted Stanfield, her family's holding and its assets, and she was his means to that end. Or she had been. Her son's birth changed that. Marriage to her now would gain Ranulf nothing.

Unless her son were dead. If Ranulf learned of her son's birth, she had no doubt she would lose two children this day. Her son's twin sister, as perfect as an angel, lay at peace in the cradle by Katherine's bed. The girl-child had been stillborn. God had given and God had taken away . . .

And now, God forgive her, the only way to save her son from Ranulf was to use the boy's dead sister.

"Sir Guy," Katherine said. "How go the preparations for our departure?"

"All is ready. Horses await us in the forest beyond the hidden passages."

Sir Guy had been in service to her family since before Katherine's birth. Other than herself only he knew of the escape passages that existed beneath the keep.

Middy, Katherine's old nursemaid, stood dwarfed by Sir Guy. "Me lady," Middy said, "You are not yet healed from the births. How will you ride?"

Katherine did not need to be reminded of the long deliveries. Her slightest movement brought pain. "I will ride because I must," she said.

"Will you not change your course an' ride with us?" Middy asked.

Katherine shook her head. "When Ranulf finds me gone from here he will leave no stone unturned in his search. To ride with you is to risk capture for my son." Katherine glanced at her daughter. "Ranulf will see that the babe I delivered this day is dead. Only we in this room know of a second babe." Softly she added, "And I must make my appeal to de Lauren in person." *She must not fail.*

"How will you send word that the keep is secure?" Sir Guy asked.

"You will know to return when the Stanfield banner flies again."

Katherine hugged her child tight. She kissed him then wiped her tears from his pale skin.

"See him safe, Sir Guy, until I can reclaim him."

"I will protect him with my life."

Katherine nodded. She expected nothing less.

Middy shuffled to the bedside and Katherine placed her child in the old woman's outstretched arms. "Go with God, my son."

Katherine watched the door close behind them. A few minutes more and they would be in the passages. She could only hope that with the battle raging outside the keep their escape would go undetected.

She slid to the edge of her bed. Clutching the bedpost, she stood, and made her way to the hearth. The June air blowing in through her window now was warm, but it had been night when her labor began, and a fire had been lit. Low flames still licked at blackened logs.

Above the hearth, behind the likeness of her father, was the map to the passages. Her father had shown it to William when he'd married Katherine. William had not been concerned with escape routes when he'd asked to see the map, Katherine knew, but with the path that led to the Stanfield jewels that were her bride-price.

The jewels could finance a kingdom. Ranulf must not find them.

She removed the map and tossed it into the fire.

At her clothes chest, she tossed in her wedding band and withdrew the ragged and dirty peasant's garb that Middy had left for her. She withdrew a cloak sewn in the blue and white colors of Stanfield. She dressed quickly then went to her daughter and knelt before the cradle. Her eyes filled with tears. Tonight, she should be sitting vigil with her child in the chapel. Instead, her daughter would be here in this room, alone. And come morning, this tiny innocent would not be laid to rest. Leaving her child was essential to the plan she and Sir Guy had devised, but now that the moment had arrived, how could she do it?

Shouts rang out from below. The clang of swords. Screams, hideous screams. Ranulf was inside. Had enough time passed for Sir Guy and Middy to reach the passages? To think not was the way to madness.

Katherine's hands trembled with the need to take her daughter's body in her arms and flee with it. But she must choose life over death. Her son's life. She leaned forward and kissed her daughter's cold lips, then draped the cloak over her. The Stanfield cloak would mark the babe as hers and satisfy Ranulf's bloodlust for her child.

Night had fallen when she emerged from the passages. Stars lit the sky. She rubbed dirt over her face, hands, and in her blonde hair. Unbound, it fell to her hips. Blowing free in the wind, it would tangle and snarl. Even now, Ranulf's men may be searching for her. Very soon, she would not be recognizable as the lady of Stanfield.

The horse Sir Guy had promised was tied to a tree in the dense growth of the forest beyond the passages. A sorry sight the animal was, Katherine thought as she seized the reins. But dressed as she was, a sturdier beast would attract attention.

Katherine untied the reins and led the horse to a fallen log. She climbed onto it and, with the added height, mounted. Pain shot through her middle. She hung across the horse's bare back, inhaling and exhaling shaky breaths; then, gritting her teeth, she gained her seat and kicked the horse forward.

De Lauren's keep was west. The quickest way there was to travel the roads, but she kept to the woods. She knew the dangers criminals posed to a woman traveling without escort. But she couldn't risk encountering other innocent travelers either, who might be able to tell Ranulf's men that a lone woman had passed this way.

Low-hanging trees filtered the moonlight. But she knew the route well. So often she'd traveled between her land and de Lauren's. So long ago. A lifetime, it seemed.

The air cooled. Owls hooted. In the distance a coyote howled. The horses' sides heaved, but she pushed him on. She stopped at a stream, and sipped from a water skin that Sir Guy had thoughtfully provided, while the horse lowered its head to drink. The poor beast had carried her for hours. Best if she would dismount and relieve him of her weight. She was afraid the animal would not last to see her to her destination. But if she dismounted, Katherine knew she'd be unable to mount again.

She pressed on. Light from a low fire glowed a short distance ahead. Someone had made camp. "Easy, my lad," she whispered to the horse. She drew on the reins to slow the animal to a walk, then led him wide of the light.

The horse emerged from the cover of trees. The first grey streaks of dawn lit the sky and she saw the familiar massive stone fortress. De Lauren's keep. She felt relief to have arrived, though she was not certain of her welcome. She dug her heels into the horse's sides.

Three soldiers rode out to her. De Lauren's men—she recognized the black and gold colors they wore. Night patrollers. Two knights flanked her while the third halted his horse in front of her. She pulled up the reins.

The knight facing her said, "State your business."

"I am—" her voice cracked. She cleared her dry throat. "I am Lady Katherine of Stanfield. I beg an audience with Lord de Lauren."

The young knight grinned. "And I'm King Henry himself." He leaned forward on the saddle horn. "Come on, sweet, try again."

Despite her altered appearance and that she would arrive without escort, she hadn't considered that she would not be taken at her word. She'd given a ring that bore the Stanfield crest to her messenger to present to de Lauren along with her handwritten note. And she had nothing now to prove her identity to these guards. Or did she . . .

Katherine removed the gold chain and cross she wore beneath her ragged clothing. She held the neck chain out to the knight. "Take this to your lord as proof that I am who I say."

De Lauren would recognize the necklace as hers. Proof of her identity, though, was not the main issue, she knew. Her messenger would have left no doubt he'd been dispatched in her name. And yet de Lauren had not come to her aid.

The knight took the neck chain and Katherine clasped her hands tightly. The chain was thread-thin, the cross tiny, yet it was more than a serf would own. Katherine thought that fact prevented the knight from dismissing her claim entirely.

The knight nodded. The soldier to her left seized her reins. They led her slowly to the keep. As they neared, the knight in front called out, "Open the gate."

Though it was barely dawn, armed soldiers strode across the courtyard. De Lauren commanded a large and powerful army, a force, she knew, not to be challenged.

She waited in the courtyard, with two of de Lauren's guards, while the third entered the castle. The sun crested the tower now, blinding her with its light. Bright spots popped in front of her eyes. Her head spun. She clutched the pommel.

"Lady Katherine."

Her blurred vision cleared. The knight came into focus. The one who'd entered the castle now stood at her side, looking up at her. He held out his hand. Her cross dangled from his fingertips. Katherine's stomach clenched. Had de Lauren sent the man away?

"Lord de Lauren will see you now, my lady."

The knot in her stomach eased and Katherine nodded.

The knight handed the cross to her, then gripped her waist and lowered her to her feet.

She clutched his shoulders. Had he not held her, she would fall onto her face. Her legs trembled. "A moment," she said.

When she took a step away from the man, he must have still doubted her ability to walk unaided. He offered his arm.

Inside the castle, the morning meal was being served. The aroma blended with the floral scent of fresh rushes that crunched under her feet. Knights at table laughed and called out coarse jests to serving maids who responded in kind. What were her own people facing this morning? Katherine tasted bile. The merriment here was obscene to her.

She was escorted up stairs and down a short corridor. The knight stopped at a door that she knew opened into the solar. He knocked once, then opened the door for her. De Lauren sat at a table. That, two tapestried chairs, and a bench beneath the window were the only furnishings. Parchment was spread out on the table, before him. He looked at her.

She waited on the threshold, but he did not bid her enter. So be it. She entered uninvited, though not far into the room. It was she who was here begging favors. She curtsied, passably she hoped, since her legs felt less than steady. "Thank you for seeing me, my lord."

De Lauren stood. She stood only as tall as his shoulders and tilted her head back to meet his gaze.

He bowed. "My pleasure, my lady."

His bow had been shallow, his tone mocking. No doubt she looked a sight. Unlike him. Five years had passed since she'd seen him. His body still attested to the rigorous training that saw him through many a fight for his life. He wore his hair shorter now, the black ends just curling over his nape. His face was leaner than she remembered, but no less handsome.

"My lord," she said. "I am here in person to request your intervention with Lord Ranulf on behalf of my people of Stanfield—"

"Your people? Widowed what, a fortnight, my lady, you waste no time in asserting your repossession of Stanfield."

Katherine licked her dry lips. "As I explained in my message to you—"

"I received no message."

That did not bode well for Robert, her messenger. She closed her eyes briefly. She had to concentrate on the fact that de Lauren had not summarily dismissed her plea. Hope fluttered in her stomach. "Two days ago, Lord Ranulf laid siege to Stanfield Keep. My late husband had taken the bulk of our forces to defend an ally to the east. Our army was badly depleted in the battle that took my husband's life. The forces that remained were not sufficient to defeat Lord Ranulf. His troops overpowered mine last evening and seized the holding."

"You say you sent a messenger to me?"

"Upon Ranulf's arrival, I dispatched a messenger, requesting aid from you."

"What of Meredith, your late husband's ally to the north?

Surely he would have rallied to your cause?" He looked into her eyes. "I find it surprising you would come to me. As you know, de Lauren and Stanfield have not been allied in five years."

Since her marriage to William. She'd broken her betrothal to de Lauren to marry William. "My lord, I could not risk approaching Lord Meredith. You may not be aware that Ranulf as well was my husband's ally."

De Lauren grunted. "Ah, yes. One jackal is dead, and the ones that remain battle each other for what was his."

Though she agreed with de Lauren's analogy, Katherine said nothing.

"Perhaps you should have paid Meredith or Ranulf a call garbed as you are at this moment. Your appearance, my lady, would raise doubt that the Stanfield wealth they seek has not been squandered."

She ignored the insult. "My lord, my cause is great—"

"Indeed."

De Lauren's eyes were cold. He might very well applaud her destruction by Ranulf. Gooseflesh rose on her skin.

"If you will not help me," she said, "then please consider the innocents at Stanfield."

He watched her in silence then said, "What will be my reward for retaking your keep from Ranulf?"

He would discuss terms. Relief made her light-headed. "Name your price, and it shall be yours."

De Lauren walked in a slow circle around her, looking her up, then down. "Your husband's demise has again made you a great heiress. Yet, I see no jewels."

Surely he did not think she'd traveled here with valuables? "They remain in safekeeping at Stanfield."

"Payment to be made after I have won your battle?"

She nodded. "Once the keep has been secured, I will obtain your payment."

"You are asking me to trust you to make good on your promise to meet my price?"

"I will gladly pay what I owe you."

De Lauren laughed, but there was no humor in the sound. "I am no longer the fool I was five years ago, to now take you at your word."

Nay, he would no longer trust her. "Tell me your terms then, and I will honor them."

De Lauren bared his teeth in a smile that chilled her. "A gesture of good faith, perhaps?" He brushed his thumb across her cheek. Dirt stained his skin. "I recall great beauty beneath this filth. Will you offer yourself?"

He would make a whore of her? She felt as if something inside her died. In a whisper she gave him the only answer she could. "If that is what it will take."

He leaned toward her. "Five years ago the only jewel I sought from the wealth of Stanfield was you." His jaw clenched briefly. "That time has long passed. While you no longer appeal, I would have Stanfield. That is my price. Marry me this day and I will liberate your people."

She'd given up the dream of marriage to de Lauren five years ago. He'd left no illusion that what he was proposing now was a second chance at that dream. Through her he believed he would acquire Stanfield. A lie.

If she told him about her son . . . Nicholas was not Ranulf. Nicholas would not harm an innocent. No matter what he stood to gain.

But his aid was conditional. He would withhold it if she told him marriage to her would gain him nothing but overseeing lands for a child who was not his . . .

"My patience wears thin, my lady. I will have your decision."

He believed she'd betrayed him when she broke their

betrothal. If she agreed to this marriage, she would betray him again. Softly Katherine said, "I will pay your price."

CHAPTER TWO

"*In nomine Patris, et Filii, et Spiritus Sancti.* Amen."

It was done. She and de Lauren were married. She would be free of Ranulf. As for de Lauren, she would be forever grateful for his intervention, despite how it was obtained, and she would do all she could to make up to him the loss of Stanfield.

The little priest completed the sign of the cross then lowered his arms and bowed to de Lauren. He rose from his knees. Her hand was atop his to receive the priest's blessing, and as de Lauren gained his feet, she teetered, and clutched his fingers. He didn't seem to notice her desperate grab; didn't even glance her way. She made it to her feet and he left her side.

She felt less than steady on her legs, due to fatigue and not pain. The worst discomfort had faded. She'd had no time to rest since her arrival at de Lauren Keep. Once she'd agreed to the marriage, de Lauren sent for the resident priest. A round-faced maidservant—Bessie she'd called herself—had offered a bath. No doubt a bath was in order, but time was wasting. Katherine had asked for a pitcher of water and had cleaned her face and hands right in the solar. Her hair needed the most cleansing. No help for that. She wound twine around it and left it to fall down the middle of her back.

The priest arrived as she'd knotted the twine. In the doorway to the solar, the small man exchanged words with de Lauren, then shook his head. She could guess a wedding without banns being read had agitated the good father. But until there was a wedding, de Lauren would not remove Ranulf from Stanfield. She was prepared to intervene herself—to plead her case, or to offer a sizeable dispensation if that was what it would take to satisfy the church—but de Lauren spoke again. The priest bowed. Katherine's stomach unclenched.

Now the wedding was done. Now they would ride to Stanfield.

Bessie held a tray out to Katherine with sweet meats, bread, water, and ale. "Some refreshment, Lady de Lauren?"

She had not eaten since yesterday, but her stomach burned. She waved away the food, took only a goblet of water. Her head pounded. How long until they rode to Stanfield?

De Lauren stood with his back to her, speaking with Stephen. During the brief wedding ceremony, she'd glimpsed Nicholas' younger brother standing at a side wall. Stephen had once been like a brother to her, too, but their camaraderie had ended when she'd left Nicholas. She'd missed Stephen.

She joined the men.

" . . . the keep is situated."

Stephen fell silent. Their eyes met. There'd been confusion there and concern for her as well as his brother when he'd questioned her following the breakup. Now, she saw only contempt. She looked away from it.

De Lauren turned around.

"My lord," Katherine said, "I would know your plans for retaking Stanfield."

"Would you?"

"I have knowledge that would enable you to come upon Ranulf unawares."

She did not want to reveal the existence of the passages. They were only useful because they were unknown. But Ranulf would spot a frontal attack.

De Lauren crossed his arms. "By all means, share this

knowledge with us."

"There are passages beneath the keep that are unknown to all but myself and commander of my guard. It is through these passages that I escaped and made my way here to you. If you would allow me, I will draw a map of the caverns."

De Lauren pointed to the table.

She went to it. De Lauren followed, and turned a sheet of the parchment over. Katherine huddled over the table and picked up a quill. She took a breath. After a few moments, she straightened. "This area, beyond the road, is forest," she said. "The hidden entrance to the keep is north, through these trees for a quarter mile, to a narrow cave." She pointed to the X she'd drawn. "You must not veer from your northerly direction. The growth is dense, barely penetrable, and conceals the cave. If you veer you will walk past it.

"The cave's entrance is a scarce slit in the stone. One of stout proportions would find himself wedged between the rock. The passage remains tight for a time, but is straight. It declines gradually, widening with the descent. Eventually, you will reach its bottom. When you begin to ascend you will know you are entering the castle."

"And where does this exit?"

"The dungeons. The only way to access them is from a secluded hall at the back of the castle. It is a distance from the living quarters. Stairs from the dungeons lead to and from that hall."

De Lauren nodded to Stephen.

"When do you ride?" Katherine asked.

"Within the hour," de Lauren said.

"My lord, I would ride with you," Katherine said. "When you claim the keep, my people will not know whether you be friend or foe. My presence will reassure them."

De Lauren looked into her eyes. She had to force herself not to step back from the malice she saw there. "You are the soul of compassion this day, as well as a font of knowledge. Aye, you will ride with us, my lady wife. I would be certain that you are not in league with Ranulf and seeking to rid him of his strongest adversary."

A trap? He thought she and Ranulf had set a trap?

Her cheeks heated with anger. "Surely you know Ranulf's reputation. Do you believe I would entrust my people to his brutal care?"

"I have yet to see if Ranulf has held true to his reputation with Stanfield. I have learned firsthand what you are capable of." He leaned toward her, close enough that his breath brushed her cheek. "Heed me well. If you have made a bargain with that devil to betray me, take the opportunity while I am occupied with killing him, and make use of the escape passages."

De Lauren nodded to Stephen and the men left.

Katherine had stopped breathing. She exhaled now. Her hands had gone cold and she rubbed them together to warm them. She had naught to concern her. When he breached Stanfield, de Lauren would see that she had not betrayed him with Ranulf.

She heard the thunder of horses and went to the window. Stable lads led the large beasts into the courtyard. Knights, with the aid of their squires, donned mail and gauntlets. Servants loaded provisions onto packhorses. The vast courtyard was quickly becoming filled with de Lauren's mighty force.

The door to the solar opened. Bessie curtsied. "I'm to take you to Lord de Lauren, lady."

Katherine thought she would be taken to the courtyard to be told they were ready to ride. But she was led above stairs. She'd spent much happy time here, during their betrothal, five years ago. She remembered the keep well and could have asked Bessie where de Lauren awaited her, then made her way there, herself.

But she followed Bessie.

Bessie led her down the narrow corridor to de Lauren's bed-chamber. She'd been inside his room once, with his mother. Step-mother, Katherine reminded herself. Lady Margaret had been Lord Anthony's second wife, and their son, Stephen, was Nicholas' half-brother.

The love in her voice when Lady Margaret spoke of Nicholas made it easy to forget that she wasn't his birth mother. That she hadn't come into his life until his seventh year. Katherine remembered how the great lady had strolled around Nicholas' room. With a laugh, she'd teased, "No doubt once you occupy this chamber with my son, the decor will improve."

The large room had been sparsely furnished with a clothes trunk at the foot of the bed, and a pitcher and basin on a chair. Nicholas' polished armor and battle gear hung on a wooden stand. Katherine had smiled and thought Nicholas did not appreciate clutter.

Lady Margaret had continued her tour. "Were you to remove the weapons from the wall, the atmosphere would be less a battlefield. I've tried for years to replace those instruments with tapestry. Nicholas has resisted me. But you my dear," she'd winked at Katherine. "My son can deny you nothing."

Remembering what she'd lost with Nicholas was painful. Katherine pushed those thoughts away.

What of Lady Margaret? If she still resided here with Nicholas, Katherine had not seen her. Probably, that was for the best. What would Nicholas' mother think at seeing Katherine now married to her son? Considering that Katherine had renounced him, she doubted the lady would be pleased.

Bessie knocked once at de Lauren's bedchamber.

"Enter."

Bessie opened the door. Katherine saw that the room was unchanged. De Lauren turned from the window. His expression was austere. Nothing had changed here, but her welcome.

Still, she was not a serf to quail at the lord's lowered brows. She met de Lauren's gaze. "You wish to speak with me, my lord?"

"It is not conversation that I would have from you."

The door closed quietly behind her.

"I will allow you no cause to seek an annulment once I have secured Stanfield," de Lauren said.

Annulment. She hadn't thought of it. But it would be his means of ridding himself of her when he learned Stanfield would not be his.

"Apparently you refused a bath and clean garments. If you believed by not bathing, you would delay this moment, be assured your appearance will not alter my course. We will consummate this union now."

The coldness in his eyes made her stomach drop.

"The bed would be more comfortable," he said. "But the wall at your back will suffice. It matters naught to me."

Again he reminded how he despised her. If he chose to, he could vent that hatred in the vilest of ways now . . .

Would he? Had he changed so much? She was afraid of finding out that he had.

If he persisted, he would soon know that she'd recently given birth. She'd wanted to wait until after the keep was retaken to tell him about her twins. While she could not tell him of her son until then, she would now have to explain about her daughter.

De Lauren crossed the room slowly and stood before her. His size and strength, that she'd once reveled in, now made her feel outmatched.

"My lord. I would have you know that yesterday I gave birth to a stillborn babe."

His eyes lowered and she guessed he was taking in her narrow waistline. She'd had a difficult pregnancy and had gained little weight. Now that she'd delivered, the only fullness she'd retained was in her breasts.

De Lauren looked into her eyes. "What is this? A ploy to forestall me?"

"Nay, my lord. I had to flee and leave my babe unburied. She is yet in her cradle at Stanfield."

"I will have proof of a birth long before we reach Stanfield."

They were standing so close now, their bodies brushed. She hadn't fed her babe since yesterday, and at this slight contact, milk spurted from her breasts.

De Lauren drew back slightly. The milk had formed patches on her gown.

"Not a ploy then," he said. "But another truth withheld until you were forced to reveal it."

No doubt he referred to her involvement with William, which she'd confessed to when her wedding to de Lauren was almost upon them and she'd had no choice. If she told de Lauren the truth of her first marriage . . . Tears pricked her eyes. She fought them back. Sweet Mary! Now wasn't the time. She could not be goaded into revealing more than she had.

"To touch you now may impede your healing," de Lauren said. "I will not risk my heirs. You may exhale, my lady. You have been granted a reprieve."

De Lauren called a halt in the woods beyond Stanfield. A chill breeze fluttered the hem of the mantle Bessie had draped over Katherine's peasant's garments before she'd left the keep. She recognized the mantle as one of de Lauren's. Black and gold, it bore his family crest on the back and on the thick broach that secured the cloak at her shoulder. The cloak covered her chin and fell beyond her toes, but more than the warmth it provided, she was grateful that her people would see her draped in de Lauren's colors, and know they were now under his protection.

Dawn was still a time away. The castle was a big, black shape in the scant light from a quarter moon. No sentries patrolled. No torches blazed. Katherine stood on her mount's stirrups, peering into the distance. There was an eerie quiet about the keep and it chilled her.

"Stephen. Hugh," de Lauren called out.

He led his men out from the cover of trees. Katherine watched them ride onto open ground. They were quickly swallowed up by the darkness. Soon after, she could no longer hear the horses' hooves pounding the dry earth. Her heart beat harder. Surely, de Lauren would not enter the keep with just two men?

Before long, she heard the horses returning, then de Lauren rode into view. Some of the tension left her body. What had he seen at Stanfield? Katherine pressed her heels lightly into the horse's flanks, urging the animal to close the distance to de Lauren. The horse was pulled back by the hand that shot out of the near-darkness and seized the reins.

"Nay, my lady," the knight mounted beside her said. "We will await Lord de Lauren here."

The knight was named Marcus. Armored as he was, she saw little of his face, but in the bright day, she'd seen his eyes were a clear green. He'd ridden by her side since they'd left de Lauren's keep. When they'd stopped to water the horses, Marcus had followed her on her brief walk to stretch her legs. She believed he was as much her jailer as her protector.

De Lauren stopped his horse in front of hers. In the filtered light she could make out his features. "My lord," she asked. "How fares Stanfield?"

"It is as quiet as a tomb," de Lauren said.

"Mayhap they await us inside," Stephen said.

De Lauren eyed her. "We shall soon find out."

Before Katherine could respond, he rode past her, deeper

into the woods, where his army awaited his instruction. This time, a dozen men followed him out from the trees. Stephen broke away from the group, but rode only to the end of the trees. Riders gathered behind him.

Katherine turned to Marcus. "Why do they not follow de Lauren?"

Marcus pointed to the sky. "Lord de Lauren's orders are to wait here until the clouds make their way to the moon. One half hour by our count. He will be through the passage then, and launch the attack. Sir Stephen will lead the remainder of our army through the open courtyard gate, to him."

When she'd asked de Lauren to retake Stanfield, she had not thought he would face Ranulf with only a dozen men.

"Thirty minutes now seems a very long time," Katherine said.

Marcus did not reply. Like him, she watched the clouds. When the moon was covered, Katherine looked to Stephen.

He withdrew his sword and shouted, "We ride!"

Soldiers rode swiftly by her. One knight took up a position behind her. Another blocked her front. Marcus was to her right. A fourth knight nodded to Marcus as he took up a position to her left.

And the waiting began again. Katherine clasped her hands tightly. Faith, but she was no good at waiting. How many of these men, forced into a battle that wasn't theirs, would lose their lives this day? How many at Stanfield were already dead? And all for the greed of one man.

A horse neighed. The sound came from beyond the trees ahead. Someone was entering the woods. It sounded like only one rider approached, yet Sir Marcus raised his sword and the circle of knights around her tightened.

"Marcus, 'tis Hugh!"

"Approach," Marcus called out.

Hugh broke through the trees, reining in hard. The horse reared, then settled. "We've secured the keep."

Katherine's tensed shoulders and back relaxed. "What of Stanfield?"

"I'm to take you, Lady de Lauren," Sir Hugh said.

The sun was a pink ball on the horizon, making the stone of the castle, and the five separate towers that rose above the walls, gleam. Her home looked magnificent; unchanged. The gate to the keep was open. Katherine rode between her escort into the vast courtyard. Her mount danced beneath her, sidestepping the body of a knight. Stanfield's blue and white mantle over his armor identified him as one of her guardsmen. More knights, all wearing Stanfield's colors, covered the ground. Severed limbs lay beside the bodies they'd been cut from. A slaughter was what she'd feared and exactly what she was now seeing.

Fire had reduced the wooden lean-tos, used by craftsmen, to ash. Tenant huts that had housed her people who lived and worked here no longer existed. Heart pounding she dismounted. Sweet Mary! Old and young. Men, women, and children in servant's garb. Dead. A babe lay on his back in a sea of his own blood . . .

"Katherine?"

Katherine fought the hand that gripped her chin and turned her head from the babe.

"Katherine!"

Her head was tilted back and she looked into de Lauren's eyes. "Breathe!" He shook her. Hard.

She exhaled the breath she didn't know she'd held.

"Stanfield is a large keep with many servants and trades-men," de Lauren said. "This cannot be all of them. The rest will be watching for your return. We must set things aright."

His message was clear: her people needed her. She nodded.

De Lauren watched her a moment more, then released her.

He gave instructions to her escort to accompany him, and the men left.

She reached for the cross she always wore around her neck, to kiss it, then remembered she'd given it to de Lauren's knight as proof of her identity. She closed her eyes for a moment in a silent prayer for her dead people, then crossed herself.

She looked to the castle. Her daughter still lay in her cradle. Finally, she would lay her child to rest.

In the upstairs hall, soldiers removed more dead. More castle servants. Though she knew she'd had no choice but to seek aid, Katherine felt guilt that she'd not been here to stand against Ranulf with them.

She entered her bedchamber. The destruction here of furnishings and fabric was absolute. But the destruction of things was inconsequential compared with the loss of lives.

She turned to the cradle and went still. The wood was in splinters. Her babe was gone.

Ranulf! She brushed away useless tears and ran next door to William's bedchamber. More destruction of property here. William's shredded and broken possessions crunched under her feet as she made her way to his bed. Her late husband had not been a man to be trusted and so trusted no one. Even here in his own home, he'd slept with a dagger beneath his mattress.

Feathers spilled from a vertical slice in the mattress. But when she stuck her hand between it and the wooden frame, she found the weapon.

Back in the hall, she descended the stairs quickly. No doubt de Lauren had Ranulf in one of the dungeons, chained to a wall. She tightened her grip on the dagger. He would soon reveal where he had taken her child's body.

She followed the narrow corridor to the dungeon stairs. No guards were posted. She reached up and grasped a lit torch mounted on the wall then descended. Hers was the only light in a blackness so thick it looked touchable.

She wanted to hear Ranulf's moans of agony from the darkness, but there were none, just a persistent drip of water striking stone and the scraping of rodents. She would apply her dagger and his screams would echo to the tower—once she found him.

She held the torch high at the iron gate of each dank, malodorous cell. Empty. Despite her resolve, her steps lagged, as she neared the oubliette, a deep pit with the width and breadth of a clothes trunk. She shone her light above the grate, but only lit the narrow mouth of the hole. She would not reach Ranulf if he were down there, without de Lauren's help.

She found de Lauren in the courtyard, crouched over a body. Stephen and two other knights were at de Lauren's side. He stood as Katherine reached him.

"I must see Ranulf."

De Lauren nodded to the soldiers, who turned and left. Stephen remained. De Lauren glanced at the dagger, clutched in her fist.

"If you are thinking to slay Ranulf with that, your vengeance will have to wait. He is not here. He and his men were gone when I entered the keep."

There had been no battle, which explained why the dead bore only her colors.

"He must be found. This day. Now. He has fled with my daughter's body."

"He has not," de Lauren said. "I ordered the babe buried."

Her child's body was safe. She felt shaky with relief. The dagger slid from her hand. "Where is my child being readied for burial, my lord?"

"She is now in her grave."

It took a moment for her to comprehend what he'd told her. "Nay!"

"It is done."

When he would have turned from her, Katherine clasped his forearm. "How dare you!" She slapped him. Her hand stung, but she had the satisfaction of seeing his cheek redden.

"I will allow you that," de Lauren said. "This once."

She ignored his warning. "You had no right to prevent me from preparing my child's body for burial." Her voice quavered and she no longer had the strength to hold his arm. Her hand fell to her side. "You had no right."

De Lauren held her gaze briefly, then signaled to a soldier. "Escort Lady de Lauren to her daughter's grave."

Katherine blinked tears and cleared her view of him. "I will never forget that you have done this."

CHAPTER THREE

De Lauren watched Katherine make her way to her daughter's grave. Her shoulders were erect, but trembled. In not allowing her to prepare her child for burial he knew he'd dealt her a terrible blow.

Earlier, he'd spotted an oak, sprouting the first buds of spring. The huge tree stood alone in Stanfield's meadow. It looked like a mighty guard keeping watch over the land, he'd thought, and ordered Katherine's child buried near it.

Katherine reached the grave, he saw, and knelt before the small wooden cross, staked into the earth there. It was a private moment. One he would not intrude on. He turned away.

Stephen came up beside him. "You had no choice but to keep her child from her, Nick. It would have been cruel to allow her to see the condition Ranulf left her babe in."

An image of the little girl's decapitated body came to de Lauren and his jaw tightened. On its own that atrocity was reason enough to send Ranulf to hell.

Stephen sighed. "In so doing, though, her mind is now set against you."

"Her mind has been set against me these five years past. I will continue to survive it."

"She was not your wife, these five years past."

"You made your reservations on this marriage clear before it took place, Stephen, I have no wish to hear them repeated now."

"I will not repeat them. I will say only that though she ap-

33

pears to have no hand in what Ranulf has done here today, I do not trust her."

De Lauren raised an eyebrow. "Think you I do?"

Stephen shook his head slowly. "Nay, but I fear that you can be made to. I know how you cared for her. That you have cared for no other since. I hoped that would not always be the case. I would see you happy, brother."

"Happy?" de Lauren said. Aye, he'd been happy with Katherine. More fool he. "You are a romantic, Stephen. Seek out a bride who will make you happy, if you must." His jaw clenched briefly. "May you not find happiness fleeting. For me, fear not, I have Stanfield. I am the happiest man in England."

De Lauren eyed his brother. "Enough of this talk. I would have a tally of Ranulf's devastation to Stanfield. Men. Servants. Livestock. Provisions. Lord Michael, Katherine's father, had a steward he thought highly of who kept records of such. See if he yet lives and can produce these accountings for us. I would present them to the king with our current numbers when Henry questions my retaliation against Ranulf."

"Think you, after all this, our king will side with Ranulf?"

"I do not underestimate Ranulf's powers of persuasion to sway the king in his favor. Ranulf is like a chameleon, forever changing his colors to suit his needs. And do not forget, I have not been in our king's favor since Stanfield fell out of my hands and to William Norris."

"Aye, the king favored you to head a strong alliance between the mighty keeps of de Lauren and Stanfield, but it has been wrong of him to blame you for that loss."

De Lauren smiled briefly at Stephen's fierce defense of him. "Perhaps. Or perhaps Henry was right. That I should have forced the marriage then. Katherine's father had given his word and would have honored the match or warred with me and our king to prevent it. Though Lord Michael doted on his daughter, he would not have sacrificed his land and his people in a battle he would not have won. Henry would have had me as his vassal to both de Lauren and Stanfield, rather than that conniving William Katherine wed, and we would not be engaged in this battle now."

"If you had it to do over, I do not believe you would do different," Stephen said. "You would not have married Katherine if you believed she preferred another."

De Lauren grunted. "Do not be too sure."

Katherine looked at her daughter's grave, and felt a stabbing pain in her stomach. The child was buried. What was done was done. But it needn't have happened this way. She could have had a last moment with her daughter. De Lauren had made sure that moment was not to be. She would not have believed him capable of such cruelty.

She'd had no choice but to appeal to him for aid. A petition to the king would have taken days for a response. If it was not intercepted. By then Ranulf would have been firmly ensconced at Stanfield with her as his lady and her son . . . Katherine dug her nails into her palms. Her son either forever exiled or as dead as his sister.

Tears filled her eyes. But what were her son's prospects now? She'd underestimated de Lauren's hatred of her, and in so doing, she had plucked her son from the jaws of one wolf and placed him on the platter of another.

This night was to be a night of celebration. With her keep again secured, she'd planned to tell de Lauren of her son, and then make haste to reclaim her child. She glanced at the battlements, where even now a man clung to the flag pole there, unfurling the Stanfield banner. Sir Guy would be watching for that banner as his signal that Stanfield had been restored to them.

She leaned forward and kissed the wooden cross, then stood. Sir Guy would be watchful, wary of some trickery by Ranulf, but de Lauren's men in their black and gold colors were even now patrolling the grounds. Sir Guy would see that de Lauren protected Stanfield and know their plan had been successful.

He would return with her child. She had to intercept him. But she would have to get away from de Lauren to do that.

She'd been escorted to her daughter's grave, then the knight had left her alone. As she made her way back to the courtyard, no one followed her. Had de Lauren called off his guard?

Where was de Lauren? All around her knights were busy carting away the dead or seeing to chores normally performed by castle servants. One man, a tall formidable redhead, sat on a tree stump while another man prodded a thick finger to a wound on the redhead's forearm. The wound oozed yellow fluid. If not treated, she could see, the knight could lose the arm.

The infection was too advanced to be an injury sustained in the hour since de Lauren and his men had been inside Stanfield. All the more reason for the wound to be treated quickly. She'd learned how to use herbs to heal from her mother and had continued on for her, treating the sick and injured of Stanfield when her mother had died. She would treat the knight after she saw Sir Guy.

She scanned the courtyard. De Lauren was not among the men there. Her tight stomach muscles eased. She could not have stood a delay in seeking out Sir Guy.

A mound of ash replaced the stables that had stood north of the courtyard before Ranulf's invasion. No Stanfield horses were about. Whether Ranulf was a thief or had destroyed the animals in his rage was unknown.

De Lauren's knights had tethered their horses to stakes set into the ground. She found the horse she'd been given to ride among the others and mounted it.

Keeping an eye out for de Lauren, she left the courtyard. A handful of crofter's cabins in the woods had been abandoned years earlier by their owners, who'd chosen the comfort and security of living behind the fortress walls. The cabins were run down, mostly forgotten, and Sir Guy had suggested the one farthest south as a place to house her son. Katherine had agreed.

She waited in the shadow of the castle while two of de Lauren's knights rode past her. She held her breath until she'd cleared the open ground and was hidden behind a wall of trees. She rode the horse at a walk, listening to the sounds around her. No human voices. No hoofbeats. She dug her heels into the mare's flanks.

The fine animal responded and broke into a swift gallop. She made good time. Before long, she ducked low, beneath a dangling branch and rode into the small clearing where the cabin was. She reined in. Sir Guy stepped out from behind a tree. He clutched a sword in his scarred fist. He sheathed his weapon, then lifted her from the horse to the ground.

"My lady, I did not expect you," he said.

"I did not expect to be here," Katherine said. "Ranulf is gone. De Lauren is at Stanfield."

"All is well, then." Sir Guy nodded, then squinted into the trees she'd ridden out from. "You are here without escort?"

"De Lauren does not know of my babe. Nor can he." Her lips trembled and she pressed them together briefly to still them, then said, "Even though he is now my husband."

"My lady?"

"There is no time to speak of it. You must continue to see to my son. I will come to him when I can and together, old friend, we will see him home."

"Aye, my lady."

Time was passing. She didn't know how long she had before she was missed, but she could not leave without seeing her child. She lifted her skirts and ran into the cabin.

Middy met Katherine at the door and knelt at her feet.

"Praise be to God, me lady. You are safe."

Katherine clasped Middy's wrinkled hands. "As we all are."

Over the old woman's head, Katherine saw another woman, beneath the one narrow window. She sat in a wooden chair, nursing the babe. So this was the wet nurse Sir Guy had selected from Stanfield.

Katherine didn't know this plump female. She'd refused William's dictate to select a nurse to attend their child after the birth. William had wanted her free to travel with him to King Henry's court, where he sought to advance his position with the king. Her husband and his ambitions, be damned, she'd thought. She'd see to her child herself.

William had surely found his place among his fellow demons, but even from the grave, it seemed, his will prevailed. She was still unable to attend her child. It hurt now seeing her son being nursed by another. She envied the woman.

The young woman's eyes widened in unmistakable fear; she plucked the babe from her breast and lifted him to Katherine.

Katherine exhaled deeply. Her face must have betrayed her. She hadn't wanted to frighten the nurse. Ranulf was the one responsible for her separation from her son. She owed this woman her gratitude.

"Pray continue," Katherine said softly. "I would not interrupt my son's feeding."

The nurse smiled, showing overlapping front teeth. In one breath she said, "He's a good eater, he is, lady. Going to be a big lad."

Milk filmed one corner of his mouth. Katherine reached out and brushed the backs of her fingers over his soft damp skin, then kissed him. "God willing," she said.

She left the cabin, and with assistance from Sir Guy, she

mounted the horse. The breeze stung her wet eyes and cheeks as she rode out of the clearing. She'd told Sir Guy that together they would find a way for her son to return to her. She had to cling to that.

She remembered the wounded knight at Stanfield and led the horse to a brook where moneywort grew. The root would draw the poison that festered in the knight's arm.

"Easy now," she whispered and nosed the horse between narrowly spaced trees. Birds soared from the branches above her. A rabbit dashed past the horse's hooves.

Katherine reined in and fitted her foot into the stirrup to dismount. She heard hoofbeats. De Lauren emerged from the trees.

How long had he followed her? Her mouth dried. To the cabin?

"You set a swift pace, my lady," de Lauren said as he halted the horse beside hers. "I was hard pressed to match it. Where are you riding to, I wonder. Or where from?"

He knew naught of the cabin. Relief left her shaky. "I have reached my destination," she said.

He raised an eyebrow. "Indeed?"

If he was hoping to catch her in a lie, in this she'd spoken truth. She dismounted and crouched in the moist soil on the bank by the brook, where the moneywort grew.

"It appears you've developed a fondness for filth since last we kept company."

No doubt the rippling water that dulled her reflection served her well at the moment, but she said, "You may recall when we kept company the threat of becoming dirty did not deter me from replenishing my supply of medicinals."

When he could take time from his duties, Nicholas had dismissed her father's escort and accompanied her into the forest, himself, she remembered. Often, to this brook. For an instant, the breeze brushing her neck became his lips.

The sensation faded and she felt bereft.

She focused on the green moneywort and explained about the knight, then asked, "Have you sought me out for a purpose, my lord?"

"I had not sought you out at all, but glimpsed you while on patrol with my knights." De Lauren leaned on the pommel. "Had I not seen the carnage at Stanfield, I would wonder if you had traveled to this isolated spot without escort to meet Ranulf."

Katherine felt her cheeks heat with anger. The blood rush steadied her. "Forgive me, my lord, if I am not grateful that my people's suffering has convinced you I am not Ranulf's accomplice." She crushed a delicate stem in her fierce grip. "He should be en route to the king's tower for his foul deeds this day. It is near impossible to accept that he is not."

A muscle throbbed in de Lauren's jaw. "He will meet his end shortly. Do not doubt it."

"Your reputation is such that I do not believe Ranulf will challenge Stanfield once word of our marriage reaches him," Katherine said.

"Think you, I will await him? That I will ignore this attack on what are now my lands and people?"

Of course he would not, she realized. De Lauren was not respected and feared because he turned the other cheek to his enemies.

"Ranulf however, poses but one threat." De Lauren straightened in the saddle and looked into her eyes. "Apparently you have no qualms about venturing beyond the walls of the fortress unescorted. No doubt, you have been secure in the knowledge that should you be taken, your late husband would pay any price for your safe return. I would advise you to curtail your inclination to ride out alone and make use of the escort I will provide for you. You are now lady of de Lauren as well as Stan-field. There are those who would seek to bring me to my knees through you. Be forewarned, any attempt by my enemies to use you against me would fail."

Katherine stuffed the herbs she'd gathered in the pockets of her cloak, then stood and brushed mud from her hem. He'd drawn blood with those words.

She kept her head lowered until she was sure her eyes and her voice would not betray her hurt, then met his gaze. "Fear not, my lord. I know full well how highly you value me."

She gained the saddle. De Lauren inclined his head for her to precede him. They wended their way out of the dense growth enclosing the brook. The forest widened and she kicked her mount into a gallop, anxious to return to Stanfield and work on restoring her home.

The forest was alive with the promise of spring. Patches of short green stems that would be wildflowers sprouted from the yellowed ground and strained toward the sun. The day was deceptively beautiful, Katherine thought.

Two knights, wearing de Lauren's colors, met her and de Lauren on the road to the keep. They reined in. Katherine saw a man in her blue and white, slung across the back of one knight's horse. She sucked in her breath. The back of the man's skull was crushed.

"Where was he found?" de Lauren asked.

The knight whose horse bore the body said, "A league north, my lord. Not long after you left us we came upon him." He held out a wad of blood-stained parchment to de Lauren and said, "We found this clutched in his fist."

De Lauren unfolded the paper, glanced at it, and said, "It would appear we have found your messenger, my lady."

Katherine closed her eyes briefly.

De Lauren nodded to the soldiers and they led the way into

the courtyard. She rode slowly by de Lauren's side, mindful of the bodies still to be removed. Blood stained the ground where others had lain.

De Lauren dismounted, tethered his horse, and went into the castle. Katherine put the sight of Robert's crushed skull from her mind. She would make a bandage from the scraps of cloth on her bedchamber floor, pummel the herb into juice to spread on the wound, and then find the red-haired knight to administer the treatment.

The ring of an anvil striking metal echoed in the distance. She passed a team of men repairing the gates to the castle, which Ranulf's soldiers had rammed into splinters.

"Aye you! Move yourself!"

Katherine knew that shout. She shielded her eyes from the sun. Livvy, the stout cook, stood pointing to a sack on the rump of one of de Lauren's packhorses. Livvy jerked her thumb at a squat lad Katherine remembered from the Stanfield stables. The boy hefted the sack on his shoulder and, staggering beneath its weight, headed toward the back of the castle where the kitchens were.

Katherine moved quickly. Livvy and the boy had survived Ranulf's attack. Were there others?

"Glad I am to see you safe, Lady Katherine," Livvy said when Katherine reached her.

"And I you, Livvy. Can you tell me of others who found safety?"

"There be ten of us, lady, what hid out in the garderobes. No one come looking for us amid that filth. Haldrake, he took charge and got us there in time." Livvy sniffed. "I ain't seen no one but from our little group until his lordship and his men come, and now yourself, lady."

"We will pray others were able to flee and will return to us shortly," Katherine said quietly.

"Lady Katherine!"

She turned at the familiar voice of her steward. On tiptoe, Haldrake stepped over a bloody patch of ground and made his way to her. As usual, Stanfield's steward was dressed as if he would at any moment be called upon to greet the king. But his fine tunic and hose were creased and dirty, and the violet plume in his cap drooped over his ear.

"My lady." Haldrake bowed low. "I am relieved to see you returned."

"Thank you, Haldrake. I have heard from Livvy that your quick wit saved our people's lives."

Haldrake lowered his gaze. "It is kind of you to remark on my small role to thwart Lord Ranulf, my lady." Haldrake bowed low again.

One of Haldrake's duties as steward was to note the comings and goings of the castle staff. "Have you any knowledge of others who've survived?"

"Not others who eluded Ranulf, my lady. But there are some who were absent from Stanfield at the time of the attack. Four kitchen maids had been out gathering berries. They saw the banner lowered and found safety in the forest. They have recently returned.

"David the woodchopper and his family are away visiting their eldest daughter, who married a lad from Wessex. They and one hunting party are expected back this night. The tanner's son and miller's daughter were engaging in a—ah—picnic at the time of Ranulf's attack." Haldrake cleared his throat behind one thin, pale hand. "The miller wishes your blessing for a marriage between his girl and the boy."

Katherine nodded absently and took a step toward him. Her eyes intent on his, she asked, "How many people in all, Haldrake?"

He shook his head slowly. "One and thirty by my count."

Katherine linked her hands so tightly they shook. Over one hundred and fifty people had been alive at Stanfield yesterday. She pressed her clasped hands to her forehead. She wasn't without blame for this massacre. It was her lack of protection of Stanfield that had enticed Ranulf. When William died, she'd put off acting on Sir Guy's advice that she petition the king for temporary enforcements until another army could be recruited. William's death had given her a freedom she'd thought lost, and she feared King Henry's solution to the problem of security at Stanfield would be to select another husband for her. She closed her eyes briefly. Her selfishness had caused this.

"I have been approached by Sir Stephen de Lauren for an accounting of Stanfield's losses," Haldrake said. "How am I to proceed, Lady Katherine?"

She lowered her hands to her sides. No doubt tales of her marriage to de Lauren were already being bandied about the keep. Her people would want to believe the rumors true. That Stanfield was again secure. They would be anticipating confirmation from her, awaiting her command of loyalty to her husband.

Her husband. She glanced at the thick ring de Lauren had taken from his finger and placed loosely on hers to seal his wedding vows. Vows made without love, she'd known, but still, as he'd spoken them, she'd hoped.

She hadn't understood then how completely he hated her. And now that she did . . .

Her neck prickled. So callously he'd buried her daughter. Given the chance, how would he use her son?

She looked up from the ring to de Lauren, who now rode out of the courtyard. Telling him of her child so he could obtain an annulment of the marriage was impossible now. They would have to remain wed. De Lauren would have to continue to believe Stanfield was his.

Until? Her throat tightened. She rubbed her eyes. They felt gritty, heavy. She'd last slept the night before her labors began. Two days had begun and ended since. Surely it was fatigue now filling her with the fear that she would not find a way to bring her son home.

For now, she would make sure she had a home for her son to return to. Without de Lauren, Stanfield would again be open to attack. She would not make the same mistake she'd made when William died, and leave Stanfield vulnerable. She needed to rebuild Stanfield's defenses. That would take time and Sir Guy's help. But she would see it done.

Haldrake stood waiting for her to tell him whether or not to provide Stephen with a tally of Stanfield's losses.

"Provide the numbers Sir Stephen requested," Katherine said. "Following the evening meal, I will announce that Stanfield has a new lord."

CHAPTER FOUR

Katherine spotted the red-haired knight in a row of other men, digging graves in Stanfield's cemetery, a flat section of land south of the keep. Ten days earlier, she'd stood and watched while William's body had been laid to rest in the tomb in Stanfield's chapel reserved for Stanfield lords.

It was an obscenity to her that William's remains had been placed there. He had been a man without honor in life. He deserved none in death.

In his last battle, she knew, he'd warred on a lord he'd been allied with. William had abandoned that alliance for one with a more powerful lord. Another ruthless act in five years of the same.

He hadn't confided the identity of this lord he favored to her, but since the defeat, she'd wondered where that lord had been when the battle had turned against William.

She'd have liked nothing better than to give the command for him to be interred with criminals who'd died out of the church's favor. That dishonor would have stripped him of the status he'd achieved—status he'd craved as much as breath. There would have been justice in that, she thought.

But there'd been their unborn child to consider. The one right thing to come from a union so wrong. In the end, she'd put her wants aside. She could not hurt the child by dishonoring its father.

She put thoughts of William from her mind and focused on

her reason for being at the cemetery. She made her way to the red-haired knight. His thick curls were matted to his forehead. He lowered the shovel he held shoulder-high and bowed, "Lady Katherine."

"I noticed that your arm is injured," she said. "I am accounted a good healer. I would treat your wound, if you will allow me."

His gaze lowered to the stained cloth that covered his arm from wrist to elbow. "I would be grateful."

She turned and walked away, leaving him to follow her. Ranulf's invasion had left her without pestle and mortar, among other equipment. She crouched and selected two flat rocks from a patch of recently overturned soil. They would serve to ground the moneywort.

In the kitchens behind the keep, Livvy and two young girls kneaded dough. Steam rose from a pot over the hearth. Katherine peered into the pot.

"I have need of a portion of this boiled water, Livvy," Katherine said. "And a deep bowl."

Livvy stepped back from the long table, centered in the room. "I got a bowl near deep enough to hold the Thames. I'll fetch it."

A few minutes later, Katherine had water, a scoop, and two clean cloths. Smoke from the hearth made the kitchens hazy. She wouldn't risk overlooking any infection. Better to treat the knight outside in the bright sunlight.

Before she left the kitchen, she placed a knife in the flames beneath the pot.

She led the knight out through the portal they'd just entered, to the coarse stone table outside, used to prepare meals when the kitchen heat became oppressive.

She unwound the dirty bandage from the knight's arm. She doused the rocks with some of the hot water, then placed a moneywort root atop one rock and ground it with the other rock. The juice in the stem mixed with the root forming a paste.

"We need this cloth cut into strips for bandages," Katherine said.

While the knight applied his dagger to one cloth, Katherine plunged the other into the steaming water. She removed it with the scoop, waved the rag a few times to cool it, then placed it on the wound to loosen the infected crusts.

"Where did you learn your healing, my lady?"

"At my mother's knee," Katherine said as she cleaned the wound.

"I confess I am grateful to your mother, who has spared me further ministrations from Sir Victor."

"Sir Victor, I take it, is the knight who administered this treatment?"

"Aye. As a physician he leaves much to be desired. Lord de Lauren's physician is at de Lauren Keep at present."

"How long have you been in service to de Lauren?"

"Three summers."

"Not so long," Katherine said.

"Nay. But I feel at home. Something I had not felt in a very long time."

"You were not content in your previous position?"

"Before the conqueror's coming, my family was Saxon with lands in Northumbria. When my father was stripped of his title and holdings, he took the only course open to him and swore fealty to Duke William. My father hadn't the stomach to war on his neighbors, but had no choice if he would not have his family reduced to beggars. Because of him, I was able to gain my knighthood regardless of my loss of nobility and am able to earn my way in the world."

It was a familiar story. Noble families, generations old, suddenly forced to swear fealty to the enemy to survive.

"I believe we've cleaned all the infection," Katherine said. "I will return in a moment."

She retrieved the knife from the hearth in the kitchen and rejoined the knight. Her teeth gritted, she laid his arm flat on the table and ran the tip of the blade down the length of the cut, searing the skin.

The stench of scorched flesh rose in the air. The knight stiffened. His arm shook. She took another root from her pocket, used it to scoop up the paste on the rock, and smeared it on his burned flesh. The knight released a breath. The root also soothed pain, she knew. She glanced up, into his eyes.

"You have the touch of an angel, my lady." His face had paled, but he spoke with a smile that rose higher on one side. "Were you not the lady of my liege-lord, I would spirit you away and make you my own."

Katherine returned his smile and reached for the cloth strips. "What, sir, no lady to call your own?"

"Alas, nay. But I am ever hopeful."

"As no doubt are the ladies," Katherine said.

He lowered his gaze from hers, but his smile remained. "You are too kind."

His humility was feigned. No doubt this man knew his appeal. Katherine laughed.

"Once the wound is bandaged, you must keep it dry," she said. "In two days, we will remove the cloth and see how the wound fares."

The knight stopped smiling, and bowed over her hand. "My thanks. A one-armed knight would be disadvantaged." He kissed her fingertips lightly. "I am called Simon, my lady. At your service."

"If it be all right, lady, I'll light a torch."

Katherine realized she'd been squinting at the lute she held, marveling over the miracle that the instrument had not been crushed beneath the boot heels of Ranulf's army. The room was now dim. She looked to the window. A sliver of red sun glowed like fire above the horizon. A shadow crept along the floor.

"We've done all we can for this day, Elspeth," Katherine said as she hung the lute back in place, on the wall in this guest bedchamber. "I imagine Livvy is becoming quite frantic over the serving of this evening's meal. I'll light the tapers. Carry a message to her that I will be down shortly."

"Aye, lady."

"And have water sent up for a bath."

Elspeth walked to the open door, but stopped on the threshold, and turned to Katherine. "Will you be wanting me to come back, lady? Since Middy's not here."

When Katherine had outgrown the need of a nursemaid, Middy had stepped into the role of lady's maid. Part of the role, Katherine remembered. Middy had no fashion sense and little talent for styling hair. Katherine had undertaken those tasks herself.

Katherine's pregnancy promised to liberate Middy from that chore. The old woman had been elated at the prospect of caring for another generation of Stanfield babes.

"Lady Katherine?"

Katherine nodded. "Aye, Elspeth. I will have need of your help."

A short time later, Katherine waved Elspeth back. "Enough."

Katherine felt a breeze on her now-bare neck and patted her skin. Elspeth had wound Katherine's hair into an elaborate coil. It felt wonderful to be free of the weight of her hair on her back.

"My lady, you look beautiful."

Katherine smoothed her palms down the front of the kirtle she wore, a sapphire blue she'd put into storage when her pregnancy advanced. She'd had the trunk brought to her chamber when she realized Ranulf had left her nothing in the trunks in her room that was wearable.

Despite Elspeth's best efforts, the linen remained creased in places. Beautiful? Hardly. But she was finally clean.

Katherine left Elspeth and went to the great hall. De Lauren's men lounged against walls, or sat at the long trestle tables, goblet in hand. She could hear the buzz of conversation.

Her own people rushed about de Lauren's men, placing goblets, trenchers, and jugs on the tables. Once de Lauren arrived, the meal could begin. And once over, she would announce her marriage.

This marriage would ensure her son had a home to return to. She'd had the right of it earlier, when she'd decided not to pursue ending her marriage at this time. Without de Lauren, Stanfield would again be open to attack. She would not make the same mistake she'd made when William died and leave Stanfield vulnerable. She needed de Lauren until she could rebuild Stanfield's defenses.

Katherine spotted de Lauren's thick-necked young squire. The lad, she'd noticed, spent his day shadowing his lord. Rare that he wasn't trailing after de Lauren. The boy would be sure to know de Lauren's whereabouts, though. Katherine hailed him and posed the question.

"Lord de Lauren is on the battlements with Sir Stephen," the squire said. "Seeing to the night watch. If there's naught else, lady, Lord de Lauren bade me deliver a message to Sir Hugh."

The boy took a step back, clearly torn between good manners and his eagerness to fulfill his duty. "There is naught else," Katherine said.

She left the hall to go to de Lauren. Some daylight remained. No torch was needed to light her path on the staircase leading to and from the battlements. At its widest, ten men could station themselves abreast, forming a wall against soldiers who would attempt to breach the battlements and take out Stanfield's archers. As she climbed higher, the passage narrowed until no more than two could fit. A defensive measure in case the stairwell was breached, she remembered Father telling her.

She'd first learned of castle defense and management from his bedtime stories, she thought with a smile. He had not intended those stories to be lessons, she knew. He'd talked of things he knew about to forge a relationship with her.

But Mother had died in childbirth during Katherine's twelfth year, and the son and Stanfield heir had died with her. Instead of remarrying to secure his line, Lord Michael had declared Stanfield would be Katherine's one day. "When the time is right," he'd said. "We will choose a man to rule your lands with you."

Father had been delighted when Katherine had welcomed de Lauren's courtship. De Lauren's lands bordered Stanfield. An alliance would strengthen both holdings. And Lord Michael had seen proof of de Lauren's strong leadership over his people, when Nicholas had taken over for his slain father, Lord Anthony, who'd been killed in King Henry's victory at Tinchebraie. Father had known de Lauren would rule Stanfield well.

Aye, Father had wanted that match, but he hadn't forced it. In a time when fathers bartered daughters for wealth and power, he'd wanted her happiness above all else.

And she'd been happy.

Then two days before her wedding to de Lauren, she'd gone to Father in the common hall. He'd sat by the hearth, setting up the chess board for their nightly game. She'd told him she would marry William Norris.

Lord Michael glanced up from the board. "What is this?"

She repeated herself. "I would marry William Norris, Father."

"Has de Lauren done aught to turn you against him?"

"Nay." She shook her head. "Nay."

"Then we will have no more talk of a marriage to Norris. Bridal apprehension, I'm told, is not unusual." Her father smiled. "While we play, I will enlighten you on the turmoil de Lauren is doubtless experiencing." He winked at her. "I know what of I speak."

Tears filled her eyes. She closed them and a moment later felt Father's calloused fingers brush her wet cheek. "Sweeting. Tell me what has distressed you."

Father would have run William through with his sword that very night if she'd told him. William's death, though, would not have enabled her to marry de Lauren. If it had, she believed she would have killed William herself.

She'd lied. Told Father she'd misjudged her feelings for Nicholas, that William was her heart's choice.

They had their first true quarrel.

"Do you not wonder why I dismissed Norris from my service? He is neither loyal to lord nor king, only to himself. His landless state consumes him. Can you not see he seeks an heiress, not a wife he will cherish? He will take no joy or pride in you, fearing you will overshadow him. As his wife, you will walk behind him, rather than at his side." Father slammed his fist onto the chess board, scattering the pieces. "I will not hand you over to such a man!"

She'd insisted and a fortnight later, in Stanfield's chapel, Father had placed her cold hand in William's.

She reached the battlements now. She blinked back tears and left the stairwell.

De Lauren stood pointing to a turret and speaking with Stephen. They were alone on this side of the battlement.

Her hair was still damp from her bath and she wore no cloak. Goose bumps sprang on her arms. She rubbed them and moved closer to the high battlement wall. She now walked in shade, but the wall cut the wind, and she felt warmer.

She reached a corner that blocked her view of de Lauren and Stephen. They were a short distance beyond the corner. She heard Stephen.

"... fortress is on a ridge. We will need to approach carefully to avoid being spotted by Ranulf's tower watch," Stephen said.

Katherine, about to step into the open, stopped.

"Marcus, Simon, and three others will accompany me," de Lauren said. "We will remove the patrol and gain entrance from the front, then open the gates for the bulk of our army. Hugh and the remainder of our men will scale the castle walls from the rear. You will remain here, Stephen."

"Leave Hugh to see to Stanfield. I will ride with you," Stephen said.

"Nay. You will protect this holding. Ranulf may be awaiting news that Katherine has returned, then attack again. It is doubtful word of the marriage has spread beyond our two keeps this soon. Ranulf left Stanfield defenseless. It is likely he still expects it to be so."

"Aye, if Ranulf doesn't know of your interest here," Stephen said. "He may return."

"I will send to de Lauren Keep for men to accompany me. Those who rode with us here will remain with you," de Lauren said. "Ranulf will not breach Stanfield a second time."

Katherine shuddered, but her fear wasn't for her home. She'd trusted de Lauren to retake her holding, and trusted him now to defend it. He was leaving a sizeable army to do that when he marched on Ranulf's fortress. He'd left men to protect de Lauren Keep as well. Ranulf's army would be at full strength, while de Lauren's forces would be divided. She was afraid for him.

"I do not like this," Stephen said. "I do not like you facing Ranulf without me at your back."

"You are needed here, Stephen."

A silence ensued, then Stephen said, his words clipped, "Aye, lord."

The wind shifted. Katherine shivered and hugged herself.

"We will march on Ranulf in two days," de Lauren said.

"Two days," Stephen repeated.

Katherine closed her eyes briefly. "Oh!" She screamed as she was yanked out from behind the corner by de Lauren. He'd moved with the stealth of a cat. She hadn't heard his approach.

She tugged her hand to free it, but he held firm, and stood looming over her. "Join us, my lady spy," he said softly.

His quiet tone alarmed her more than a shout. She knew him, knew the softer he spoke, the greater his anger. But she was no spy. At least, not the way she believed he meant it. She'd been eavesdropping. She flushed with embarrassment over that. But that was the extent of her crime.

"I am no spy. I sought you out so we may serve the evening meal. I overheard your words with Stephen. That is all."

He watched her in silence, his eyes intent on hers. She blinked quickly, tugged her hand again, but de Lauren did not release her.

"I am guilty of eavesdropping." She sounded breathless, and forced some strength into her voice. "Nothing more."

His gaze stayed fixed on her. She felt like a butterfly pinned to a board, but kept her eyes on his. Finally, he relaxed his grip, holding her hand loosely between his fingers. She slid it out.

"Take great care, Katherine," he said. "That you do not push us both to a point of no return."

Back in the hall, Katherine led de Lauren to the lord's table, on a dais, overlooking the common room. She signaled to a serving girl to relay the message to Livvy that the meal could commence, then took her place to de Lauren's right.

De Lauren's squire went to stand at the wall, behind de Lauren. When de Lauren reached for his goblet, the boy sprang forward to fill the cup with wine. As an afterthought, it looked to Katherine, the lad tilted the jug over her goblet.

"Lady Katherine cannot abide grapes," de Lauren said. "Fill her cup with water, Anson, then find your meal."

De Lauren had surprised her with that remark. Katherine didn't think he'd remember that grapes made her vomit.

Stephen took a seat to de Lauren's left as a serving girl placed a platter of meat pies and vegetables on the table. Despite de Lauren's ample provisions, Katherine had ordered a simple meal, served cold. Gerald, the flutist, had been found hiding in the well, but there would be no music. Stanfield would pass this night in mourning.

She and de Lauren shared a trencher. Katherine eyed the pie he sliced for them with distaste. She couldn't fit a bite into her stomach. It felt weighed down by rocks since her encounter with de Lauren on the battlements. She'd made no sound, she thought, but he'd detected her presence. He was now more suspicious of her.

De Lauren ate, for the most part, in silence, nodding occasionally to Stephen. He glanced from her to her untouched food, but made no comment. He ended his meal a few minutes later. It was time. She stood.

She didn't need to call for attention. She saw John the tanner tap David the woodchopper on his shoulder, then point to the dais. Word spread quickly among the gathering after that.

There'd been an air of anticipation among her people since she'd escorted de Lauren to the lord's table. They watched her now in silence, eyes wide. She felt de Lauren's gaze on her as well.

"Yesterday," she said, "during Lord Ranulf's invasion, I sought aid from Lord de Lauren. That is how Stanfield came to be under his protection. While at de Lauren Keep, his lordship and I were wed."

De Lauren listened as Katherine's people obeyed her command and pledged themselves to him. Many accompanied their oaths with horrific tales of Ranulf's brutality.

"His lordship be looking for you, Lady Katherine," John Tanner said. "He were sure someone knew where you'd hid and that you'd be given up." John smoothed back the few hairs that remained on his head. His protuberant eyes bulged further. "No one here would give you up to Ranulf, my lady. I be thinking Lord Ranulf, he figured that much out for hisself and lost his head."

Gerald, the flutist, cleared his throat. "I couldn't see nothing, hidden as I be in the well, but I could hear. Screaming and begging as the soldiers talked of sawing off limbs and poking out eyes, then went and done it." Gerald choked then cleared his throat again. "T'were sounds I ain't never going to forget."

"Lord Ranulf, he ordered the land salted so's nothing would grow," Livvy said. Her hands were clasped at her ample belly, so tight the knuckles protruded. "He called for the salt but then yelled, 'nay.' Said he wouldn't salt land that would soon be his."

A short while later, when the last of Stanfield's people had sworn fealty to him, de Lauren refilled his wine goblet and climbed the stairs to the battlements. He nodded to several of his guardsmen as he made his way to a spot by the wall where he would be alone.

Stars lit the sky. Moonlight bathed the land in a soft glow that hid bloodstains, ash, and pits dug into the earth from the hooves of Ranulf's charging destriers. He couldn't see the devastation, but it was there just the same. De Lauren's grip on the goblet tightened. While he still breathed, Ranulf would not have Stanfield.

De Lauren heard footsteps and turned. Stephen came up

beside him and braced his palms on the stone wall.

"I thought I would find you here," Stephen said.

"Predictable am I?"

Stephen shrugged. "On occasion to a brother who knows you well." Stephen inhaled deeply. "Ah, fresh air. 'Tis welcome to clear the stench of the day. I have found myself a willing wench and will soon be abed."

De Lauren smiled. "I will not expect you at first meal, then."

Stephen laughed. "No doubt there is another female about, eager to please the lord of the keep."

"Mayhap," de Lauren said. "But I will not make her acquaintance this night."

"Will you seek out your wife?"

De Lauren eyed Stephen and said quietly. "You overstep, brother."

"I cannot apologize for it," Stephen said, but he flushed. "I do not know what game Katherine plays, but I fear her traitorous heart. You would do well not to forget you caught her spying on us this very evening."

"I forget nothing."

"How did you know we were being overheard? No sound came from that corner."

Nicholas raised his cup to his lips and caught the fragrance of the wine. "From her scent," he said. "The wind shifted and carried it."

"Ah, perfume. Then you knew our spy was a woman."

De Lauren nodded. He didn't add that he knew that woman was Katherine. That she still sprinkled rose petals in her bath. And that the blend of roses and her skin's own natural fragrance gave off a scent he could never mistake.

CHAPTER FIVE

Katherine knelt beside de Lauren on the cold stone steps leading into Stanfield Keep. The sky was pink with the dawn. Morning dew made the land glisten.

Four steps above her, Father Juttan raised his arms in the sign of the cross. He was blessing the army of knights and foot soldiers about to depart for battle with Ranulf. Katherine clasped her hands tight, and added her own prayer for their safe return.

With the blessing completed, de Lauren stood. She rose with him. He turned to her. "In my absence," he said, "Stephen is in command. I have left instructions that no one is to leave the keep until my return. Not even you. I will not allow you to indulge your impulse to venture beyond the protection of the fortress when that impulse risks Stanfield."

"These are my people. I would not endanger them."

"Then we are in accord."

De Lauren turned away from her and descended the steps to his horse. Stephen joined him there. The brothers exchanged a quiet word, then clasped arms briefly. De Lauren mounted.

"God speed, my lord," Katherine murmured.

Stephen climbed the steps and stood as she did, watching de Lauren leading the knights and foot soldiers from the courtyard.

"Will he send word, Stephen?"

Eyes narrowed, Stephen turned on her. "And what word do you seek? That you have lost another husband in battle?"

"I could never want Nicholas' death."

"Unless you would gain from it. Was your plan to manipulate Nick into marriage, and add de Lauren Keep to your worth? I will remind you, my new sister, that I remain my brother's heir—title and holding—until you present him with a son. If Nick should die before that happens, you will have no more than you had before this marriage."

"I planned no marriage." She shook her head and whispered, "You know naught of what you speak."

"I know that five years ago you used Nick to ensnare William Norris, the one you favored. Now you are using him in this battle with Ranulf of Warbrook." Stephen's voice throbbed with emotion. "Were I my brother I would have left you to Ranulf. Like to like. The decision was not mine to make, however, and so here we are. Know this, Katherine, if my brother falls in this game you play with Ranulf, I vow, you will not long survive him."

He stalked by her, kicking up a breeze in his haste to be away from her. She'd made a powerful enemy in Stephen. De Lauren, she knew, was not a man to be influenced by others. But Stephen had his brother's trust and love. Both could be strong weapons against her. She could not underestimate them. Stephen would wield them well when Nicholas returned. She shivered in the slight breeze and clutched her elbows beneath her thick fur-lined cloak. When Nicholas returned . . .

De Lauren drew his horse to a stop. Eyes narrowed against the setting sun, he peered at Ranulf's keep on the rise in the distance. An additional tower was being added to the keep. That made six. Ranulf prospered. Prosperity gained, no doubt, by preying on the defenseless. As Stanfield had been.

De Lauren clenched his jaw. Not long now and he would have Ranulf at the point of his sword. Patience. Patience. He'd been telling himself that since he'd led his troops from Stanfield, forcing himself not to push the men beyond their endurance to make the day's ride to Ranulf's holding sooner. De Lauren needed his men rested. Ranulf would not go quietly to his death.

De Lauren had spent the last two nights observing Ranulf's castle defenses. From this spot in the trees beyond the keep, de Lauren found what he'd been looking for. A weakness.

Despite the glare of last night's full moon, one small section of the high curtain wall that enclosed Ranulf's castle had remained in deep shadow. De Lauren nodded in satisfaction. Tonight, two at a time, a contingent of his men would scale that wall.

De Lauren rode back through the trees to where he and his men had made camp. Though he could not see them, he knew men were positioned in the branches above him. Scouts ready to sound the alert should Ranulf's men venture this way.

In the camp, knights sat sharpening their blades, or tossing rocks between two trees in a game of skill. Anson ran to de Lauren as he drew his horse to a halt. De Lauren tossed the boy the reins and dismounted, then went to Hugh, who was leaning against a tree, watching the play. A shout rang out. Marcus slapped a few coins into Simon's palm.

"We go tonight," de Lauren said to Hugh. "We will launch our attack at dusk before the moon rises to give us away to the tower watch."

Hugh nodded and straightened from the tree. The light filtering through the branches above him bleached his thinning blonde hair near white. "It is almost dusk now. I will give the word."

Again, they made no cook fire that would reveal the presence of a campsite. De Lauren ate lightly with his men from the provisions they'd brought with them, then the knights departed to don their armor.

De Lauren donned the breastplate with the crossed swords that were his coat of arms, but declined the similarly decorated helm. He could conceal the breastplate, but not the helm. He could not risk the emblem being identified before he was ready to announce himself.

A lone owl hooted in the distance. De Lauren looked to the sky. No moon, but a scattering of stars gave off a soft light. 'Twas time.

Once he'd breached Warbrook Keep, Hugh would lead the rest of the army to the battle.

De Lauren led Marcus, Simon, and seven other mounted knights from the camp, then he and Simon separated from the others. The remaining knights also broke off in pairs. They were five groups of two altogether.

De Lauren had observed guards stationed to the north, south, west, and east of Ranulf's fortress. De Lauren's teams had each been assigned a station and would dispense with the guards there. He and Simon took up their own position in the woods.

"They come," Simon said quietly.

De Lauren peered through the dense growth at the approaching guardsmen. The two patrol guards were his and Simon's to dispatch. One rode slightly behind the other. Simon pointed to the rear guard, a burly man with a mop of curly hair, then to himself. De Lauren nodded.

The guards drew nearer. Close enough that de Lauren could hear the clip-clop of their horses moving at a walk, but not close enough to make out more than the men's muffled voices.

Ranulf's guards circled wide of the holding. From what de Lauren had observed earlier, the guards kept a distance from the trees that encroached on their route—the trees where de Lauren and Simon now waited.

The guards were as close as they would get. De Lauren nodded to Simon and the two men charged out from the trees.

De Lauren rode toward the guardsman in front. He expected the man to halt, draw his sword, and engage in battle. Instead the guardsman kicked his horse forward. De Lauren gave chase. When his horse was parallel to the other, he launched himself from the saddle, onto the other man. He struck him from his horse. The guard grunted on impact, but he too, wore a breastplate, and de Lauren felt the jolt as well.

They rolled in the dust. The man had the wide chest of a barrel and would not be pinned. He drew his dagger from his waist, aiming high. De Lauren seized the guard's thick wrist and twisted, turning the blade inward, away from himself. He used his other arm like a bar, pressing it against the guard's throat.

Their raised arms trembled. De Lauren forced the blade back, back, into the guard's neck. Blood splattered de Lauren's chin.

He wiped his face, rolled the guard's body over and took the man's cloak, draping it about his own shoulders.

Simon gained his feet as well, and did the same with the cloak of the guard he'd killed. The cloaks were the red and green of Ranulf's house and concealed de Lauren's own yellow and black.

De Lauren looked to the keep. "Ranulf awaits," he said and mounted his steed.

At the gate, de Lauren called up to the tower guard, "Open!"

The twin gates slowly swung apart. De Lauren and Simon rode between them.

Shouts rang out from the back of the holding and de Lauren knew his men had topped the curtain wall. Ranulf's castle was now under attack from the rear.

De Lauren's men, led by Hugh, swarmed into Warbrook's courtyard. Ranulf's knights drew swords and advanced on de

Lauren's army to defend the keep.

De Lauren flung Ranulf's colors from his shoulders. He raised his sword and shouted, "No mercy!"

"My lord, we've searched the entire holding. Ranulf is not about."

De Lauren nodded to Marcus. Proof of his men's thoroughness was all around him. The battle had raged throughout the night. The smell of death rose from the bodies strewn on the rush-covered floors.

Not all of the bodies belonged to Ranulf's men. De Lauren's knights went about now collecting their own dead for transport back to de Lauren Keep.

De Lauren had allowed one of Ranulf's guardsmen to live. The man sat on the floor in the great hall, amid the bodies of the men he'd fought beside. A length of chain used to pen the dogs at night linked his wrist to a loop in the wall.

De Lauren stood over the man now. The guard's pale, sweating face, blanched further. "You live to deliver my message to Ranulf," de Lauren said. "Tell him de Lauren is now lord of Stanfield, wed to Lady Katherine one week past. The lady and the holding are lost to him. And tell him when he raises his head from the hole he hides in, I will lop it off."

The guard's prominent Adam's apple bobbed up and down, and he nodded quickly. Outside, de Lauren's men had assembled the castle people. The servants were old men, and women whose young children now buried their faces in their mother's skirts. De Lauren eyed the group. A sorry lot they were, with their ragged clothing hanging on near-emaciated frames. Severe punishment, indeed, for these people to be tied by law to Ranulf of Warbrook.

Ladies, probably the wives of the fallen knights by their costly attire, huddled together in the sharp wind. Clouds covered the morning sky. A storm was brewing.

Absent was the lady of the keep, whom de Lauren knew had passed away recently.

De Lauren nodded to Hugh.

"You may leave," Hugh said to the servants. "Lord de Lauren does not prey on the innocent." He turned to the ladies. "You will receive safe escort to Warbrook's closest ally, Fenwick Keep."

The servants scattered, leading the barnyard animals with them. Eight of de Lauren's knights departed with the ladies.

"We await your orders, lord," Hugh said.

"Light torches," de Lauren said.

A short while later, fire had devoured the tenant huts, lean tos, and barns. Smoke rose from the ashes.

"Finish it," de Lauren said to Hugh.

Hugh staked the de Lauren standard into the ground before the castle steps.

"My lord, we were not expecting you," Gerard of Montrose said.

Ranulf Warbrook nodded to Gerard, a lord who at thirty plus two years was Ranulf's own age. Gerard, who'd once stood tall and sturdy as an oak, like Ranulf himself, now appeared as if a breath would bring him to his knees. Disease ate away at him. Patches of his skin were routinely cut away, yet the sores returned.

Gerard appeared more gaunt than when last Ranulf had seen him. Montrose Keep was a holding Ranulf had long coveted. When Gerard passed on, Ranulf would petition Henry for control of it.

"I trust I have not come at an inopportune time?" Ranulf asked.

"Nay. Nay, Ranulf, you are always welcome."

Ranulf sauntered into Montrose's great hall, keeping pace

with Gerard whose step was greatly slowed. The scent of fresh rushes was in the air. Light from the many torches mounted on the walls illuminated rich tapestries and glinted off jewel encrusted ornaments.

A fire burned in the hearth. Ranulf loosened the ties at his throat that secured his cloak. He followed Gerard to the two armchairs set across from the flames and selected the one farthest from the heat. Gerard, Ranulf noticed, took a coverlet from the back of the chair and spread it across his lap.

"So tell me, my friend," Gerard said. "What brings you my way and at this late hour?"

Of Ranulf's allies, Montrose Keep was the greatest distance. Ranulf had traveled the last four days, since his attack on Stanfield, stopping at each of the neighboring keeps looking for Katherine. These lords were Stanfield's allies. Katherine may well believe she could seek protection from one of them. Ranulf hoped that was the case, for if she put these allegiances to the test, she would find she stood alone. Not since her father had ruled Stanfield would men rally against the house of Warbrook.

Ranulf accepted the goblet a buxom serving maid offered, then lifted his gaze from her cleavage to Gerard. "I need to know if Katherine of Stanfield has been in contact with you."

Gerard reached for the steaming cup of tea the maid set on a table by his chair. "Nay. Am I to expect word from her?"

If she had not reached Montrose by now, Ranulf believed she would not come here.

She continued to elude him. Ranulf clenched his fist, then slowly uncurled his fingers. "Should she send word or arrive here—"

"We will certainly detain her," Gerard said.

Ranulf nodded. "My thanks." He drained his goblet and gained his feet.

"The hour grows late," Gerard said. "Will you and your men

not spend the night?"

"As much as I would enjoy a trouncing at the chess board," Ranulf said with a smile, "I would begin the return journey to Warbrook."

"I am glad of your visit, Ranulf, however brief." Gerard glanced away, raised his hand and waved it as if embarrassed. "I have been concerned about you. Since your lady Celeste's passing."

Ranulf lowered his gaze and drew out a silence.

"Forgive me for being artless in prodding a still fresh wound," Gerard said, shaking his head.

"Naught to forgive," Ranulf said. "Now, I must be on my way." Ranulf stood. "My respects to Lady Grace."

"She will be sorry not to have seen you," Gerard said.

"Another time and soon."

Ranulf mounted his horse. He had a small contingent of men with him. He led them out through Montrose's gates, riding at a trot, until he'd cleared the hilly terrain surrounding the keep. Once on the open road, Ranulf spurred his horse into a full gallop.

Gerard had mentioned Celeste. Ranulf sneered. He had not thought of his late wife since the day he'd buried her.

Each night of the last two months of her life, he'd visited Celeste in her bedchamber. Ranulf's physician, Burton, greeted him at Celeste's door, bowing low.

"You have not allowed my lady wife to die, yet, have you Burton?" Ranulf had asked.

Sweat trickled down the temples of the stooped physician and he shook his head quickly. "Nay, my lord. She lingers."

"Excellent. Leave us." Ranulf took his place in the armchair by Celeste's bed. A branch of candles flickered on a bedside table. Ranulf could see her features, sharply outlined by deep hollows beneath her cheekbones. Her skin appeared translucent.

He'd ordered the candles lit at all times. He wanted to see Celeste clearly when he visited her. More, he wanted her to be able to look upon herself. To see the leeches gorging on her bare arms.

She lay on the massive four tester, her face as white as the coverlet on her pillow. Her once-glorious black hair hung limp.

She resembled a corpse. She would soon become one. But not yet.

Ranulf took one of Celeste's long black strands between his thumb and index finger. He leaned in close, brushing his lips against her ear. "Celeste," he whispered. "I am here, my love."

Celeste whimpered. As always of late when she heard his voice. Good. Pain and fear had not yet taken her mind.

Six years he'd been wed to her. The daughter of a baron in France, she'd come to him with a handsome dowry of gold and foreign lands, and she was one of seven children born of the same mother. The only daughter. He'd confirmed this and further investigated her lineage before offering for her. As far back as Ranulf could determine, Celeste's female ancestors had birthed well and often.

And Celeste, like the female ancestors she sprang from, was no fragile blossom. She was taller than most of the women of his acquaintance, but, while not given to fat, had the voluptuous curves and broad hips of a breeder.

His face went hot, and he yanked the hair he held. She had not bred even one son.

He stared at a leech, swelling with Celeste's blood. When their first wedding anniversary had also marked the fact that they were childless, Ranulf had demanded Burton cure Celeste of her inability to carry children. Burton had prescribed bloodletting in short bursts to cleanse Celeste's system of impurities. The treatments had done naught.

Six years later, Ranulf's nursery remained empty. Three,

sometimes four, miscarriages in one year. After each aborted pregnancy, he'd instructed Burton to increase the duration of the treatments.

Her last miscarriage had been two months ago. Her final failure, he'd decided then. He'd instructed Burton to begin another course of bloodletting. And never issued the order to stay the treatment.

His French wife had deceived him with her appearance, her fertile lineage, and her tearful promises of "next time" following each failure. Duplicitous bitch. Ranulf had made sure her death was a long one.

She'd lasted longer than he'd expected. Ranulf bit back on his molars briefly. Would that she'd sustained his sons so well as she sustained herself.

He unclenched his fist and caressed Celeste's cheek. Her skin felt cold, and dry as wax.

"Congratulate me, Celeste," he said. "I am to be remarried. Katherine of Stanfield is my intended."

He would marry Katherine, joining Stanfield to Warbrook, becoming the most powerful house, second only to the king. And she would give him an army of sons.

Her fertility and her ability to carry her pregnancy to term was fact. While at court, William Norris had shared glad tidings of his impending fatherhood with Ranulf. Ranulf paid William a visit shortly after, and confirmed Katherine was gently round with child. Proof that she'd carried to full term had lain in the cradle at Stanfield.

He would not be cheated again. Katherine would fill his nursery, and enrich his holding with the addition of Stanfield, and then, she, too, would die, freeing him to take another heiress to wife.

"My lord . . . "

Had he imagined Celeste's voice? He wasn't certain she'd

spoken above the drip drip of her blood striking the silver pans beneath her arms.

"My lord . . . Kill me, and have done with it, I beg of you." She tilted her head with an effort that winded her, and looked into his eyes. "If you ever had a care for me, Ranulf, grant me this mercy."

She hated the bleeding, he knew. Each time he'd ordered the treatment, she'd pleaded with him on hands and knees not to subject her to the leeches.

"Mercy, my lady? You ask for mercy. I will grant you the mercy you have shown my offspring these many years. Burton!" Ranulf shouted.

The door to the chamber slammed opened. Burton scurried in, head bowed. "My lord?"

"See that Lady Celeste is nourished, that she may live to see another sunrise."

Celeste had been dead going on four weeks now, Ranulf thought. By week's end, Warbrook would have a new lady.

Ranulf drew his horse to a stop and signaled his men to make camp for the night. They rose early, riding hard through the day and night, reaching Warbrook Keep two mornings later.

Ranulf drew his horse to a stop in Warbrook's courtyard. What was this? He gaped at the bodies and devastation to the keep, and then spotted the standard staked into the ground at the castle steps. Crossed swords. De Lauren. Ranulf clenched his fist.

Inside was more destruction—the tapestries of likenesses of Warbrook lords hung on the walls in tatters. Ranulf's eyes watered from the stench of rotting corpses that littered his hall. Among them sat one soldier, chained to the wall like a mongrel dog.

Ranulf approached the soldier, whose name he couldn't

recall, and cast his long shadow upon the man. The soldier trembled.

"My—lord," the soldier stammered. "Lord de Lauren bade me give you a message."

Ranulf fixed his unwavering gaze on the man at his feet.

"De Lauren said—" The soldier's voice cracked. He swallowed then resumed speaking. "Tell Ranulf that de Lauren is now lord of Stanfield, wed to Lady Katherine one week past. The lady and the holding are lost to him. And tell him when he raises his head from the hole he hides in, I will lop it off."

Ranulf's cheeks heated with anger. He drew his sword and drove it to the hilt into the soldier's belly.

"My lord, do we ride on de Lauren?" Gavin, commander of Ranulf's guard, asked.

Ranulf's grip on his sword whitened. "Nay."

As much as it galled him to admit it, the balance of power between him and de Lauren had shifted drastically in de Lauren's favor since his marriage to Katherine. Though Ranulf had crippled Stanfield's defenses, it still had the wealth to re-arm and until that was fully accomplished, Stanfield would draw on de Lauren's significant resources. Only a fool would war on de Lauren now.

History had repeated itself. Five years earlier, Ranulf had found himself threatened by an alliance between de Lauren and Stanfield. He'd squelched the threat then. He would do no less now.

Ranulf narrowed his eyes. The answer to this wedding between de Lauren and Katherine was a funeral.

"Find Ellis," Ranulf said to Gavin. "Bring him to me."

Gavin went in search of the other knight. A few moments later, Ellis entered the hall.

"You wished to see me, my lord," Ellis said. The knight bowed slightly.

Ellis had ridden with Ranulf in search of Katherine and still wore his mail. His cheeks were red from the hard ride.

"I have an assignment for you, Ellis."

"I live to serve, my liege. Who is it you wish me to kill?"

"Nicholas de Lauren."

CHAPTER SIX

De Lauren rode from Warbrook Keep to de Lauren Keep to bury his dead. The funeral service for his fallen soldiers was brief and conducted under a slow drizzle. After, de Lauren spent time with the families, settling small dowries on daughters and presenting sons with their father's swords. The presentations were a tribute to the slain men, and marked de Lauren's pledge to see their sons attain their own knighthood. God willing, it would be so.

It was evening when de Lauren finished the presentations. He dined with Sir Walter, a seasoned knight, who had fought alongside de Lauren's father and who was presently in command of the keep. All was in order, as de Lauren expected it would be.

He updated Walter on the attack on Ranulf, then said, "On the morrow, send men to the convent to collect my mother."

With Ranulf a threat, de Lauren would not allow Mother to remain beyond the protection of the keep. De Lauren could not say he was displeased at cutting Mother's time at the convent short. Though if she was not at prayer there, she would be here at home. De Lauren sighed in frustration at that thought.

It'd been two months since he'd seen her. How was she faring? He looked to Walter. "When you collect Mother from the convent, escort her to Stanfield rather than here."

Walter swallowed a bite of partridge. "I will see to it."

Mother knew naught of his marriage. He retired to his solar

to write a letter to her that he would send with her escort. He lifted the coverlet back from the narrow window. The rain that had fallen steadily throughout the day still pattered against the stone.

At his writing table, he picked up a quill. He had an additional letter to write. To Henry. The king would be none too pleased about a wedding without his consent. De Lauren knew he had no justification for the hasty marriage. He could have liberated Stanfield and then petitioned Henry for Katherine's hand. No doubt Henry would reach the same conclusion. Were he informed of Ranulf's attack . . .

De Lauren decided he was not going to tell the king about Ranulf. He would deal with Ranulf himself.

What to put into the letter, though? He was going to have to strive for a certain diplomacy in the tone while he presented the marriage as a fait accompli. Henry could undo the marriage if he so chose.

De Lauren's grip on the quill tightened. Damned if he would have that.

One week later de Lauren rode into Stanfield's courtyard. The day was dark. A hard rain had left the courtyard resembling a quagmire in places.

Katherine was standing on the castle steps. Her hair was back from her face, coiled atop her head. A rose-colored kirtle hugged her body. De Lauren realized he was staring. He scowled, and looked away from her.

All around him was evidence that Stanfield's residents had not been idle in the time he'd been gone. In the distance, one barn had been erected. His soldiers stood on ladders now, building a frame for a second one. He inhaled the sharp tang of smelt. The blacksmith was conducting his business.

Stanfield's extensive gardens had been trampled to dust in

Ranulf's attack. Too late to replant now and expect an autumn harvest, yet some re-seeding had taken place. Women, bearing jugs, sprinkled water over newly tilled earth.

Stephen's skills did not extend to the day-to-day management of a keep. Katherine would be responsible for this turnabout, de Lauren knew. He'd seen proof of her skill at overseeing the management of this keep during their courtship.

Now, he, too, would see about restoring Stanfield. Ranulf had fouled Stanfield's store of game. Hunting parties needed to be dispatched if Stanfield was not to rely on de Lauren Keep for its meat this winter.

Stanfield's army had to be rebuilt. The keep was secure with the men de Lauren had taken from his own holding. But like all of Henry's vassals, Stanfield was expected to maintain its own army. If summoned, Stanfield's troops would march to defend the throne. Stanfield was a wealthy holding, and had housed over one thousand men, one of the largest armies under Henry's command. Henry needed to be able to count on that army.

De Lauren dismounted. Stephen closed the distance between them at a brisk pace and clasped de Lauren's shoulder. "Glad I am that you are back, Nick."

"All is well here?"

"Aye. There are a few matters I would discuss with you, but none that cannot wait until you've had a meal, and rested." Stephen grinned wide, showing deep dimples. "Mayhap a bath."

Doubtless he needed that. He'd ridden hard. De Lauren rubbed the back of his neck. Sweat and dirt matted his tunic to him. His horse smelled better. De Lauren told his brother of the battle at Warbrook and that he'd just come from de Lauren Keep to bury their dead.

Stephen's lips firmed briefly, then said, "Tell me Ranulf is also counted among the dead."

"Ranulf yet lives," de Lauren said. "He was not at Warbrook Keep."

"Damn Ranulf for being away from the keep. That bastard has the devil's own luck." Stephen was quiet for a moment then said, "Unless he was forewarned of your attack."

"If so, I shall mount that spy's head on a pike when I find him."

"Or her?" Stephen asked softly, inclining his head toward Katherine, standing on the castle steps.

De Lauren focused on her. They'd found her eavesdropping before the march on Warbrook Keep. No doubt Stephen referred to that incident. Stanfield had endured much from Ranulf. Still, de Lauren would not dismiss the fact that Katherine had known when he planned to attack.

De Lauren eyed his brother, then repeated, "Or her."

Katherine was in the great hall when a young knight who looked as if he hadn't yet felt his first razor informed her that the tower watch spotted de Lauren.

She'd been crazed with worry when de Lauren had left Stanfield to battle Ranulf, terrified that she would receive word that he'd been killed. Though she'd not cared for William, the memory of hearing of his death in battle from Sir Guy was still fresh in her mind. She'd feared receiving a similar message about de Lauren. Clutching the knight's forearms she asked, "The watch has identified de Lauren. Specifically?"

"Aye, lady, he leads the troops."

Relief left her shaky.

In the hall, women stood polishing the pewter ornaments blackened by smoke in Ranulf's attack. Katherine left them to it and dashed to the castle steps.

She did not approach de Lauren, but hung back, taking in the sight of him. Dirty. Unshaven. He wore no armor, only his mail. Mud was caked in the links. If there was blood, she couldn't distinguish it. But he sat erect in the saddle, a sure indicator that he had no severe injuries. He was here. And he was whole. Katherine said a prayer of thanks for that.

Stephen reached the castle steps as she did. Their gazes met briefly, but he did not acknowledge her. They'd spoken of nothing that didn't pertain to castle business since their hostile exchange the day de Lauren left for Warbrook Keep.

Knowing his brother was safely returned, and victorious in that battle, she'd thought would have allayed Stephen's suspicions that she was plotting against de Lauren with Ranulf. Apparently, not.

De Lauren and Stephen stood talking in the courtyard. Stephen's voice rose. She overheard him say that Ranulf had not been at the keep when de Lauren attacked it, and further suggest that she may have forewarned Ranulf of the attack. She sucked in her breath, outraged. She wanted Ranulf dead at her feet.

De Lauren's gaze met hers. His voice did not rise. She could not hear what he was saying to his brother, but she caught his warning in the hostile look he gave her as clearly as if she'd heard it. She looked away from it.

Stanfield's gates hung open. De Lauren's return to the keep meant his order that no one venture beyond the fortress walls would no longer be in effect. If not for her inability to leave the keep, she wished de Lauren would leave again. With him at Stanfield, and no longer occupied with besieging Ranulf's keep, she feared he would be ever more alert to her comings and goings.

Each time she left Stanfield she took a risk. A fortnight had passed since she'd last seen her son. It seemed an eternity.

She looked to de Lauren again. His presence at Stanfield threatened all she held dear, still, her heart picked up its pace at the sight of him.

"Lord de Lauren! My lord!"

The man who'd shouted rode hard through Stanfield's gates. He did not slow his pace, despite the courtyard traffic of mounted knights, foot soldiers, and castle staff, pushing carts and leading animals. The rider carried the king's banner.

"My lord!"

De Lauren turned away from Stephen. The rider hauled back on his horse's reins, yanking the animal to a stop that kicked up mud.

"I bear a message from our king!" the rider said.

De Lauren had been expecting a reply to his letter informing the king of his and Katherine's marriage. Henry had wasted no time.

"Bring your message inside," de Lauren said.

He dismounted, and climbed the castle steps. Katherine was still on them. She looked like a ray of sunlight on this dark day. He didn't care for the comparison.

"Accompany me," he said as he passed her.

The castle was quiet. First meal was long over. Castle staff and soldiers were about their duties.

De Lauren went to the solar. With no sunlight to penetrate the narrow window, the room was dim. Anson lit tapers, beating back the shadows, then went to stand at the door.

The young bearded messenger was breathless, and perspiring heavily, de Lauren noted. Henry was ever one for drama. Whatever his reply to the marriage, clearly the young man had been given orders to dispatch it with all due haste.

"My lord," the messenger said. He bowed then handed de Lauren a folded parchment sealed with wax bearing the king's insignia.

De Lauren broke the seal, and read the missive. A bid for

Katherine and himself to join Henry at court right away.

A bid? De Lauren grunted. Hardly that. It was a summons, and well he knew it.

"Anson," de Lauren said to his squire. "Escort the messenger to the kitchens. Bid cook to see to his meal while he awaits my reply to the king."

Katherine stood by his side, hands folded in front of her. He handed her Henry's missive. She lowered her eyes to the parchment.

"We are to go to court," she said. "Why?"

"The king will render his verdict on our marriage."

"I hadn't thought of it," Katherine said. "Of course, the king would be displeased by a wedding without his sanction."

Henry would ask about consummation, de Lauren knew. That the marriage was unconsummated would give Henry ease in dissolving it. No risk existed that Katherine would birth a bastard in a few months' time.

"No doubt it grows tiresome for our king, sanctioning the hasty marriages of the Stanfield heiress," de Lauren said. "Tell me how did our king react to your father's petition to marry William Norris but days before you were to marry me?"

"King Henry was not pleased, I understood from Father, but sanctioned it. At that time, though, our king had not been presented with a wedding after the fact."

Nay, Lord Michael had adored his daughter. He would not have jeopardized her happiness by providing the king with an excuse to overturn the marriage.

"Enjoy this visit to court," de Lauren said. "I will do my part to ensure we will not return any time soon."

"I will not miss King Henry's court."

"It is my understanding that William Norris adored court life."

"William visited our king often. I rarely accompanied him."

De Lauren hadn't expected that. Hadn't expected Katherine would want to be separated unduly from Norris.

Norris had been a fool in not insisting Katherine accompany him. Her presence at his side would have surely helped him further his ambitions. De Lauren had attended court with her and Lord Michael to obtain Henry's sanction on their betrothal. The endless party that was court life strained de Lauren's patience. He'd stood back, just watching her. She'd been dazzling.

The memory soured. "Prepare yourself," he said to Katherine. "We leave at dawn."

Katherine left the solar. King Henry's summons could be the key to bringing her son safely home.

Rather than going to her bedchamber to instruct Elspeth on what to pack for court, Katherine left the keep, and went to the newly erected stables.

"A dismal day for a ride, Lady Katherine," Donny the groom said. He saddled the spirited grey mare Katherine had ridden from de Lauren Keep, and since come to favor. Donny pushed his cap back from his forehead and smiled at her.

"So it is," Katherine agreed.

She mounted and rode into the courtyard. The gates to the keep were open, but guarded. Men-at-arms stood ready to close the gates should the alert be sounded. Archers watched from the tower. Beyond the curtain wall, a handful of knights rode patrol.

"I will escort you, my lady."

The knight who'd spoken was Sir Marcus, the knight she'd come to think of as her jailer/protector since the ride to retake Stanfield.

" 'Tis unnecessary. I shall not venture far into the woods," she lied.

Sir Marcus did not look pleased by her response, but nodded. Clearly de Lauren had meant what he said about an escort being her choice.

She rode to the cabin. Sir Guy lowered her from the horse. She updated him on de Lauren's attack on Warbrook Keep, and that Ranulf had not been at his holding.

"I will not be at ease until Ranulf is dead," she said. "De Lauren will see this done."

"Aye," Sir Guy said. "It appears Ranulf will trouble us no more. Yet we are not hastening to return to Stanfield."

Katherine closed her eyes briefly. "Nay, we are not. Nor can we." She clasped her hands in a tight grip. "I cannot trust de Lauren with my son's life. De Lauren will have Stanfield. I fear, at any cost."

Sir Guy was silent for a moment, then said, "And when de Lauren has killed Ranulf for you?" Lines creased the skin around Sir Guy's hooded eyes. "What of de Lauren? How will we be rid of him?"

I could never want Nicholas' death. Her words to Stephen replayed in her mind. "De Lauren and I have been summoned to court. It is quite possible the king will oppose this marriage, which occurred without his sanction, and dissolve it. De Lauren would no longer have claim to Stanfield then. My son would be safe.

"If the marriage is undone, I will tell the king of my son, Stanfield's rightful lord, and appeal to him to secure the keep until we can rebuild and stand on our own."

Again, she felt the stab of regret that she had not asked the king to secure the keep when William died, and thereby left Stanfield vulnerable to attack. She hoped the king would install one of his vassals to oversee the holding until her son attained his majority. A vassal, not a husband for her, was still what she wanted. Since her son's birth, she was no longer an heiress. No longer a prize. Noblemen would now look elsewhere for their bride. She would remind the king that she was no longer desirable for marriage, and hope he would assign a vassal to Stanfield, and remove de Lauren.

If King Henry dissolved her marriage, all would be well.

It was what she needed, but Katherine felt an ache in her chest with that thought.

"Time passes, Sir Guy, and I would see my son."

Inside, the babe slept in a corner on a pallet. The wet nurse sat beside him on the dirt floor. She moved aside and Katherine knelt over him.

"He's grown," she said.

"Aye, he's putting on weight."

Katherine blinked back tears and lifted him into her arms. He squirmed, opened his eyes, and wailed. Katherine laughed. "Ah, already you assert yourself as lord of the manor. My apologies for disturbing your sleep."

"Oh, aye, he lets you know right enough what he wants." The nurse laughed. "And what he don't want. Spits his milk right back at me when he wants to let me know he's had enough!"

Eyes on her son, Katherine asked, "Does he sleep well at night?"

"Wakes up about three times to feed, but then goes right back. Good as you please."

The door opened. Katherine felt a bony hand on her shoulder. Middy.

"He likes when you sing a little something to him," Middy said.

"Has he smiled yet?" Katherine asked.

"Oh, aye," the nurse said. "He's a happy lad. And a strong one. He'll hold your finger if you give it to him."

Katherine stroked his palm with her small finger. His hand

closed around it. Her throat clogged with tears. "He has excellent grip."

"The boy looks like you, my lamb," Middy said, using her pet name for Katherine.

Katherine saw the resemblance as well. The fair coloring, the shape of his eyes, his slight upturned nose. He was clearly hers. Sweet Jesu that resemblance terrified her. If Ranulf or de Lauren found him, there would be no denying he was her son.

"Me lady, I been thinking the boy needs a name," Middy said.

Katherine had known she would give him her father's name since first setting eyes upon him.

She lowered her head, and kissed the small, plump cheek. "From this day forward, you will be known as Michael of Stanfield."

Katherine rode away from the cabin. King Henry had to end her marriage. She could not long endure this separation from her child.

She heard a horse riding hard behind her, then the horse and rider dashed by her. The rider bounced in the saddle. The man had clearly lost control of his mount. She kicked her own mount forward. Her mare overtook the old nag easily, but before she could snatch the reins, the horse reared, throwing its rider. The man landed on his back on ground covered by twigs and stones.

His tunic had torn down the front, baring his lightly furred chest. A cross, not unlike the one she usually wore, but in silver and bent at the tip, hung to his breastbone.

Katherine dismounted, and crouched beside him. Blood oozed from a shallow cut at his temple. The man's eyes opened, settled on her, then narrowed in pain. He raised himself onto an elbow, groaned, and reached to the back of his head. When he removed his hand, blood stained his fingertips.

"If there is blood, 'tis a good sign," Katherine said softly. "It is likely your injury is superficial."

The man blinked. His large brown eyes were clear. Another good sign.

"Can you stand?"

"I believe so."

"Let me secure your mount, and then we will get you to your feet."

The horse had stopped as soon as it dislodged its rider. The beast had given her all in that run. Her coat was wet with perspiration. Her flanks were heaving. Each panting breath jiggled a trio of bells attached to a string around the horse's neck.

Katherine looped the horse's reins around a low-hanging branch. With her arm at his waist, the man gained his feet. He swayed, and stumbled against her. Katherine staggered, gritted her teeth, and kept both herself and him standing. Eventually, with her weight at his back, he mounted.

He was clearly dizzy as well as in pain. "My home, Stanfield Keep, is a distance from here," Katherine said. "But if you will accompany me, we will tend to your injuries there."

"My head hammers."

"Be at ease, I am a healer, and have prepared many a remedy for men who've imbibed too much, and complained of hammers in their heads." Katherine smiled.

"If it would not trouble you overly, I would be thankful."

He wore tattered but clean breeches and tunic, befitting one of limited means, she saw, yet his speech was refined.

She set a slow pace, watching him, in case he slumped in the saddle. He kept his seat. At Stanfield's gates, she pointed to a young knight with a narrow mustache. "Follow me."

She led the knight and the injured man to the castle steps, and dismounted. "Assist this man to the hall, sir." She faced the injured man. "I will gather my medicinals, and join you shortly."

A few minutes later, Katherine again crouched beside the man. He sat in the arms of the thick padded chair Father had favored for their chess games. Father had been a giant of a man and had the chair built to accommodate his great size. This young man looked like a sparrow being cuddled by a bear.

She cleaned the cut at his temple and another behind his right ear. He hadn't vomited or complained of nausea. His pupils were not enlarged. Katherine applied a soothing balm to the injuries and left them open to dry in the air.

She smiled. "A good night's rest, and I believe you will be as you were."

"I am certain you are correct, Lady de Lauren."

"Ah, so you know who I am."

"Aye, lady. Sir Frederic, the knight who assisted me, told me."

"May I also know your identity?"

Clutching the chair, he gained his feet. "Forgive me. I am Ian, my lady." He bowed. Lowering his head must have cost him. Katherine winced as he did.

"Pray take your seat, sir."

A maid arrived with a tray bearing wine and ale. "I do not suspect you are concussed," Katherine said. "But I would prefer that you refrain from spirits for today at least. Tea, for our guest," Katherine said. "I will have the same."

"I am not a drinking man. I am more than happy to comply," Ian said. "First, though, if I may, I would like to see to my horse. Clara and I have traveled a long way. I would see to her comfort."

De Lauren joined them. "No need. Your mount has been stabled."

"I am in your debt," Ian said.

85

" 'Twas my lady who was your Samaritan, I understand," de Lauren said.

"Your lady? Then you are—"

"De Lauren."

Again, Ian stood, and bowed.

De Lauren crossed his arms. "Where do you join us from?"

"A small village. As yet unnamed. Guildford is the nearest town."

"You are a ways from home," de Lauren said.

Something akin to pain passed across Ian's eyes, Katherine saw.

"That village is no longer home to me, my lord." Ian's Adam's apple bobbed. "I find I am excessively weary. If I may, I would rest for a bit."

"My squire will locate a pallet," de Lauren said, and inclined his head to Anson who stood by a wall.

"Last meal will be served in an hour," Katherine said. "I will send someone to fetch you." Ian did not walk away.

"Is there aught else?" Katherine asked.

"Has Stanfield a resident priest?"

Katherine nodded.

"Would it be possible for me to speak with him?"

"Anson will escort you," de Lauren said.

When they were alone, de Lauren turned to her. "Your patient's injuries do not appear extensive. I expect he will be fit to travel by morning."

"I expect so," Katherine said.

An hour later, Katherine took her place by de Lauren at the lord's table. The serving maid Katherine sent to Father Juttan's chamber returned with a message from Father that he and Ian would not partake of last meal.

Stephen had eaten and left the table. A servant refilled de

Lauren's goblet while others cleared the hall tables for the night. Katherine was about to leave the hall herself, and see how Elspeth fared with the packing, when Father Juttan called out from the steps to the dais.

"Lord de Lauren. Lady Katherine. May I have a word?"

"Be seated, Father," de Lauren said.

Father Juttan nodded his thanks, and took a seat opposite de Lauren.

"I would like to ask your permission, my lord, to invite young Ian to extend his stay at Stanfield."

"Why do you wish this?"

Father Juttan rubbed his sagging jowls. "The young man is troubled, my lord. I believe he would benefit from some time among us."

"What is the nature of his trouble, Father?"

Father Juttan's watery eyes widened. "He came to me in confidence, my lord."

"These are unsettled times," de Lauren said. "I will exercise caution."

De Lauren had kept his tone quiet, but firm. He would have his answer, Katherine knew.

Father Juttan nodded. "Ian is in truth, Brother Ian, a monk. Has been for some years, though his youthful appearance belies that. He has recently come to question his path."

"How so?" De Lauren asked.

The priest frowned, and the skin on his forehead puckered. "He has fallen in love with a young woman. He is in torment, lost between two worlds. I can say no more without breaching the sanctity of the confessional."

"Where was he headed before he encountered Lady Katherine?"

"He is a man without direction, I'm afraid. His aim was to distance himself from the woman. If not for you, my lady, I fear he would not have survived long in his present state of mind."

"I would speak to Katherine, Father. You will have my decision shortly."

Father Juttan nodded. "Thank you."

Father Juttan left the table. De Lauren said, "Precisely where did you encounter this Ian?"

She'd been but a short distance from the cabin. She could not tell de Lauren that, and risk him wondering if she had reason for venturing so far from the keep. She would have to lie, say she was close to Stanfield. Katherine licked her lips. If de Lauren chose to ask this question of Ian, her lie would be revealed.

"I had left the thicket from which I obtain my supply of larkspur."

"In which direction was Ian traveling?"

The same direction as she. Away from the cabin, but in this she could tell the truth. "North."

"Did he mention a destination to you?"

"Nay."

She should have left Ian to that destination! She'd brought him to Stanfield for treatment not thinking beyond the moment, and compromised all she and Sir Guy had done to secure her son.

Ian had to be away come morning.

" 'Twould have been uncharitable for me to leave him, injured, in the woods," Katherine said. "But he will recover by morn, and as you explained to Father, these are unsettled times. We know naught of this man, but what he has told us."

"Unsettled times, indeed. But as you have proven, my lady, not uncharitable. I am inclined to grant your priest's request." De Lauren looked into her eyes. "Unless you have another objection to sway me."

Katherine felt her stomach tighten, but held his gaze. "I have voiced my thoughts on this matter." She stood. "There is much to do if we are to leave for court at dawn. Good eve, my lord."

Chapter Seven

At dawn, Katherine rode behind de Lauren out of Stanfield's courtyard, onto wide, open road. Twenty knights rode escort in V-formation: nine men to her right, nine to her left, two at the rear. Dressed in gauntlets and mail, and mounted atop thick-legged stallions many hands high, the knights were prepared for battle should Ranulf or another threat arise.

It had rained yet again overnight. The horses splashed through ruts now filled with water. Fog misted the air. De Lauren kept his horse to a canter. Katherine exhaled a short, quick breath. The three-day trip to court would not be made in three days at this snail's pace.

She removed a glove, and pressed her fingertips to her throbbing eyes. She'd slept little, following a hellish evening in her bedchamber, waiting for de Lauren to retire for the night to the lord's room, next door. Afraid that he was with Brother Ian, learning that she'd not met up with the monk where she'd claimed.

De Lauren had not sought her out, but went directly to his chamber. Unlikely then he'd discovered her lie. Still, she'd fretted. There was still the morn. Time enough for him to learn the truth then.

He hadn't, though. *He hadn't.* Now, they were away from Stanfield. And when she returned from court, de Lauren might no longer be her husband. He would no longer be concerned with where she'd met up with the monk. Michael would be safe.

And she would be safe. She needed de Lauren gone from her life for her own sake now, as well as her son's.

Katherine lowered her hand from her eyes, and replaced the glove. She glanced at de Lauren's broad back, erect in the saddle. Lying in bed last night, she'd heard him preparing for his own bed through the door that connected the lord's and lady's chambers. Heard him, nay listened to him. To his curt dismissal of Anson who would linger to fuss, which she knew Nicholas hated. To one boot, then the other, thud to the floor. To water slosh against the sides of the wooden tub. Despite all that had passed between them recently, she'd listened, and remembered when she'd loved him above all else, and knew that love returned.

The bed would be more comfortable, but the wall at your back will suffice. She closed her eyes on that ugly scene following their wedding. He had no tender feelings for her. To love him now would give him a weapon he would use to destroy her.

She could not go on living with him. King Henry must undo this marriage.

De Lauren turned off the road, into the forest. She nudged her mare's right flank with her heel, directing the horse to follow. The knights rode single file on each side of her.

Marcus, riding to her left, drew his sword and used it to push aside low-hanging branches. Birds screeched then soared from the trees.

De Lauren stopped by a shallow stream where the water raced over smooth colored rocks. They were traveling light. Necessities, only, de Lauren had ordered. No squires, or servants. The knights saw to their own steeds. Marcus helped her dismount, then led her horse and his own to the water.

Sir Hugh watered the packhorse while Katherine set out

meat, bread, and cheese. The knights helped themselves, then stretched out beneath the trees to take second meal. Katherine ate by the stream. She crouched to rinse her hands in the rippling water as Sir Simon joined her. He held up two skins, and a wooden cup.

"Ale, my lady," he said. "Or mayhap water? I heard you cannot stomach wine."

"Water, please." She took the cup he filled. "How fares your arm, Sir Simon?"

"You are an accomplished healer, my lady. A meager scar is all that remains. Alas."

If his deep sigh was meant to convey disappointment, it was belied by a glint of mischief in his pale grey eyes. Katherine sipped, then smiled. "Alas, sir?"

"Aye, my lady. A jagged, puckered scar to attest to my bravery in battle would win me much from the ladies."

Katherine laughed. "I shall keep that in mind, sir, should you ever need my attentions again."

Simon grinned his crooked smile.

"And what attentions would those be?" De Lauren said from beside Katherine.

His words were clipped. She glanced up at him. He was angry, she realized. "Medical attentions, of course. I treated Sir Simon's injured arm." Katherine handed the cup back to Simon. "I have had my fill. Thank you, sir."

Simon bowed, and took his leave.

"If you will excuse me as well, my lord," Katherine said, smoothing the front of her cloak with her palms. "I would examine the roots growing along this bank for possible medicinal value."

"You could have subjected those roots to a thorough study, had you not spent your time beguiling my knight."

His face was taut with anger. She felt anger as well, now.

"You impugn my honor without cause. You go too far, my lord."

"I think not. I recall your attraction to landless knights." He looked into her eyes. "You are my wife, now. Never forget that."

She laughed softly, without humor. "I assure you, my lord, our marriage is ever at the forefront of my mind."

"Our next stop will be at dusk, at Merton Keep, where we will pass this night. If you would see to your roots, do so now. We ride in five minutes."

The fog lifted in the evening. De Lauren spurred the horses on, but they'd lost several hours due to poor visibility, and did not reach Merton Keep until nightfall.

In the glow of a star-studded sky, Katherine saw Merton's four towers. A section of the otherwise smooth curtain wall was jagged. She wondered if it had been built or repaired in haste, when craftsmanship would have been secondary.

Sir Victor, who bore de Lauren's standard, raised it high. The gates swung open.

In the courtyard, servants rushed out of the castle, taking the reins from de Lauren's dismounting knights.

Sir Marcus helped her to the ground, then shadowed her as she made her way to de Lauren.

A slight man with a trimmed brown beard and thinning hair rushed out of the keep, reaching de Lauren as she did. "My lord! A pleasant surprise!" The man smiled. "And you have brought a lady?"

"This is Katherine, my lady wife, Alec," de Lauren said. "Lord Alec Merton, Katherine."

Lord Merton wore a purple tunic of rich linen, and a thick gold neck chain with a pendant the size of a goose egg.

"Felicitations on your marriage, my lord." Merton bowed to Katherine. "Enchanté, my lady."

Katherine curtsied.

Lord Merton led them into the castle hall. De Lauren's knights followed. Pallets lined the floors. At night, the hall became sleeping quarters for the castle staff. Now, servants kicked the pallets into corners, and snatched tables from against the walls. A husky man carried a flaming torch, lighting the ones on the walls.

Within moments, the hall was bright. Maids brought trenchers, jugs, and goblets to the tables. The food smelled of strong spices.

"Doubtless you are overcome by fatigue, Lady de Lauren," Lord Merton said. "I know naught what is keeping my wife."

"Pray do not concern yourself," Katherine said. "I am sure she will arrive in due course."

Lord Merton nodded. His gaze lifted to something behind her. Katherine turned. A very pregnant woman in a deep blue kirtle slowly descended the castle steps. Katherine saw her in profile. Dark hair. Dark eyes. The woman was beautiful.

"Lord de Lauren. Welcome," the woman said, reaching out to him.

De Lauren bowed over her hand. "My apology for our untimely arrival, Lady Edwina."

"No apology necessary, my lord, of course."

"Edwina, Lord de Lauren visits us with his new lady," Lord Merton said.

Lady Edwina turned to Katherine, revealing the other side of her face. A scar arced across the skin from cheekbone to jaw and had not knitted well.

"Lady Edwina," Katherine said. "Thank you for receiving us. I hope to return your hospitality one day soon at Stanfield."

"Stanfield?" Edwina paled. "You are the lady of Stanfield?"

Lady Edwina's sudden pallor alarmed Katherine. "Indeed, I am."

Edwina's hand rose to her scarred cheek. Her eyes filled with tears.

"De Lauren, what are you about?" Merton said.

Lady Edwina was crying softly.

"Pray tell me what has distressed you?" Katherine asked her.

Merton's gaze narrowed on Katherine, watching her now as if she were something foul.

"Your Lord William Norris of Stanfield approached me to form an alliance," Merton said, his voice hoarse with emotion. "While I was away leading my troops on the king's business, Norris used this friendship to gain entrance to the keep, and attacked. He underestimated my knights, however, and could not take the holding." Merton lifted a trembling hand to his wife's face. He lowered her arm, baring the scar. "In his rage, Norris ordered this."

Katherine felt sick for what these people had endured from William. "I am sorry," she said. "I am so sorry."

"Do you dare stand here asking forgiveness?" Merton shouted.

De Lauren stepped between Merton and Katherine. "Lady Katherine asks for naught. She has done naught that requires your forgiveness."

Sir Marcus and three other knights advanced until Katherine was enclosed between them. The remaining men formed a line on either side of de Lauren.

"Marcus," de Lauren said. "Escort Lady Katherine from the keep."

Marcus placed one hand on the hilt of his sword and clasped Katherine's wrist with the other. The knights surrounding her clutched their swords as well.

Merton held up a hand. "Nay, Nicholas. Nay." The red color that had flooded Merton's cheeks faded. "You have the right of it." Merton shook his head slowly. "Your lady is no more responsible for Norris' deeds then my lady is for mine."

Lord Merton was wrong, Katherine thought. She did share blame for William's actions. She had placed Stanfield's resources in his greedy hands.

"I have not forgotten your help following that dark time, Nicholas," Merton said. "I would see this right between us, my friend. We are honored to have your lady here." Merton turned to his wife. "Edwina, ready our bedchambers for Lord and Lady de Lauren."

Following a tense meal in Merton hall, Katherine walked beside de Lauren up the wide castle steps. She went by the lady's chamber, onto the lord's with him. Inside the room, she turned on him.

"You knew. You rendered aid following William's attack. You knew what he had done, yet, you brought me here where my presence could only hurt these good people. Had you no other allies in the vicinity where we could have lodged this night, we were well prepared to sleep on the road."

"Lord Perry is my ally. Perry Keep is but three miles north."

"Yet we are here? Why? Sweet Mary, can you tell me why?"

De Lauren's voice was cold. " 'Twas time Stanfield's lady saw for herself what her noble house has become under William Norris' rule."

Dishonorable. Unscrupulous. Treacherous. Tears burned her eyes. Aye, she knew well that with her marriage to William, she'd destroyed all her father and what Stanfield lords before him had spent their lives building.

"Think you, you have revealed something about William that was unknown to me?" She wiped her wet cheeks with the back of her hand, and straightened her shoulders. "Be assured, I knew what manner of man William was when I married him and if I had it to do again, I would do the same."

She left the chamber, slamming the door behind her.

De Lauren let her go. She had known Norris' character, still, she'd married him. She had thrown away her birthright for love of that man. Jealousy tightened de Lauren's gut. He slammed his fist against the door. Norris was dead and yet de Lauren longed to run him through with his sword.

He'd brought her to Merton Keep to see her shock and revulsion over Norris' actions here. He'd wanted to show her how Norris' rule had besmirched Stanfield. He'd wanted her to see that she'd compromised her land and her people with that marriage.

She'd seen and still she'd said if she had to do over, she would marry Norris anyway. Clearly, she considered marriage to that bastard worth any price.

De Lauren gritted his teeth. Regardless of what he'd told Merton, Katherine was to blame for Stanfield's dishonor. De Lauren held her accountable. God willing, their children would one day rule the two holdings. But first, de Lauren would see William Norris' taint removed from the name Stanfield. Katherine's love for Norris be damned.

Three days later, de Lauren led his knights through the gates to the king's palace. From there, he and Katherine were escorted into the king's receiving room. Henry Beauclerc sat on his throne on a dais in the opulent chamber. Some time had passed since de Lauren had seen him. Henry's dark eyes looked startling against his sallow complexion.

The footman who'd escorted de Lauren and Katherine to the king bowed, and backed out between double doors. They were not alone with Henry. Lords and ladies in what de Lauren called full "peacock" regalia filled the space.

"Lord de Lauren, and the lovely Lady Katherine."

Henry's booming voice was honey-smooth, and he was smiling. A shallow smile that did not reach his eyes. A subtle display by Henry of his displeasure, de Lauren knew. And the second one in the short time they'd been inside the palace. The first one had been his command to have them brought to him immediately upon their arrival, rather than being shown where to refresh themselves.

So be it, de Lauren thought. He, too, would see this matter done.

"Approach," the king said.

De Lauren extended his arm to Katherine. She placed her hand atop his and they made their way up the carpeted walkway.

"Leave us!" The king shouted.

The lords and ladies responded to Henry's sharp tone as if they'd been struck, bowing to him quickly, then making hasty exits. The door closed behind the last serving maid. Henry eyed de Lauren. "You are wed."

De Lauren bowed his head briefly, then met Henry's gaze. "Aye, sire."

Henry turned to Katherine. "Such haste, my lady, are you enceinte?"

Katherine's cheeks turned pink as she rose from her curtsy. "Nay, Majesty, I am not with child."

"When will you know if a child will result from the marriage?"

"The marriage is unconsummated," Katherine said.

Henry raised his thick brows.

Katherine lowered her gaze briefly, then licked her lips.

De Lauren realized she hesitated to reveal the reason for nonconsummation of their marriage. Recalling the stillborn birth was painful, no doubt, but he saw no hurt in her eyes.

"Prior to wedding Lord de Lauren," Katherine said. "I delivered a stillborn babe. I am in a period of recovery."

"Not a marriage in truth, then," Henry said. "Tell me, Lord de Lauren, why I should not dissolve this union, made without my sanction, and arrange another match for our Lady Katherine."

De Lauren saw the promise in Henry's eyes. He would do this. He would make an example of them. Make her a prize to be awarded to one of his favored nobles at his whim.

De Lauren would not let her go to another man. To gain Henry's sanction, he had to show the king that this union benefited him.

"The reason you approved this match five years ago, sire, remains true this day," de Lauren said. "De Lauren and Stanfield combined, under my command, would make your position in the east invincible."

Henry's hawk-like eyes gave away nothing. He drew out a silence, then said. "You will both remain here at court while I decide the fate of this marriage."

Chapter Eight

"And o' I go.

On to fulfill love's promise!"

If she had to listen to one more verse by Lady Arabella, one of the queen's ladies in waiting, Katherine thought she would lose her mind. She left the little group of six gathered around Arabella, now applauding, and went to the window overlooking the queen's private gardens.

Lush red roses bloomed by a man-made pond. Vines climbed a trellis that marked the entrance to a maze the queen delighted in.

Ten days since Katherine and de Lauren had come to court. Immediately following the king's interrogation, King Henry had ordered her escorted here to the ladies' chambers, where she would reside during her "visit."

Ten days and the king had yet to render his verdict on the marriage. Her life was on hold until he made his decision.

She could not predict the outcome. King Henry could be ruthless in the face of defiance. De Lauren had acted on his own authority by wedding her. The king could punish de Lauren by taking Stanfield from him. But would he? Katherine rubbed her forehead. Henry was a practical man, and to unite Stanfield and de Lauren holdings, he might overlook de Lauren's breach.

"Lady Katherine?"

A bird bent its head over the pond to drink. Katherine turned away from the window to the footman who'd spoken.

"Last meal is being served. I am to escort you."

She joined de Lauren at the king's long table as she had each evening. She was among the last to arrive. The festive music stopped. A trumpet blared, heralding the arrival of the king. As one, the lords and ladies crowding the hall rose to their feet and stood until King Henry was seated. Henry liked to draw out a moment of attention, Katherine had noticed. For herself, she was impatient for another night to be over so she might be one step closer to going home. She had to suppress the urge to tap her dainty lavender slipper against the floor.

Finally, the king raised his arm. Chair legs scraped against the floor as people retook their seats. The music resumed.

De Lauren stood by her chair until the footman seated her, then took his place beside her.

Last meal was the only time in the day when she saw de Lauren. As one of the queen's entourage, she did not roam the palace unescorted. Unchaperoned. She could not see de Lauren if she'd wanted to.

King Henry had effectively separated them. Treating them as if no vows bound them. Mayhap the king began as he meant to go on, and planned to make their separation permanent.

A servant set a platter with goose, venison, and vegetables before de Lauren. A deep laugh rose above the buzz of conversation. The king's laugh.

Katherine swallowed a small bite of the goose. Succulent and well-spiced, but she had no appetite tonight. She set her spoon by the trencher. Moments passed.

"Is the goose not to your liking?" de Lauren asked.

His voice startled her. They'd spoken little since their argument at Merton Keep.

"I am not hungry," she said. "I expect the lack of exercise has affected my appetite."

The queen's ladies spent their days over their embroidery, sitting in the gardens, and composing and reciting verse and song.

"Tomorrow you will remedy that," de Lauren said. He sliced venison with his eating knife. "The king has called a hunt, and has invited the ladies along." He studied her closely. "You have paled."

No doubt she had. Her stomach felt hollow. "I find myself recalling the last time we hunted in the king's woods." Five years earlier during their betrothal.

"That drunken fool Bantam is no longer permitted to hunt, you will recall." De Lauren's voice grew cold. "And this time, there will be no doubt but that we will remain with the rest of our party."

'Twas her doing that they'd not stayed with the others during that hunt, five years ago. Her folly. A mistake Nicholas had paid for.

De Lauren cared naught to be reminded of why he and Katherine had not remained with their hunting party that day. The king's jester was introduced. De Lauren turned his attention to the small stage servants had pushed into the center of the room.

"Lord de Lauren?"

De Lauren glanced over his shoulder at the footman, now standing behind him. The servant crouched by de Lauren's chair and pitched his voice slightly above the jester's. "Sir Hugh asks to see you, milord. Right outside the doors, he waits for you."

De Lauren nodded his thanks. He'd told Hugh and the other knights to watch for Ranulf's arrival at court. As he left the king's table, he wondered if Ranulf had been seen.

Outside, Hugh stood beneath a flaming torch on the wall. He

was alone. De Lauren closed the door on the laughter and applause coming from the room he'd just left.

"I believe I have learned where Ranulf was when we attacked Warbrook Keep," Hugh said when de Lauren reached him. "With Lord Gerard Montrose, seeking Lady Katherine."

"You know this for fact?"

"From Lady Gwendolyn, sister to Lady Montrose."

Gwendolyn and Hugh were lovers, de Lauren knew. Her pillow talk had proven reliable in the past.

"Gwen is presently here at court," Hugh said, "but was visiting her sister the eve Ranulf arrived at the keep. She was present during first meal when her sister asked Lord Gerard about Ranulf's late night arrival."

"Lady Gwendolyn said that Ranulf expected Katherine to be there, awaiting him?"

"Nay, lord. I speak naught against Lady Katherine. Gwendolyn knows only what I have told you." Hugh shook his head. "She said naught of a rendezvous between Lady Katherine and Lord Ranulf."

Hugh looked appalled at the notion, de Lauren saw. He would have liked to feel the same outrage on Katherine's behalf. To know for a certainty that her loyalty was true. Once, he would have slain a man who'd suggested otherwise. Now . . .

Had Katherine sent a message to Ranulf warning him of the impending attack on Warbrook Keep? Had she planned to meet Ranulf at Montrose, then was unable to leave Stanfield when de Lauren ordered the keep secured until his return?

She was hiding something about Brother Ian. De Lauren didn't doubt she wanted the monk gone from Stanfield. Which he couldn't comprehend since she'd brought the man to the keep, herself.

He would see the matter of this marriage settled, de Lauren thought. Then he would find his answers about Katherine.

De Lauren nodded to Hugh, then returned to the great hall. As he reached his chair, Katherine stood.

"I am for an early night," she said. "I have made my excuses to our king. I bid you good eve, my lord."

Without waiting for him to reply, she brushed by him and hurried from the hall.

She could not rout that hunt of five years ago from her mind. Inside her room, Katherine turned again on the bed. In the morning, Nicholas would be hunting in the king's forest. As he had five years earlier . . .

"Come, Nicholas, we shall not be missed," Katherine said.

She glanced over her shoulder at him, and nudged her horse away from the others in their hunting party, leading the animal deeper into the woods. De Lauren shook his head, but followed, as she knew he would.

"A few minutes only," he said as he rode up beside her. "There are too many eyes here at court. I won't have your reputation sullied by wagging tongues, should we be discovered alone."

She looked up at him, a sidelong glance. "We are but a fortnight from wedding, my lord. I say, let them talk."

De Lauren groaned. "Bewitching eyes, and that saucy mouth. Good Christ, Kate, I vow, 'twill be the longest two weeks of my life."

She laughed. He took the reins from her hand, drawing her horse and his to a stop. They were in a clearing, beneath a canopy of lush, green leaves. Katherine smelled lilacs.

De Lauren moved his horse alongside hers. The animal snorted and pawed the earth at being near her mare. He controlled his mount. He slid one hand up her arm, over the bell-like sleeves of her cloak, to her shoulder. He drew her close and brushed the thumb of his other hand across her lower lip. "Saucy mouth," he said in a near whisper.

His lips were an inch above hers, and her heart beat harder, anticipating his kiss.

His eyes lifted to something behind her. She was about to see what had drawn his attention when he shouted something she didn't catch. And pushed her from her horse.

She hit the ground hard, shook her head, and looked up at him. He was slumped across the saddle. An arrow was embedded in his chest . . .

Katherine woke, screaming. Tears and perspiration blinded her. She couldn't breathe.

She flung the coverlet from her, then stumbled to the window. She stood there, hugging herself, gulping cold air.

"Lady Katherine? Are you alright? I thought I heard you scream."

The soft female voice came from the now open door. Letitia, who occupied the next chamber, slowly entered, carrying a lit taper.

"Lady Katherine?"

The sky was moonless. Katherine knew she stood in darkness. "I am at the window."

Lady Letitia, a timid blonde of ten and six years, raised the candle and studied Katherine with her wide innocent eyes.

"Are you ill, lady?" Letitia said.

Katherine pushed damp hair back from her face. Her hand shook. "A dream, that is all."

"Would you like me to sit with you for a time? Mayhap until you sleep again?"

"It has passed," Katherine said. "I am sorry I disturbed your rest."

"I am glad you are recovered. Good night, my lady," Letitia said.

The young woman made her way back through the door, closing it softly behind her. Katherine stayed by the window, staring out at the darkness. The dream had passed yet the horror of that day had not.

In that instant, five years earlier, she'd thought de Lauren was dead . . .

From the ground where he'd pushed her she saw the arrow imbedded in his chest, and scrambled to her feet. But as she ran to him, his eyes closed, and he slid from the saddle. Her heart felt as if it had stopped.

Then he said her name.

She knelt over him. He was on his back on a bed of moss, his face pale and glossy with sweat. His cheeks too cool against her palms. The arrow pierced him above the heart. Only half the shaft was visible. The rest was imbedded in him. Impossible to remove it. His blood would spurt from the hole, onto her hands . . .

No mail covered his chest. Just a tunic on the warm spring day. In the king's guarded woods what need had he for mail? Tears fell onto her cheeks.

"Kate." He opened his eyes, found hers, and squinted up at her. "Kate. Hear me."

His voice sounded thin. His words overly spaced.

"Look to the trees," he said. "Any movement?"

She blinked, and half- stood. He pulled her back to her knees with a swiftness that took his breath, then kept her hand tight in his.

"The archer may be within the trees waiting to see how we fare," he said. "Stay here. Look from here. Keep my horse between you and the trees."

She did as he bade her. No wind blew, and all was still.

"Mayhap he did not tarry once his aim proved true," de Lauren said. "But we can take no chance that he lays in wait for you to raise your head. Lead my stallion out of this clearing. Keep the horse between you and the trees that concealed the archer. When you are out of here, mount, and ride south. Our hunting party rides south. Go to them. Stop for no one."

She shook her head. "We will go together. I will ride behind you lest you fall."

He didn't reply. Didn't tell her he was unable to mount.

"Take my dagger."

It hung on the left side of his belt, as always. Easily reached, yet he didn't retrieve it for her. He held her fingers with his right hand while his left lay limp, palm up on the moss. His sword hand.

Tears burned her eyes. "I will not leave you."

But he wanted her away, and knew what to say to gain her compliance.

"You can do naught for me here. Seek help."

She rode away from him, then, terrified that when she returned, she would be too late.

She exhaled now, a deep, shaky breath and shuddered, remembering that frantic ride.

King Henry had investigated the incident. Lord Bantam, a man often deep in his cups, had separated from his own hunting party, and was discovered drunk a short distance from where de Lauren was felled. Bantam, like many of his fellow nobles, had his crest carved on the shaft of his arrows. One of them was removed from de Lauren's chest. The king determined Bantam had sent the arrow astray while intoxicated.

Katherine knew the truth.

Several boar were caught the next day by the hunting parties, each group vying for the king's favor with the largest number of kills. The lords returned to the palace, cheering their successes. Their ladies heaped praise. Katherine now found the sport repulsive. She was glad to see the event end.

Back in her room, she sat while Colleen, the freckle-faced maid assigned to her, finished styling her hair.

Katherine had another reason for wishing the hunt over. Lady Millicent. The curvaceous young widow flirted outrageously with de Lauren throughout the course of the hunt. Sidling her mare so close to his that de Lauren's destrier nudged her mount.

Lady Millicent, appearing to slide from the sidesaddle, shrieked. When de Lauren righted her, she clung to him like a leech. To Katherine's eye, he hadn't extracted himself from the voluptuous lady quite as quickly as he could have.

In the past, Katherine had found such flirtations comical. But then, she'd known de Lauren loved her, and because of that love other women held no appeal for him.

He'd appeared to find Lady Millicent appealing, however, and Katherine felt a stab of hurt, watching him with her. Had he escorted the lady to her room after the hunt?

Someone knocked on the door. Colleen answered it, then admitted a footman. Katherine pushed painful thoughts of de Lauren with Lady Millicent from her mind and focused on the evening ahead. The footman was here to escort her to another evening meal that would be followed by another frivolous evening. She'd been away from Stanfield more than a week longer than she'd anticipated. Each wasted day here gave Ranulf another day to learn of her son.

She followed the groom. Instead of leading her to the king's hall, she was taken to King Henry's receiving room. Her stomach fluttered. Had the king decided about the marriage?

The groom closed the double doors behind her. De Lauren stood by the wall. She looked to the throne. Vacant. She and de Lauren were alone. The room was warm, cloying. Flowers, on several small tables, gave off a strong perfume that blocked any other scents in the chamber.

"The king is not here," Katherine said softly.

De Lauren raised an eyebrow. "Anticipating your freedom from me?" He crossed his arms. "Have you considered my replacement? Mayhap a withered old man who cares naught how he uses his beautiful young bride so long as he begets an heir." De Lauren grunted. "Or a lord who will vent his anger over each frustration on his lady."

Aye, if not for her son, her position would be precarious, indeed. She knew many of King Henry's vassals. Could name several who fit de Lauren's descriptions. Depending on the king's anger, she could have very well found herself wed to another man she despised. Thinking of it chilled her.

De Lauren's eyes became intent on her. "If Henry rules against the marriage, know that will not be the end of it. I will challenge the man Henry names to be your husband to an outrance. It is my right as Henry's vassal. I cannot be refused. And be assured, I will win."

An outrance. The worst form of tournament, fought with few rules. Often the combatants were severely maimed, or killed. Katherine grew colder. "Faith, but you want Stanfield very badly to consider such an option."

"Never doubt it."

Not many men would be bold enough to accept a challenge from de Lauren, Katherine knew. Though, for the prize of Stanfield, some may take the risk. A lord, unable to fight for himself, had the option of selecting a champion to represent him.

She would not allow an outrance. As soon as the king annulled this marriage, she would tell him of her son.

The door in a side wall opened. Two footmen backed in, bowing. King Henry followed, and made his way up the dais to his throne. When he was seated, he dismissed his servants. Katherine walked by de Lauren's side up the aisle to the foot of the dais and paid her respects to her king. When she raised her head, the king's dark, unblinking eyes were on her.

He watched her a moment more then turned his hard gaze on de Lauren.

"Lord de Lauren," King Henry said, "you married our Lady Katherine without my sanction. You will lose much this day as a result."

De Lauren did not respond.

"You will increase Stanfield's and de Lauren holding's forces each again by half. Effective immediately, and for the next three years, Stanfield's taxes will be trebled and all prosperity—crops, animals, income derived from the sale of such—will be forfeit to the Crown.

"This match serves the Crown. The marriage will stand. But you will gain naught from this union, other than the lady, until that time has passed."

The marriage will stand. The king's words echoed in Katherine's mind.

De Lauren bowed his head to the king.

"Lady de Lauren," King Henry said.

"Majesty?" she said softly.

The king stroked his bearded chin. "It would not displease me were you to name your firstborn son Henry."

CHAPTER NINE

"Increase our own army and Stanfield's by half again. Treble Stanfield's taxes, and forfeit all Stanfield's prosperity to the Crown for the next three years. A staggering sum," Stephen said, shaking his head.

At dawn, three days later, de Lauren had led Katherine and his knights through Stanfield's gates back from the king's court. Now, he looked across the long table in Stanfield's solar to Stephen, who sat on a ladder-back chair, and thought Stephen was correct. Henry had demanded an imposing fine. The king sought to make an example of him to his other vassals, de Lauren knew. He'd made no appeal on his own behalf, though. Indeed, he would have paid more to keep Stanfield.

"You may have saved much had you informed King Henry of Ranulf's deeds here," Stephen said.

"I expect the time will come when Henry will learn of all that has transpired between Ranulf and myself, but not before I've dealt with him."

Stephen nodded. "That bastard must be attended to. He is still."

"For the moment," de Lauren agreed. "Ranulf is no coward. Nor is he a fool. He will strike, do not doubt it. But he will not be goaded into moving in haste. Neither will we await his leisure."

"What is your plan?"

"To determine the status of Ranulf's alliances. Hugh and Victor have remained at court to learn what they can of Ranulf's affairs. We seek to learn if there is discontent in Ranulf's ranks that we may use against him."

"If meetings need to be held, I will meet with Ranulf's malcontents on your behalf."

De Lauren shook his head. "Nay. If our inquiries prove fruitful, I will meet with Ranulf's vassals."

Stephen leaned forward in the chair. "Any information we glean is not infallible. There is naught to ensure that one of Ranulf's allies may not seek a meeting with you as a ruse to lure you to your death."

"I will take no undue risk, Stephen. Thus far, Hugh has learned that Ranulf went to the keep of his strongest ally, Gerard of Montrose, seeking Katherine. I will know why Ranulf sought her there."

"Think why, brother!" Stephen came out of his chair, knocking it to the ground. "She is in collusion with Ranulf to destroy you!"

De Lauren eyed his brother. "I will learn the truth of Katherine's dealings with Ranulf, do not doubt it."

Stephen's fair cheeks reddened. His lips thinned briefly. "I pray that truth will not come to you too late."

Stephen yanked the solar door open and strode out, ramming into Haldrake, who'd been about to knock. The old man toppled back against the stone wall of the corridor.

De Lauren watched his brother grip Haldrake's forearms, beneath a magenta tunic, and assist Haldrake to his feet.

"My apologies, Haldrake," Stephen said.

"No harm done, sir."

An instant later, Haldrake stood alone at the open door. He tapped on the wood.

"You wished to see me, my lord," Haldrake asked.

De Lauren met the old man's gaze. "Come in."

Haldrake righted his collar, and patted the top of his mane of silver hair. He closed the solar door behind him.

De Lauren pointed to the chair Stephen had vacated. Haldrake righted it, then perched on the end of the seat, brown-spotted hands clasped on his knobby knees.

"King Henry has decreed that Stanfield treble its annual taxes," de Lauren said. "The Crown has determined Stanfield pay this sum." De Lauren handed Haldrake a parchment.

"I will see to it at once." Haldrake glanced at the paper and blinked. "My lord, this amount is based on Stanfield's income prior to Lord Ranulf's attack."

De Lauren had read Haldrake's accountings of Stanfield's assets when he'd given them to Stephen. Despite financing countless offensives, Stanfield had prospered in the last five years. Much as he wanted to, de Lauren could not deny the numbers. William Norris had made sound decisions regarding Stanfield's resources.

Haldrake frowned. The sagging skin around his eyes sagged further. "Forgive me, my lord, but if we submit current accountings, the latter figures would reflect significantly less pay out."

And the king would question why Stanfield's resources were suddenly depleted.

"You have the right of it, Haldrake," de Lauren said. "But we will make restitution based on Stanfield's wealth prior to the attack."

Haldrake bowed his head. "As you wish, of course. My lord, henceforth do I refer matters of Stanfield's economics to you?"

Haldrake's tone was a little high, de Lauren noticed. Desperation perhaps? No doubt the steward doubted his new lord's judgement after this decision with the tax calculation.

"Was it not your practice to refer economic matters to Norris?" de Lauren asked.

"Lady Katherine made such decisions in the past."

"In Norris' absence?"

"At all times," Haldrake said.

De Lauren raised an eyebrow.

Haldrake licked his lips. "Lord William took on the task of managing the keep's finances following Lord Michael's demise." Haldrake cleared his throat. "Lord William's skill, however, lay in other areas, and Lady Katherine assumed this duty."

De Lauren grunted. So Norris had been inept, and Katherine had been obliged to save the day.

" 'Twas not a role she took on lightly, my lord." Haldrake's words came fast. "Nor was it her intent to usurp Lord William's authority. If I may be so bold, my lord, Lady Katherine acted only out of concern for her people."

Haldrake was sputtering now. Perspiration shone on his brow. De Lauren realized his features had tensed in his last thought of Norris. Haldrake seemed to fear he'd painted Katherine in a negative light that would bring the new lord's anger down on his lady.

"Be at ease. All is well Haldrake," de Lauren said. Five years earlier, de Lauren had planned that Katherine would manage Stanfield by his side. He hadn't changed his mind about that. "Inform Lady Katherine of my wishes in this taxation matter. Henceforth, refer matters to us both."

Haldrake bowed and left the solar. The air in the room had staled from a morning of closed-door meetings. De Lauren went to the window and pulled back the coverlet. A soft breeze carried the scent of flowers from the white blooms of a bush that grew beneath the window. The noon sun lit the meadow and Katherine walking across it.

Without blinking, he watched her. Her hips swayed softly in her pale blue gown. She wore no circlet, as she had at court. When at home, she dispensed with the formal trappings of her station. A practice he'd noticed from their courtship, five years earlier. One that she'd maintained.

Her hair was now coiled atop her head, baring her neck but for a long curl that spiraled to the pulse point in her throat. A butterfly-light caress against the soft skin with his fingertips would make that pulse throb. And if he touched her there with his tongue . . .

De Lauren blinked sweat out of his eyes. Christ, his hands tingled, recalling the feel of her. Afternoons by their favorite brook in Stanfield's woods, he'd glimpsed Katherine's passion and wanted naught more than to throw honor to the wind.

His eyes narrowed. He'd honored Katherine, aye. Would not deflower her until she was his lady before God and man. Later, after she'd broken their betrothal, he'd wondered if she'd gone from his embrace to Norris'.

De Lauren closed his eyes against the horror of that image.

When he looked to Katherine again, the wind had molded her gown to her. De Lauren traced each curve with his eyes. He'd lied on their wedding day when he'd told her she no longer appealed to him. Five years ago he'd wanted her as he'd wanted no other woman. That had not changed.

He wanted her, and she was his. A few more days, she would be healed from the birth, and in his bed.

He would learn Katherine's secrets outside the bedchamber as well. He would know the truth of her dealings with Ranulf. One way would be to tell her of Ranulf's decapitation of her babe. But he could not do it. Even to turn her against Ranulf, he could not tell her that.

There was other pressure he would bring to bear. Beginning this eve.

Katherine entered the great hall for last meal. Laughter rang out. She looked to the source. John Tanner, Kervil, the candle maker, and their women. Her own people. With their safety assured, Stanfield was fast becoming the happy place it had been before Ranulf's attack. Despite the ill between herself and de Lauren, she was grateful to him for that.

De Lauren sat at the lord's table. Katherine nodded to Livvy to begin serving, then joined him there.

He stood as she reached him, holding the chair beside his as she sat. He'd been alone at table before she'd joined him. Where was Stephen? De Lauren's suspicion of her was like a sliver beneath her skin, always prodding. He watched her now, studied her, she thought, out of his dark, deep-set eyes. She didn't relish the prospect of passing the meal alone with him.

Katherine pleated a linen wiping cloth set by her trencher. "Will Stephen not be joining us this eve, my lord?"

"Nay. His presence is required elsewhere."

No help from that quarter to keep de Lauren engaged, then.

"We shall not partake of this meal, alone, however. I have invited a guest." De Lauren's gaze left hers briefly, then returned. "Ah, he arrives."

De Lauren's menacing tone had her heart racing. She looked to the door: Brother Ian. Katherine felt something crawl up her spine.

A moment later, Brother Ian stood at the foot of the dais. De Lauren called out, "Brother Ian, do join us."

Katherine inhaled a shaky breath. What game was de Lauren playing with her now?

Brother Ian bowed, "My lord. My lady."

He climbed the steps slowly, then bowed again, before taking the seat de Lauren pointed to, opposite his own.

Two serving girls placed steaming trenchers heaped with pheasant, boar, and vegetables swimming in a thick pepper-scented sauce on the table. Katherine nodded as portions were placed on her trencher.

Anson appeared at de Lauren's elbow and filled his goblet with wine, then Katherine's cup with water. Too soon after, Anson and the servants backed away. The buzz of conversation in the hall, and the clack of trenchers and cups striking the wooden tabletops, was not enough noise to prevent talk at the lord's table. She wished it were.

"How are you enjoying your stay with us?" De Lauren asked, as he reached for his goblet.

Brother Ian cleared his throat. "Stanfield's people are of the most gracious." Ian bowed his head. "I am truly blessed by your hospitality, my lord."

"I am not long to Stanfield, myself," de Lauren said. "In my short time here, I have come to the same opinion. Stanfield's people are indeed gracious, mirroring their mistress in that respect. I'm sure you will agree."

"I will, indeed," Brother Ian said.

"My cheeks grow overly warm with such praise," Katherine said. "Pray taste the boar, Brother Ian. Livvy, our cook, has improvised a new recipe." Katherine sliced a portion of the rare beef herself and left her seat to serve the monk. She wanted to hurry his meal and send Brother Ian on his way.

"My thanks, my lady," Brother Ian said.

Katherine nodded and returned to her chair.

As Brother Ian picked up his eating knife from beside his trencher, de Lauren said, "Tell us of your travels, Brother."

Katherine's mouth dried, yet she dared not pick up her goblet and reveal that her hands were shaking.

"I must confess, my lord, until a few weeks ago, I had traveled little. Truth to tell, I lack the constitution for it." Brother Ian's cheeks pinkened. "I am a homebody at heart."

"How fortunate that my lady wife must venture far afield from Stanfield to replenish her medicinals." De Lauren looked to Katherine. "What herb did you say you were seeking the day you encountered the good brother, Katherine?"

Katherine's mind went blank. What had she told him when he'd first asked her? She cleared her throat. "Larkspur."

"Ah, larkspur." De Lauren sliced pheasant on his trencher. "Where does that grow?"

"By streams," Katherine said, keeping her answer vague.

De Lauren swallowed then nodded. "That is where you met up with the good Brother? By a stream?"

Katherine's heart pounded. She had not been anywhere near water. "Nay, I had collected the flower by that time."

Brother Ian crunched a crust of bread, then dabbed a cloth to his lips. "I am not a skilled equestrian, I fear. My horse unseated me shortly after I left an abandoned crofter's cabin I'd come across and spent the previous night in."

"A crofter's cabin?" de Lauren said.

Perspiration broke out on Katherine's spine. She was going to lose the few bites of pheasant she'd choked down. If de Lauren took it into his head to ask the location of the cabin Brother Ian had stayed in, or worse ask the good brother to escort him to it, de Lauren may very well stumble onto Michael's hiding place.

"Aye, my lord," Brother Ian said.

De Lauren eyed Katherine but said to Ian. "And fortune smiled on you yet again when you encountered my lady."

"Indeed, it did," Brother Ian said.

Katherine squeezed the wiping cloth between her trembling fist.

De Lauren pushed his trencher back from the table's edge. Katherine licked her lips. De Lauren was implying that she'd not met Brother Ian by accident, but by design. She had to get a message to Sir Guy to flee. Last meal would end swiftly now. Her people would soon take to their beds. De Lauren, though, did not retire early. She'd have to wait him out. When he was abed, she would leave Stanfield through the secret passages and make her way to Sir Guy.

A guard approached the dais and bowed. "The tower watch has identified a traveling party bearing your colors, my lord," the guard said. " 'Tis Lady Margaret."

De Lauren's mother. Katherine was grateful for any means that would divert de Lauren's attention from the monk, but Lady Margaret's arrival also meant de Lauren would not find his bed anytime soon.

De Lauren hadn't seen his mother since he'd bid her goodbye for her visit to the convent. He was looking forward to the reunion.

Shortly after the guard had reported the traveling party, an escort of de Lauren's knights rode through Stanfield's gates. De Lauren went to his mother and lowered her from her horse, onto the flattened grass of Stanfield's courtyard.

Stars lit the sky. She removed the hood of her voluminous black cloak, revealing the black headdress she wore beneath that completely concealed her hair. De Lauren hated that thing. Hated that she felt compelled to wear it. He would not dwell on it, however, and mar his joy at seeing her.

He bowed to her. She clasped his wrists in a grip that pinched him. She watched him. Her soft eyes seemed to be drinking him in. He was used to this close scrutiny from her after a period of separation, and gave her her time. Usually, though, it was he who was arriving—from battle—standing before her while she assured herself that he was safe. A necessary separation, unlike the reason she'd been away from De Lauren Keep.

Again, his thoughts turned, and again, he forced himself to concentrate on the fact that she was here.

He'd been seven years old, when his natural mother had died. His memories of her were not unpleasant, yet whenever he thought of "mother" it was this woman now standing before him who came to his mind.

She wrapped her arms around his waist in a fierce hug. Stephen joined them, and she subjected him to the same study and the same show of affection. Stephen bent for her kiss. He'd inherited her fair coloring and refined features.

"Mother," de Lauren said when she'd released Stephen, "may I reacquaint you with Katherine. As I wrote, she is now my lady wife."

Katherine stood a few paces behind him. She stepped forward and curtsied to Lady Margaret. Head bowed, Katherine held the pose. "Welcome to Stanfield, my lady."

Lady Margaret clasped her gloved hands together and licked her lips in an obvious show of nerves. She was the dowager lady of De Lauren Keep. So long since she'd fulfilled that role, though, de Lauren feared she no longer thought of herself that way.

"Mother?" de Lauren prodded her gently.

Her step lagging, she went to Katherine and kissed her lightly on the cheek. "And I welcome you, my daughter by marriage."

"You must be tired, my lady," Katherine said, regaining her feet. "Your room is prepared and a light meal will be served to you there, if you wish it."

Lady Margaret nodded. De Lauren intervened. "I am aware the hour grows late, but I would very much like to sit with you at table, Mother. Katherine will you arrange this?"

"Certainly," Katherine said. "If you will excuse me, my lord?"

De Lauren nodded and Katherine left.

"Bishop Whittaker will also require accommodations," Lady Margaret said quietly.

Whittaker. De Lauren eyed the bishop riding through Stanfield's gates, his ivory robes fluttering in the breeze. De Lauren would have liked nothing better than to escort the so-called holy man away from Stanfield—away from Lady Margaret. It galled him that because he loved his mother, he could not.

De Lauren looked to Anson. "See to it."

A handful of servants remained by the lord's table. Stanfield's people were preparing for their beds, stacking tables against the walls, laying pallets over the rush-covered floors. De Lauren nodded to Anson to top up his wine.

"If the boar is not to your liking, my lady," Katherine said, "Cook will prepare whatever you like."

De Lauren's gaze went to Lady Margaret's trencher. A slim slice of bread on it and a small mound of barley. Eyes narrowed, de Lauren took in Whittaker's plate. The bishop was seated to Lady Margaret's right. De Lauren grunted. Thick slices of boar overlapped the edges of the trencher.

"My lady wife is a healer, Bishop," de Lauren said. "If you are in need of a digestive aid following your meal, do seek her out."

Whittaker's pinched face narrowed further as he pursed his lips for a moment. "I consume only what is needed to meet my physical requirements, my lord."

"It would appear your physical requirements are much. Apparently unlike the bodies of your faithful flock," de Lauren said, pointing to his mother's plate.

"Nicholas, please," Lady Margaret said. "It is my transgression that has me eating plain fare this evening. Pray, do not concern yourself."

Not concern himself? Without her cloak, he could now see she'd lost more weight from a body that could ill afford to. De Lauren felt anger building inside him. "What transgression, Mother? What has our good bishop found fault with this time?"

Lady Margaret's cheeks pinkened. She glanced around the table, then whispered. "Please, Nicholas."

"As you know, my lord," Bishop Whittaker said. "The secrets of the confessional remain sacrosanct. I am your mother's confessor. God's representative. She accepts my penance as from Him."

De Lauren's grip on his goblet tightened. "Aye, my lady mother's confessor you most certainly are. But God's representative, I do doubt that."

"One day, my lord, you will go too far." Bishop Whittaker swallowed the last of his wine. "My appetite has soured. I will take my leave now. My lady Margaret, will you join me in prayer?"

Lady Margaret nodded and rose to her feet.

De Lauren released a deep frustrated breath and clenched his fist.

The bishop stood and made the sign of the cross over the seated people. To de Lauren he said, "I will pray for your soul, my lord."

De Lauren eyed the bishop. "You would do well, Bishop, to pray for your own."

A full moon lit the courtyard. No breeze. Katherine, peering down from her bedchamber window, would have liked a little wind to rustle leaves or carry the sounds of night creatures to the guards stationed about the castle. She needed to mask her own passage out of Stanfield.

Her people were abed. Last meal had ended hours earlier. A tense meal that for once did not owe its tension to her relationship with de Lauren. His focus had been on his mother and on the bishop.

Katherine had been startled by the change in Lady Margaret's appearance in the five years since she'd last seen her. Then, Lady Margaret had favored jewel-tones, a reflection of her vibrant personality, Katherine had thought. This night, she wore a tent-shaped gown that hung on her. And it was in unrelieved black, like the austere headdress she wore.

The great lady had been a whirlwind the last time Katherine had seen her. Issuing commands during the final fitting to Katherine's wedding gown. Father had done his best to show enthusiasm over samples of material for her gown and sketches of floral arrangements, but had been sorely out of his element. Lady Margaret had stepped in to fuss over the bride, and had made the absence of Katherine's own mother bearable.

The lady Katherine had seen tonight was no whirlwind. Indeed, she appeared as if a breeze would fell her. Katherine frowned, not caring for that thought.

A thud came from de Lauren's room. Katherine returned her attention to him. Had his boot struck the floor? Was he finally preparing for bed? She'd waited long for de Lauren to retire. Was still waiting. So much time passed, she wondered if he would seek his bed at all? Or, instead, had he found a willing woman to pass this night with?

She thought again of the lovely Lady Millicent who'd flirted with de Lauren at the king's court. Watching him with her, she'd felt as if something heavy had landed on her chest, making her fight for breath. Thinking of him with one of Stanfield's women now, she felt the same pain.

Better for her if he were away from his room this night. No chance then that he would hear her slip out of her own room.

Time was wasting. She left the window, went to the trunk at the foot of her bed. Inside was the peasant's cloak she'd worn the night of her flight from Ranulf.

Bootsteps. In the corridor. In de Lauren's room. She heard his muffled voice as he dismissed Anson. The thud of the heavy door being closed.

Impossible for her to leave now. Before de Lauren slept. She bit her lower lip. She had no choice but to wait him out.

Katherine stayed crouched by the trunk. The moon rose higher. Enough! She could wait no longer. She curled her fingers around the coarse wool cloak and—

A creak. She looked to the door that adjoined her bedchamber to his. It was being opened. Rarely had that door been used since she'd occupied this bedchamber. From their wedding night, William had found no warmth or welcome in her bed. If not for his desire for a legitimate heir, she had no doubt he would not have sought her out at all.

She blinked as the door came fully open. De Lauren stood in the space.

CHAPTER TEN

De Lauren stood in the doorway between their chambers. Katherine, crouched by the open trunk, went still. Had he found her out? Impossibly read her mind, and her plans to be away this night?

He crossed the room to her. Katherine released the peasant's cloak she gripped, letting it drift back atop the other clothing in the trunk.

He looked into her eyes. "I will have now what I purchased weeks ago with my sword arm. Disrobe, my lady."

So she had not been discovered. De Lauren did not know she'd meant to be away this night. Nay, his reason for being in her room had naught to do with her leaving Stanfield. She felt the strength returning to her limbs in relief, but his words replayed in her mind. *Disrobe, my lady.* She'd known this marriage would become one in truth. The king's sanction had deemed it so. De Lauren would see this done, removing any question of his possession of Stanfield. Aye, she'd known, but . . .

His jaw was tensed, that, and the hard glint in his eyes made him look as if he were marching into battle rather than contemplating making love with her. Her stomach tightened.

Five years earlier, she'd imagined making love with de Lauren with a maiden's curiosity and budding passion. And with great love between them. There would be no love in this coupling. De Lauren brought only anger and hatred to this moment.

She felt hatred herself now. Hatred for William, who'd brought herself and de Lauren to this point.

"The fire returns to your eyes," de Lauren said, crossing his arms. "No longer do you appear the uncertain virgin bride to stir my sympathy."

Anger heated her cheeks and she stood, bringing them almost toe-to-toe. She tilted her head back and looked into his eyes. "I would not stir you in any manner, this night, my lord."

De Lauren clenched his jaw briefly. " 'Tis your ill fortune that the one you would stir is in his grave and I am not." His voice lowered. "If you require assistance in dispensing with your garments, I will relieve you of them."

A threat or a promise she wasn't sure, but if he meant to humiliate her, she'd not give him that power. She was Katherine of Stanfield and she'd stand tall and proud before him. Keeping her eyes on his, she slid her gown over her shoulders. She lowered the bodice. Down her waist. Past her hips. She released the garment. It pooled at her feet. She raised her chin, and stood, unmoving.

De Lauren's eyes on hers were hot enough to burn. He reached for her and she braced, not knowing what to expect from him, yet prepared to show him she would not be cowed. But he cupped her shoulders gently, with a tenderness she'd thought never to feel from him again. She wanted to feel nothing from this coupling, a defensive measure to protect her heart from him. But that very tenderness undermined her defenses as nothing else could.

He brought her flush against him. She could feel his tensed muscles and his every shallow breath, and her pulse quickened.

His gaze lowered to her body. His nostrils flared and his grip on her tightened. His desire belied his earlier statement that he no longer found her appealing, and it thrilled her.

His calloused hands skimmed down her arms, then moved on, slowly, so slowly, leaving no skin untouched. 'Twas no mistaking who held her. She knew de Lauren. Her heart and her body recognized him. Her flesh heated. For the first time in five years, she felt desire.

So long since she'd touched him. She tugged at his tunic. De Lauren dragged it over his head, dropping it on the floor, atop her gown and chemise. The rest of his clothing followed. She stared at the horizontal scar above his heart, left by the arrow. For an instant she couldn't breathe. She splayed her hand over the ridged flesh, and pressed against his heart. She felt it beating strong and sure.

At her touch, de Lauren sucked in his breath. He threaded his fingers in her hair, coiled above her head. Dimly she heard the pins strike the stone floor. Her hair fell around her. He sifted his fingers through it and held her head between his wide palms. His eyes narrowed on her. He seemed to be studying her features, then his mouth covered hers, open and hot. She clutched his neck to hold him there.

Faith, how she loved this man . . .

His arms wound around her, and he lowered her onto their discarded garments.

After, her body still warm from his, he got to his feet.

Katherine braced herself on her elbow. "Nicholas?" It was a question, spoken in a near whisper.

He did not reply. Eyes wide, Katherine watched him make his way to the door between their bed chambers. He swung it closed behind himself.

She stared at the closed door, unable to breathe, and when she did, her breath came out in a rush. It was over. He'd assured his claim to Stanfield, and left. Making love with de Lauren had felt like love. For a few glorious moments, she'd believed he felt it, too.

And she'd believed in the dream of a future with him.

'Twas de Lauren's hatred of her that made him a danger to Michael. If de Lauren loved her, she could bring Michael to him. Aye, he would have no cause to use her son against her. Indeed, she knew, he would give his life to protect her child as surely as he would to protect her. If de Lauren loved her . . .

She closed her eyes. Tears slid from between her lids. Clearly, he did not.

De Lauren finished his patrol of the grounds and rode to Stanfield's gates. The sun peeked from behind clouds and he squinted in the sudden brightness. He didn't care for the heat that came with the light and swiped his arm across the sweat that sprang on his forehead.

A horse with a wagon was stopped outside the gates. Two men and one woman stood beside it. A third man stood talking with Sir Grant. All wore worn though clean clothing. De Lauren wondered if they were of Stanfield, and had only recently learned their home was again secure.

De Lauren reined in beside his knight. "Grant?"

"My lord," Sir Grant said. "This troupe of entertainers beg entrance."

De Lauren's horse stomped its hoof. De Lauren squeezed lightly with his knees on his horse's flanks to keep the animal in place.

" 'Tis their want to perform in exchange for a meal and a night's lodging," Grant said.

The idea of an evening spent listening to inane bards and jests set de Lauren's teeth on edge, but his men would welcome the leisure. One performance, however, would mean only the guards off duty tonight could watch. For all the men to take in a show, several more performances would need to be added. De Lauren addressed the man who stood nearest Grant. A tall, slightly stooped fellow with a habit of frequent blinking, de Lauren noted.

"If you amuse this eve," de Lauren said to the man, "we will accommodate you for a fortnight."

The man smiled wide and inclined his head. "We will surely please you, your lordship. I warrant it!"

De Lauren nodded and rode into the courtyard. Anson ran to the horse, tugging a gangly pup at the end of a rope. The pup looked large enough to be a horse's offspring, de Lauren thought. As de Lauren dismounted, he tossed Anson the reins. As the boy reached for them, the rope fell from his hand. The pup darted off. Katherine was the first person in the pup's path. She'd stepped off the castle steps. It leaped up on her, knocking her on her backside.

Anson stopped and stared, wide-eyed, open-mouthed for an instant, then ran to Katherine. The horse moved as well. De Lauren seized the reins and drew the animal to a halt.

"My lady, forgive my carelessness! Are you hurt?" Anson asked.

Clearly, she was not. The dog tried to work its way into her small lap, and she laughed.

"I am well, Anson. Fear not. Is the dog yours?"

"Aye, lady. I found him this morn, making his way through Stanfield's gates."

Anson extended his hand to Katherine. She eased the dog's head back from her face, and placed her hand in the squire's.

On her feet now, she ran her palms down the front of her pale lavender skirt. De Lauren watched the descent of her hands, feeling his body warm and harden. He wanted to run his hands down the petal soft skin beneath her skirt, as he'd done last night.

He hadn't been able to sleep after making love with Katherine. Unable to rout her from his mind. She'd been all he remembered and all he'd fantasized.

And after, with his lust satisfied, he'd wanted naught more than to hold her against him and never let her go.

The way he used to.

He'd clenched his fingers into white-knuckled fists to stop himself from reaching for her and then taken himself from her when the need for her became more than he could bear.

Those times when he'd held her tightly in his arms had been a lie, when she was betrothed to him and in love with William Norris.

Naught more than a lie . . .

Katherine glanced away from Anson, up into de Lauren's eyes. His gaze was chilling. She turned from it and welcomed the warmth of the sun on her face. She'd seen hatred in his eyes countless times before when he'd looked at her. Still, it hurt. Absurd. After last night, a mere glance should not wound her. But it did.

"Lady Katherine! Lady!"

Katherine turned at the sound of Livvy's voice, grateful for the distraction from de Lauren. Livvy was stomping across the courtyard. Two birds fluttered up from Livvy's path.

Livvy reached Katherine and her pudgy hand latched onto Katherine's. "You got to come, please, lady, my youngest, Jane, she's labored yestereve and this night away, and the babe ain't showing no signs of coming out."

The women of Stanfield delivered each other's babes. Katherine was only called to help with a birth if one of Stanfield's midwives became concerned.

"Let me fetch my medicinals," Katherine said.

At a little tenant hut, Livvy's daughter, Jane, a girl of ten and six lay with her eyes glazed. Her dark hair was matted to her scalp with perspiration. Her abdomen was well rounded on her otherwise slender form.

Katherine went to the water pitcher, washed her hands, and examined Jane. A moment later, she straightened away from the girl, and frowned. The babe would not be making its appearance anytime soon.

Another contraction seized Jane. Her eyes rolled back in her head so only the whites showed. She made a low, keening sound of agony. It was all she was capable of with the strength she had left. Katherine bit her lip. Mayhap not enough strength to see this babe delivered.

Katherine washed again quickly, went into the bag she'd brought, and withdrew a leaf of ground pine and a stalk of poppy. She tore the leaf into small pieces then sprinkled them into a cup of water. She broke the stalk over the cup, letting the milky sap ooze into the liquid. She'd used this herb combination successfully before, though only a handful of times. By God's grace, most of Stanfield's women delivered their babes in due course.

"Help her to sit, Livvy," Katherine said. Jane slumped against her mother. Katherine pressed the cup to Jane's white lips, and said, "Drink."

After, Katherine placed the empty cup onto a small wooden chair by the bed. What she'd just given Jane would induce contractions. The babe would come sooner because of the ground pine.

She pushed her hair slowly back from her face. And the poppy would dull Jane's pain. The church proclaimed that pain during childbirth was women's atonement for Original Sin.

Katherine hoped God would forgive her her interference.

Two hours later, Katherine cradled Jane's squalling little girl in her arms. " 'Twas you causing all this fuss," Katherine said with a smile. "How glad we are to finally meet you."

Katherine hugged the newborn, felt the solid weight of her. The babe's crying grew frantic. Katherine kissed the child's forehead then gave her to her mother for feeding.

The door thudded against the nearby wall. A young man filled the doorway. His eyes were huge in his pale face.

"There you be, Basil, now that all of it's over!" Livvy said. But she was grinning, her plump face flushed. "Go on then, to your family."

Basil joined his family on the pallet and Katherine slipped out of the hut.

Clouds had gathered again in the time she'd been with Jane, blocking the sun at the moment. She strolled back toward the castle, on a tree-lined path where several huts that belonged to Stanfield's hunters were grouped together. She heard children's high-pitched laughter.

Her arms felt empty with Jane's daughter no longer in them, and Katherine hugged herself. She wanted to fill her arms with her own children. Her daughter lay in Stanfield's graveyard, forever beyond her reach. And her son—she tightened her lips—she would not let that be true of her son.

She had to see Sir Guy. He had to be warned that de Lauren knew where she'd met the monk. She picked up her pace to the stables, and saw de Lauren riding out from them. She rubbed her forehead. With de Lauren out of Stanfield, she could not ride to Sir Guy. She could not risk being spotted while on her way to or from the cabin. Her shoulders tensed. She rolled them. When de Lauren returned, she'd go to Sir Guy.

Hours later, Katherine paced the length of her chamber. The light wrapper she wore swirled around her ankles. Outside her window, the sky was dark. De Lauren had not returned. The day had passed and she'd had no opportunity to slip away and see Sir Guy. Where was de Lauren? So long ago he'd ridden out from the stables. She'd watched below stairs for his return until thirty minutes ago. Time for last meal was fast approaching. The need to bathe and dress for that had forced her to her room. Mayhap for the better. Had she come upon de Lauren as soon as he returned, her face may have betrayed her anxiety.

"Oh, my, this is a right beautiful gown," Elspeth said, lifting the cream-colored dress from Katherine's clothes trunk.

"It will serve," Katherine said without interest.

"I met them entertainers. One of them men—Devon's 'is name," Elspeth said, shaking out the gown. "He's sweet on me. Spent most of his afternoon following me around at me chores."

Katherine's gaze went back to the window. She'd left it uncovered, open to the sound of hoofbeats in the courtyard below that would mark the return of de Lauren and his men. She heard nothing.

Her tight stomach burned with the fear that he'd gone out to look for the cabin Brother Ian had mentioned, and that the delay meant he'd found Michael.

"He's a troubadour, Devon is," Elspeth said, "and new to the troupe, according to Moll, the only woman in their group. He got taken on real recent like, after they found the man who did do the singing, knifed. Moll says they was real lucky to get Dev. Good singers is hard to come by." Elspeth giggled. "He's a handsome devil. I don't mind telling you, lady, he sets me blood to boiling, and not just on account of the way he looks." Elspeth held the gown to her chest. "He talked to me, really talked to me. Asked me about me. Not like Donny." Elspeth gave a wrinkle in the gown a hard swat. "Donny, all he goes about is sticking his hand under me skirt, every chance he gets." Elspeth smiled, showing a slight overbite. "After tonight's show, Devon's going to take me for a walk." Elspeth sighed. "I must confess I can't wait for the show to be over."

Katherine agreed. She wanted this entire night over. God

willing, de Lauren had not found Brother Ian's cabin and morning would bring with it another chance for her to slip away and see Sir Guy.

"I got the wrinkles out, lady. If you be ready?" Elspeth said.

Fifteen minutes later Katherine descended the steps to the hall. People were seated, awaiting the beginning of the meal. Laughter, conversation, and the smell of ale drifted up to her. Someone thumped on a pared-down barrel.

The lord's table, though, was unoccupied. No de Lauren. As she thought that, the outside doors swung open, and she saw him with Stephen, Sir Grant, and several other knights. De Lauren's dark hair was damp, combed back from his face with the ends beginning to curl over his nape. His black tunic and breeches looked fresh. He'd obviously washed and changed clothes somewhere other than his bedchamber. Since the other men also looked groomed, she figured they'd all washed in the knight's quarters.

If de Lauren had found Michael, doubtful he'd have taken time for a bath before coming to her. The throbbing in her temples eased.

De Lauren and Stephen took their places at the lord's table. Other than that brief exchange of glances earlier, she'd spent no time with de Lauren since last night. She'd taken her meals deliberately later than she knew him to take his, wanting to give herself time to get control of her emotions. She would wrap herself in a cloak of pride, and not show him how much he'd hurt her when he'd left her on their discarded garments last night.

Lady Margaret and Bishop Whittaker joined de Lauren and Stephen. Katherine descended the remaining steps to the hall, then signaled to Livvy to begin serving last meal.

Katherine was glad of Bishop Whittaker's presence at table.

De Lauren's focus was on the man seated beside his mother, and not on her.

"Lady Katherine? Might I have a word with you?"

It was Livvy calling out from the foot of the dais, and she carried Jane's newborn. Katherine nodded and Livvy climbed the steps to the platform.

Livvy huffed, catching her breath. "With your permission, Lady Katherine, we're going to name this wee one after you."

"I would be delighted," Katherine said.

Livvy went on to tell the circumstances of the babe's birth. "My Jane was failing, but you saved her, sure enough, lady." Livvy sniffed. "You saved 'em both."

" 'Twas God's will that prevailed, mistress," Bishop Whittaker said. "Not herbs or any handling by a mere mortal." His lower lip curled. "To suggest otherwise would be to endow our lady Katherine with powers equal to God's."

His dark gaze fixed on the cook without blinking. Livvy's mouth opened but she said naught, and fear widened her tiny eyes. Katherine knew Livvy had not meant to imply that Jane's safe delivery was not due to God, and she turned to address the bishop and ease his concern.

"Of course, Your Grace, it is God's will that Jane and her babe are with us this night," Katherine said.

The bishop looked to Katherine. "We shall see."

The church was powerful. If the bishop chose, he could make a formal accusation against her, Katherine knew, and call into question whether or not this child had had a Christian birth. The consequences of a nay decision could cost the child's life, and her own. An unsettling thought, even though she knew her methods were not of the devil.

By calling her methods into question, the bishop might frighten her people away from modern medicines so they would not come to her for treatment. At the moment, that was her main concern. She could not let that happen. She needed to explain her practices to the bishop, and looked to him again. His gaze, though, was not on her, but on de Lauren. The bishop's eyes had widened slightly, and brightened in what looked to Katherine like malice.

De Lauren's eyes, too, were trained on the holy man. "What are you implying, Bishop?"

"I imply naught. I am but God's humble servant. Devoted to caring for the immortal souls of His people." The bishop's gaze narrowed in a calculating look. "I will, of course, investigate the matter of this birth and ascertain that, indeed, 'twas God at work this day and not the demon."

In a low deadly tone, de Lauren said, "Tread lightly, Bishop. My mother's skirts shield you only so far."

The bishop's face reddened at the insult. "I will take my leave of you."

He drew himself up and made the sign of the cross over the people at the table, then left them. His robes rippled out behind him with his swift stride.

The bishop had spoken out against her, Katherine thought as she watched his exit. He planned to investigate her for practicing the devil's work. Yet, his enmity had not been directed at her but at de Lauren.

CHAPTER ELEVEN

Another day had passed and Katherine had not spoken with Sir Guy. She'd dared not leave Stanfield last night in case de Lauren decided to come to her as he had the night before, and found her gone.

'Twas a new day and he had not done so, but the opportunity was lost. She had no notion if he would choose to come to her this night. She could not anticipate him, and because of that could take no chance and leave Stanfield after dark. She was going to have to find a way to go to Sir Guy when she knew de Lauren would not seek her out.

As she finished dressing, she believed the opportunity she sought was at hand.

From her bedchamber window, Katherine saw de Lauren training with his men in the lower bailey. The dawn sun glinted off the men's armor. The clang of swords rang across the courtyard.

De Lauren parried a sword thrust by Stephen, and at the blink of an eye, countered with a downward sweep. Five years had passed since she'd watched him train. He was skilled, beautiful to watch. She remembered telling him that, and smiled. She'd earned a change of subject for that compliment, and then she'd said, "Teach me defense."

His eyes had narrowed on hers, gauging that she'd spoken in truth, no doubt, then he'd nodded. Time after time, he'd stood at her back, with his hand on hers adjusting her grip on a dag-

137

ger. Raising her arm high, he'd angled the blade, until she'd mastered a deadly upward sweep. She hadn't thought she could love him more than she did, but her feelings for him climbed another height when she saw he'd taken her request seriously, that he'd respected her enough not to fob her off with a token effort.

She leaned against the wall, unable to look away from him, remembering that time. But as always, her memories of what they'd once shared left her feeling empty. She forced her thoughts out of the past and turned away from the window.

A quarter hour later, armed with the small satchel she kept her herbs in, Katherine nodded to one of de Lauren's guards and rode out of Stanfield's gates. Sunlight struck her face. She shielded her eyes with her hand until she'd crossed the road and was in the woods where trees filtered the bright rays.

A training session lasted for hours. If she hurried, she could reach Sir Guy and be back at Stanfield while the sun was overhead. She would be back in time for second meal. De Lauren might not learn she'd even left Stanfield.

" 'Tis done!" De Lauren called out to his men, ending the training session. Swords lowered. Spears were stuck into the ground. Anson ran forward and handed de Lauren a wiping cloth. De Lauren passed it over his face, then draped it across his shoulders and made his way over the hard-packed earth to the castle.

Anson followed him to his room. The boy dumped buckets of warm water into the tub by the hearth, then went to the trunk to lay out clothing.

"Desist," de Lauren said. He wanted a quick bath without his squire underfoot. "Leave, Anson. Take my wine flagon and refill it. And take your time about it."

De Lauren had finished bathing and dressing when Anson

returned. At his nod, the boy filled a goblet with wine then set the jug in its usual place on the small table in the chamber.

De Lauren dismissed Anson to polish his armor, then, goblet in hand, fetched writing materials from his trunk and took a seat at his writing table. He knew what he wanted to write, yet held the quill above the parchment, contemplating Katherine.

She was hiding something about her meeting with Brother Ian. De Lauren grunted. Was that who the man partaking of Stanfield's hospitality was? 'Twas time to know for sure. He was going to add another inquiry to Hugh and Victor's list at court. He wanted to know if a man fitting the monk's description was in service to Ranulf.

'Twas still to be determined if Katherine had ties to Ranulf. If so, mayhap she and Ranulf had engineered the tale of the monk to position a man loyal to Ranulf at Stanfield. De Lauren did not believe her tale of venturing so far from Stanfield for larkspur. She'd erred by telling him that, forgotten that he'd escorted her many times on her forays for that flower in the past, and knew they grew in abundance very near Stanfield.

If she'd contrived a tale for the good brother, she should have taken better care to inform the monk of her habits.

De Lauren planned to add a side trip to Hugh and Victor's stay at court. They would find out what they could about the state of Ranulf's alliances, then travel to the small town outside of Guildford, which Brother Ian had claimed as his birthplace, and verify the monk's identity.

If the monk was found to be Ranulf's man, de Lauren would have proof of Katherine's alliance with the Warbrook lord.

De Lauren snapped the quill with that thought.

He set the two quill pieces on the table, then went to his trunk and fetched another nib to write with. He drafted his message to Hugh and Victor, and then left the parchment there.

The soft breeze coming in through the window would dry the ink.

The door was flung open. De Lauren turned from the window, and raised an eyebrow at Stephen, who charged into the room.

"Trouble, Nick," Stephen said. "Katherine went riding this morning. Nesbitt, on watch, remembers seeing her leave. The mare you gave her has been found by our patrol. Alone."

De Lauren led a contingent of his men into the woods. According to Sir Nesbitt, Katherine had ridden south. De Lauren relayed her direction to his men with instructions to "fan out."

He'd examined Katherine's mare quickly, thinking its condition may reveal how it happened to return without Katherine. The horse's coat had been damp with sweat. Clearly, she'd been on the move awhile. Twigs and leaves stuck to the horse's grey coat, and a few nicks marred the skin, probably from low-hanging branches. Otherwise, the animal was unhurt.

He'd been looking for puncture wounds from an arrow or dagger that would indicate an attack. He'd found none, but 'twas still possible Katherine had been set upon, and unseated without injury to the mare. She was an excellent horsewoman, and this animal was swift. 'Twould be difficult indeed to overtake her, and vault from one horse to hers.

Difficult, though not impossible.

In the trees above him, birds twittered. Squirrels scurried out of his horse's swift path. The growth thickened. De Lauren slowed his mount. He could hear his men's shouts, but could no longer see them.

Stephen rode up behind him, and with a nod, they rode deeper into the trees.

"Think you she may have come this far?" Stephen asked, reaching for his water skin.

She'd encountered the monk farther south. De Lauren was heading there. "Aye," he said to Stephen and offered no further explanation.

They rode in silence again, after that. The shadows on the ground lengthened. 'Twould soon be dark. De Lauren slowed the horse to a walk. His men would be returning to Stanfield at dusk where he would meet them. If Katherine had not been found, torches would be lit to continue the search at night.

" 'Tis possible she's been taken," Stephen said quietly. "Or set upon by brigands."

De Lauren did not respond. That thought was burning a hole in his stomach. Katherine in the hands of brigands may be worse than if she were held by an enemy lord. An enemy may seek to bargain for her release. Unlikely a brigand would know who he held, and by the time he learned her identity and that she could be ransomed, she may be so ill-used her captor would fear de Lauren's retaliation and kill her.

"Water up ahead," Stephen said. "The horses need to drink, Nick. Nick?"

After a moment, de Lauren nodded.

They stopped briefly at a stream, then rode on. De Lauren heard a swish, like branches moving. He clutched the hilt of his sword in its scabbard, and yanked hard on the reins, turning the horse in the direction of the sound. Katherine stepped out from behind bushes. De Lauren took his first deep breath in hours.

Clearly, she'd concealed herself, only revealing herself when she identified de Lauren and Stephen. De Lauren took in her appearance. A rent in the front of her pale green gown exposed her to mid thigh. Her skin there was not marked, nor was she hurt anywhere he could see. Her movement was unhampered. Still, he needed confirmation from her.

"Are you hurt?"

She shook her head. "Only my pride, I fear. The mare

unseated me as if I were but on my first ride."

"What happened?" Stephen asked.

A strand of hair escaped from the thick loop at her neck, and fell across her cheek. Katherine pushed it back from her face. She looked to Stephen. "A snake sprang up from beneath the patch of leaves Louisa trod on. She was startled. I was caught unawares and I found myself seated on the ground, watching her flee into the trees. How came you to be here, my lord?"

"Your mare was spotted. By my patrol," de Lauren said. He recalled the horrors he'd imagined had befallen her while he'd been searching, and felt fear burn his stomach again. That he felt such fear for her angered him. His voice harsh, he said, " 'Tis fortunate my guardsman observed your direction when you left Stanfield, otherwise more time would have been spent looking for you. As it was this search cost us most of this day."

She raised her chin. "I would have eventually made my way home. I was headed in that direction, until I heard horses approaching. I secreted myself until I identified you."

"I have not the time nor patience to embark on another expedition such as this one. Henceforth Marcus will escort you whenever you feel a need to leave Stanfield."

Katherine's eyes glittered with anger of her own. "I ask you to recall, my lord, you gave me leave to gather my herbs, alone. The matter of an escort was to be my choice."

Her defiance in refusing escort made him wonder where she rode to that she didn't want him to know about. His anger climbed another level, and with it came hurt that wherever she'd gone, she'd been plotting against him.

"I gave you the choice of an escort before I took you to my bed," he said coldly. "Even now, you may be with child. I will not risk my heir."

Katherine's eyes widened on him a moment. Her hand splayed across her abdomen, then the fingers curled there and she said softly. "A child." She turned away from him, but not before he saw her eyes close tight as if in acute pain.

At the thought of bearing his child? De Lauren's jaw clenched and then another possibility struck him. Was she recalling the recent loss of her daughter? If so, how would she feel about another pregnancy?

"Stephen, I would speak with Katherine alone," de Lauren said. "Ride on. We will join you."

Stephen nodded and turned his horse in the direction they'd come from. De Lauren dismounted and went to stand behind her. "I realize you yet suffer the loss of your daughter," he said. "Another child will not replace her, but 'tis my hope you will take comfort in the children we will have. God willing our sons will grow strong to rule Stanfield and de Lauren holdings."

Katherine faced him. She'd paled and her eyes were huge in her face. "If God is unwilling," she said. "If there are no sons from our union . . . "

She appeared stricken.

" 'Twill be as God decrees," he said softly. "Daughters would not be amiss."

'Twas the truth he gave her. Certainly, he didn't work without the thought of leaving all to his sons, one day, but should God bless them with daughters, he would not be disappointed. Girl-children, mayhap with their mother's wit and smile. Nay, he could not be disappointed with that.

He'd thought his answer would reassure her, instead she paled further. Was there something about the birth she had not told him?

"Is there a reason you suggest we may not have children?" he asked gently. "Was all well with your daughter's birth?"

She drew out a silence, then said, "I can give you no children, my lord." She turned and went to his horse.

She'd spoken in a bleak monotone. Clearly resigned to her

fate, and it shook him. How could she be certain? What had transpired during the birth? He wanted answers, but he'd seen tears in her eyes, before she'd turned from him. She appeared shattered by this admission. For the life of him, he could not press her.

He would learn who attended her during her daughter's birth, and find his answers there.

A child! De Lauren's child. Riding in front of de Lauren on his stallion, Katherine could think of naught else. Night had fallen. Moonlight silvered the trees around them now and lit their path. De Lauren's arms were around her, holding the reins. The horse pranced over a fallen log. She rocked back gently, against de Lauren's chest, and his hold on her tightened.

A child with de Lauren. She'd not considered the possibility of pregnancy until he'd raised it, and then she'd felt a surge of love so strong it stopped her breath. And then the reality of her situation reasserted itself. If she and de Lauren had a child, Michael would never be safe. His own sibling would be his enemy.

Siblings battling for wealth and power was not unheard of. It was whispered that King Henry had killed his elder brother William Rufus to gain the throne of England. Henry then went to war against his brother Robert over Normandy. Robert was defeated and imprisoned.

The thought of her own children becoming enemies turned Katherine's stomach.

If she and de Lauren had no children, would he accept her son as his own? Heart pounding, she'd posed a question to him, "If God is unwilling . . . If there are no sons from our union . . . " He'd thought she referred to bearing him only daughters, and she could risk saying naught more.

She and de Lauren could not have made a child yestereve.

Her timing was wrong. Blessedly wrong, and yet . . . She felt an ache in her chest, near her heart.

There would be no child from that coupling. What about the next? De Lauren wanted an heir. He would not desist visiting her bed until she was with child.

Just as ground pine brought on contractions, it would bring on monthly courses, aborting pregnancy. Katherine shivered with the abhorrent thought. She'd wanted no child of William's, but once she'd learned she was carrying had never considered ridding herself of it.

Ground pine was not an option. She had to ensure she did not become pregnant. She'd given William a wintery reception. Five years of marriage had resulted in but one pregnancy. If she made de Lauren as unwelcome in her bed as she'd made William, would de Lauren, too, distance himself from her?

She was going to have to make it so.

She'd not reached Sir Guy before the mare had unseated her. Two days had passed since that failed attempt, and Katherine had still not found a way to leave Stanfield undetected. Each day that passed left Michael at risk. There was an alternative. One she had no taste for. She frowned. But she could wait no longer. De Lauren commanded she leave Stanfield escorted. Escorted then she would be.

She filled an ale skin from the supply kept in the storehouse, took two metal cups from the kitchens. A stop at her bedchamber, then she headed for the newly erected stables.

Inside the barn, Donny tossed a saddle over de Lauren's horse. The animal snorted, and nudged off the green hat Donny favored, revealing his bald scalp. Donny chuckled. "There now, don't be trampling me hat."

The barn door thudded to a close behind Katherine.

Donny glanced over his shoulder. "Afternoon to you, Lady

Katherine I'll have Louisa saddled for ye, straight away. A right fine day for a ride."

"Lovely day."

"I'll send word to Sir Marcus that you be going riding," Donny said.

"That is not necessary," she said. "I but seek a bit of light exercise and will remain within shouting distance of the patrol guards." A lie, of course.

Donny chewed the inside of his cheek. "Begging your pardon me lady, but it be me head, if Lord de Lauren finds out I saddled Louisa here for you, and let you ride off alone. His lordship's right protective of you."

Katherine did not respond to that.

Donny whistled to the lad raking out the stalls, then sent the boy to inform Sir Marcus of her plans. Donny was one of her people, yet that was no longer enough for him to blindly do her bidding. Since his arrival at Stanfield, de Lauren had become the authority figure, rather than she. She'd commanded her people to swear allegiance to William as well. Still, they had followed her. William had not won her people's trust or loyalty as de Lauren had.

With Donny's help, she mounted and left the stables. Marcus, on his own mount, awaited her by the open gates. Men at arms stood ready to close them should the alert be sounded. Archers watched from the tower. Beyond the curtain wall, a handful of knights rode patrol.

They inclined their heads as Katherine passed them, leading Sir Marcus into the woods. She took him a fair distance from the keep, to a quiet spot where wild flowers sprouted. She could smell their sweet fragrance.

"I should like to stop here for a bit," she said.

Marcus leaped from his horse to the ground and lifted her from her saddle, then went to lean against a tree. His negligent pose was misleading, she knew. His gaze roamed their surroundings.

Katherine knelt amid the flowers, picking randomly. None here were useful to her. She was passing time. A short while later, she pocketed the flowers and gained her feet.

"I have brought refreshment," she said. "Sir Marcus will you join me?"

"I thank you."

Katherine untied the ale skin and the cups from her saddle. She poured for Marcus and for herself. He held his cup, but did not lift it to his mouth. Clearly his good manners would prevail, and he would not drink until she had. She raised the cup to her lips, careful that the liquid did not slosh to the rim and touch her lips.

Marcus downed his ale. Katherine leaned forward to refill his cup.

"No more, for me, my lady. I must keep my wits about me."

To press him further would arouse his suspicion. She stood, and taking her cup with her, again crouched amid the flowers. Marcus turned and started back to his post at the tree. Katherine emptied her ale in a patch of Baby's Breath.

A quarter hour later, Marcus yawned. She glanced over her shoulder at him. He shook his head and rubbed his knuckles into his eyes.

"Lady Katherine . . . "

Marcus slid down the tree trunk, and plopped onto the leafy ground.

"I am ill," he said.

Katherine brushed her palms together to clean the dirt from them, and slowly approached the knight.

"Take heed." Marcus blinked quickly. "I am useless to you." His words were slow and slurred. "Ride hard for the keep, my lady."

His head lolled onto his chest.

"Sir Marcus?" She crouched beside him and shook his shoulder gently. "Sir Marcus?"

She'd added poppy to the ale skin. One cupful of ale, by her count, contained enough poppy to keep him senseless for perhaps two hours. It would have to be long enough.

Katherine eased him onto his back, on the ground, then went to her horse. Her foot in the stirrup, she glanced back at the knight. In his present condition, Sir Marcus was vulnerable. Should he be set upon . . . Katherine shook her head. She had no choice. She mounted and rode to the cabin.

Sir Guy was walking toward the cabin when she rode up. Two rabbits dangled from his hands. He set the rabbits on a rock and lowered her from the horse. "Much time has passed, my lady, since your last visit. I have feared aught has gone amiss."

Katherine quickly brought him up to date. "I fear, Sir Guy, that de Lauren will venture out this way and come upon the cabin and Michael." She told Sir Guy de Lauren was suspicious of her encounter with Brother Ian. "We can take no chance. You must flee."

"Aye, we will move."

"Where to?"

Sir Guy shook his head. "I know naught at the moment."

Katherine paced a small section of grass. Certainly Guy needed time to plan, but she would lose her mind if she did not know where her son was. "We must meet again, after you have relocated. I must know where you have secreted my son."

"Aye," he said. He rubbed his square jaw. "Since we cannot make a definitive date to do so, I will return to this location one week hence and every Tuesday thereafter. I will remain here until sunset."

"I will come to you when I can," Katherine said. "I would see my son, then you'd best be away."

Katherine held her child, cooing and speaking to him while Middy and the nursemaid collected their belongings, then reluctantly relinquished her child to their care, again.

From atop her horse, she watched Sir Guy, the women, and her son ride into the forest. When they were no longer in view, she tugged the reins to turn her animal about for the return trip to where she'd left Sir Marcus. A twig snapped. Katherine tensed, and glanced behind her. The mare snuffled and tossed her head, anxious to be away, Katherine believed, but she held the reins taut, and the horse in place. A fox darted out from the trees, and leaped over a fallen log, rustling a patch of leaves in its path. Otherwise, all was silent. She was alone, and exhaled deeply.

"Come, Louisa. The hour grows late. Let us ride with all haste."

Marcus was as she'd left him, sprawled on the leafy ground. Faith, she was grateful that no ill had befallen him. She knelt beside him, and shook his shoulders.

"Sir Marcus? Sir Marcus?"

The knight's eyelids fluttered, then opened. His bright green gaze was glazed for an instant then cleared, and he looked up into Katherine's eyes. Katherine smiled. "You have slept the afternoon away, sir. I trust you are refreshed."

Marcus bolted to his feet, knocking Katherine down. He moved his head from side to side wildly, and drew his sword.

"We are alone, Sir Marcus," Katherine said softly. "Be at ease. We are alone."

After a moment, the tension left the knight's body. He sheathed his sword. He lowered one hand to her, and rubbed his abdomen with the other.

"Does your stomach pain you?" Katherine asked.

"Aye."

Upset stomach was a side effect of poppy. "I will prepare a treatment of lettuce when we return to Stanfield. Are you fit to ride?"

Marcus stretched out his arm, and stood with his palm flat against the tree trunk. "Ale has never affected me adversely." He shook his head. "I have no excuse, my lady."

She did not want him blaming the ale for his condition. "It would appear you are overset by a stomach ailment. I, too, drank ale, as you will recall, yet I am fine."

"I left you unprotected. Had we been attacked . . . "

"Naught occurred. We will say no more of it."

Marcus shook his head. "Lord de Lauren—"

"Need not know you took ill. You will recover and we will continue as we have. You cannot be held accountable for illness."

Dangerous to have drugged him, of course. But she'd had no choice. She could not be certain Marcus would keep this incident from de Lauren. Marcus' code of honor and fierce loyalty to de Lauren might compel him to tell this tale. If he did . . . perspiration broke out on her spine. Fear sweat. De Lauren would not be manipulated, as Marcus had been.

She would press the matter no further with Sir Marcus and risk arousing his suspicion.

De Lauren learned which women performed midwifery from Haldrake. The list was not long, just four women and if complications arose, Katherine was summoned. Who, though, would have been called, if complications had arisen during Katherine's birth? De Lauren rubbed a hand down his face, and entered the kitchens. Livvy, the cook, also acted as midwife, and was the first name on his list. He hadn't wanted to call attention to his inquiries by sending for her to come to him in the solar. For that same reason, he hadn't asked Haldrake to find out this information. If possible, de Lauren didn't want to arouse speculation about Katherine's delivery and hurt her further. So, he sought Livvy out, himself.

She sat on a stool, stirring a steaming pot that hung above the flames in the hearth, and rocking a cradle with her foot. Whatever was in the pot smelled strongly of onion.

A gangly lad sat on a stool, slurping soup from a trencher. Two young girls sliced vegetables at a corner table.

De Lauren reached Livvy. Her hand stopped in mid stir. She lowered her foot from the cradle and stood to bow to de Lauren. "My lord?"

"The evening you spoke of the birth of your granddaughter," de Lauren said. "you prepared a dessert that Lady Katherine particularly enjoyed." De Lauren could not recall what had been served that night, but the excuse to seek Livvy out would serve.

Livvy's moon face beamed. "Aye, my lord, that would be raspberry pie."

De Lauren nodded. "I believe my lady remarked that her taste for it has only recently returned," de Lauren lied.

"She hadn't a want for much of anything in the last months before her babe was born." Livvy made the sign of the cross. "Poor wee thing."

"Were you with Lady Katherine, during her time?"

Livvy shook her head. "I surely would have been. I'd done anything I could to help me lady, but Middy attended her." Livvy dabbed at her eyes with her apron.

Middy. Katherine's old nursemaid. He'd forgotten about her. Katherine held great affection for the old woman, as he recalled. Yet, he hadn't seen her since his arrival at Stanfield. 'Twas possible she'd perished in Ranulf's attack.

"I wish that dessert served following today's last meal," de Lauren said.

Livvy straightened her shoulders. "O' course, me lord."

De Lauren nodded. He dispatched Anson to find Haldrake and bring him to the solar, along with the accountings of Stanfield's dead since Ranulf's attack. De Lauren needed look no further back than the attack since the old woman had been alive to attend Katherine's delivery on that day.

Haldrake arrived within moments of de Lauren's request, toting a cumbersome tome.

"How may I be of service, my lord?" Haldrake said.

De Lauren pointed to the table. Haldrake set bound papers beside an inkwell. Anson left, closing the door behind him.

"Do you know my lady's former nursemaid?"

"Middy, aye," Haldrake said.

"Consult your records. I would know if she perished in Ranulf's attack."

Haldrake's thick silver brows drew together as he opened the tome. "I don't recall entering her name here, my lord."

Haldrake passed his finger beneath each entry. Finally, he'd reached the last name on the last page, and shook his head. "Her name is not here, but nor is she at Stanfield?"

'Twas possible not all people were accounted for after an attack. Had Middy been a noble lady, de Lauren would have considered that Ranulf had taken her as a hostage to be used when he saw fit. De Lauren did not believe Katherine's attachment to the old woman, however, even if Ranulf knew of it, would move him to take her with him. He would know the old woman would not be a means to force Katherine to give him Stanfield, the prize he sought. 'Twas possible the woman escaped and had yet to return to Stanfield.

Until he found proof of it otherwise, de Lauren would presume that the woman lived.

"Make inquiries, Haldrake, ask if anyone recalls seeing Middy on the day of the attack. Do so with utmost discretion. My lady holds great affection for her. I would not see Katherine upset by what we may learn of the old woman's fate."

Haldrake bowed and left the solar. De Lauren turned to the window. The time might come when he would have to go to Katherine to get the answers he sought. He would exhaust every other attempt first.

De Lauren was still in the solar when Haldrake returned.

"My lord," Haldrake said. "I have but one report to make and I fear it is inconclusive. Camilla, one of the laundresses, claims to have seen Middy at the time of the attack. Camilla recalls this because she'd been looking for a place to hide, and saw Middy go into the storage room. Camilla called out to the old woman, then followed. The storage room, however, was empty. Camilla maintains that Middy vanished. There is only one exit from that room, my lord. Camilla may have imagined the event, in her upset."

Nay, the laundress had not imagined seeing Middy, de Lauren knew. There was not but one exit from the storage room. He'd led his men into the keep from the passages below through a concealed door in that room. Clearly, the old woman knew about that door.

"One other thing, my lord." Haldrake cleared his throat. De Lauren thought the old man appeared embarrassed. "Camilla claims Middy did not enter the storage room alone. She claims Middy was accompanied by Sir Guy du Monde."

CHAPTER TWELVE

The laundress claimed to have seen Sir Guy enter the storage room with old Middy. De Lauren was still contemplating that information the next day. He left the table in the solar, where he'd been reviewing his plans for increasing his armies as the king commanded, and strolled to the window.

Dusk was a while away, yet the day had darkened. Clouds scudded across the sky. 'Twould rain, and soon.

When Sir Guy was not found among Stanfield's living or dead, de Lauren believed the knight had perished in Norris' attack at Fanshawe, which had killed Norris himself. Apparently not.

If not for the fact that the laundress claimed Middy and Sir Guy had vanished from inside the storage room, which accessed the hidden passages below the keep, de Lauren may very well have dismissed her tale. He'd gone out of his way to speak with Guy during his betrothal to Katherine. He'd wanted to form his own assessment of the knight who held the powerful position of commander of Stanfield's guard. De Lauren had come to respect Guy both as a commander and as a man. Unthinkable that he would leave Stanfield, and Katherine, and flee to safety.

Yet, Guy had been seen entering the storage room with the old woman. So, if he was not abandoning his post, could he have been acting under orders? 'Twould take an order, de Lauren believed, for the knight to leave Stanfield while under attack. With Norris dead, only Katherine had the authority to command Guy. Had she ordered him to escort the old woman to safety?

If he'd safeguarded Middy, weeks had passed since the attack. Guy would surely have learned Ranulf was no longer at Stanfield. Since he and Middy had not returned, 'twas possible they were dead.

De Lauren's patrol, though, had covered miles of ground, and repeatedly, since that first ride to Stanfield. His men had come upon a few of Stanfield's people, in hiding, and returned them to the keep. But they'd discovered only one body off Stanfield ground; the messenger Katherine had dispatched to De Lauren Keep.

Ranulf would certainly not have taken time to bury Guy and the old woman, had he met up with them. If these two people were not dead, then where were they?

A knock on the door drew his attention. That would be Katherine and Haldrake. They'd set this time to review their progress on restoring Stanfield.

"Enter," de Lauren called out.

Anson opened the door, then stepped back from it for Katherine to enter. Haldrake followed her into the room.

An hour later Haldrake lowered the sheets of parchment he held.

"The combined efforts of your men, my lord," Haldrake said, "and Stanfield's remaining hunters, have done much to replenish what was lost in the attack. Stanfield will be well-housed for the upcoming winter."

Lightning streaked across the sky. Rain pelted the stone. De Lauren heard children's laughter in the hall, and smiled briefly to himself. Aye, Stanfield was slowly but surely being set to rights.

"I will, of course, keep you apprised, my lord, my lady," Haldrake said.

De Lauren nodded. "I have naught else, Haldrake." De Lauren turned to his lady. "Katherine?" he asked.

She shook her head.

Haldrake bowed and left the solar. Katherine glanced up at de Lauren from her seat beside him. Her hands were clasped in the lap of a blue-green gown. "I would thank you for all you have done for my people, my lord," she said.

"My people also, my lady. To fully restore Stanfield, however, we need to replenish the population. My knights are a temporary solution, fulfilling roles as farmers and general laborers. Their skills do not excel in those areas, nor would I have them become proficient in them. I have given thought to inviting people from de Lauren Keep to relocate to Stanfield. As an inducement, I would offer larger parcels of land than are currently being worked at de Lauren. I will not insist, but I believe the promise of increased income from larger portions of land will attract takers. What think you?"

" 'Tis a sound notion," Katherine said.

She'd sounded wistful, he thought, as if naught would come to pass. Did she doubt he meant what he said? The possibility annoyed him.

" 'Tis my intent to build a town," de Lauren said with some force. " 'Twill have a trade center. Such is sorely lacking in our part of this country, leaving us to send out our own to restock or to do without until the traveling merchants return."

Katherine leaned forward in her chair. "I recall your plans for such—on the land betwixt our two holdings. There is more than ample land there for a town." She was silent for a moment, then said, in that same wistful tone he'd heard earlier. "To have a trade center. Neighboring keeps would benefit, as well. Such a town would be most welcome." She raised one blonde brow and smiled. "I wonder, my lord, if the idea for a town took hold of you the day de Lauren's sugar supply was late in arriving and cook served unsweetened biscuits."

De Lauren grinned. "They were naught more than hard bread."

She laughed. "With your sweet-tooth, my lord, 'tis a wonder your teeth are sound."

"Mayhap you would care to sample the strength of my bite!"

He snatched her hand from her lap, brought it to his lips, and kissed her palm. He met her gaze. Her eyes were wide on him. Her lips slightly parted. He lowered her hand from his mouth and moved toward her.

Lightning lit the room for an instant. A crack of thunder followed.

A shout of "Fire! Fire!" came from the hall.

De Lauren released her. He rubbed a hand down his face and left the solar.

Lightning had struck a barn. Katherine stood beneath the overhang that led into the castle, her arms around her to guard against the chill in the air. With the help of the driving rain, de Lauren and many other men had extinguished the fire quickly. Smoke curled into the air from the barn. Grooms led the now homeless horses to another barn.

How could she have spoken aloud her thoughts of the day de Lauren had tasted the unsweetened biscuits? What had she been thinking in the solar earlier? She hadn't been thinking. When he'd moved toward her, she should have backed off. Instead, she'd leaned into him. Had the fire not sparked, would she have recalled that she and de Lauren must have a marriage in name only?

Her stomach felt coiled tight as rope. He'd hurt her after making love, by leaving her on their discarded garments, yet that incident had not killed her love for him. Better if it had.

"Beggin' yer pardon, Lady Katherine? A word if ye please?"

She'd not heard Timothy, the shepherd approach. He stood beside her now, crushing the brim of his hat with his blunt fingers.

"Certainly," Katherine said.

"I've come to ask yer leave to marry Frances. She's Harold the candle maker's widow."

Such a request was normally made to the lord once a month, when he held court. William had heard all disputes and proposals, after Father died, but William's fees for granting his permission made Stanfield's sessions very brief. Her people could ill-afford to pay half the crops that remained after they'd given their due to their lord, or to part with their only piglet. She'd argued with him over that, but to no avail. He would have seen their people with no income from their efforts at Stanfield, reducing them to slave labor.

She'd put the word about through Haldrake that the people go to her with their concerns. Now she was married to de Lauren. For as long as that marriage was in effect, he was Stanfield's lord, and such decisions fell to him. That chafed, giving up another measure of her responsibility to her people. But unlike William, she knew de Lauren would do right.

"Does Frances also seek this marriage?" Katherine asked Timothy.

"Aye, lady."

"I will speak with her on the morrow," Katherine said. As was her practice, she would confirm that Frances did indeed want this marriage. Timothy nodded and bowed, and then she stood alone again.

De Lauren and the other men were now crossing the muddy courtyard back to the castle. Last meal would commence soon. The entertainers would perform after. And after that . . .

A few nights ago, she'd wished the night over, so morning would bring with it the chance to see Sir Guy. Now, she would have the evening go on and on. Her head throbbed at the prospect of retiring for the night. She was very much afraid de Lauren would seek to finish what they'd started in the solar.

He did not, though. Dawn lit the sky, and de Lauren had not come to her. Katherine tossed off the coverlet, grateful to see the sun. She washed and dressed and broke her fast, then set out to speak with Frances, the woman Timothy the shepherd wished to take to wife. After last night's rain, the scents of grass and mud and the trio of pigs, now crossing the courtyard with Katherine, filled the air. Good scents. Scents of life.

"Are you for the stables, my lady?" Sir Marcus said as he fell into step beside her.

The forest would be ripe with nature's own scents, Katherine thought with a smile. A ride would have to wait. "Not at this moment, sir," Katherine said.

They skirted a puddle. Jane approached them at a run and stepped into their path, so close that Marcus rocked back on his heels to avoid colliding with her. Jane fell to her knees at Katherine's feet and raised her hands in supplication.

"The bishop, he's got me babe."

Tears coursed down Jane's cheeks. Her body shook with the force of her crying.

"What?" Katherine asked.

"He means to find out if the devil had a hand in the birthing. Please, lady, I beg you, tell him that ain't what happened."

"The bishop has the child now?"

"Aye, he be at my hut." Jane clutched the hem of Katherine's yellow gown. "Please lady, please tell him."

Katherine knew some of the methods used by the church. Trials were conducted, trials that were often impossible to pass. An accused may be tied hand and foot and placed inside a sack weighted down with rocks, then flung into the lake. If the individual floated to the top, alive, then he was judged not guilty of a crime against God. If he did not surface, then the church would deem God's justice had been served. Despite the sun on her back, she shivered.

Katherine stepped away from the sobbing Jane, lifted her skirts, and headed for the hut at a run. She heard Marcus call out to her. She ignored him, leaving him to follow or not.

A crowd had gathered on the road in front of the hut. She could not see beyond the people who stood elbow to elbow, but she heard a man's choked voice say, "My lord bishop, please, is there not another way?"

Katherine stepped into the crowd. Her people cleared a path for her, and she saw the man who'd spoken was Basil, Jane's husband. Tears glistened on his cheeks. Jane ran out from behind Katherine to Basil.

The bishop stood on the muddy path, in direct sunlight. With the sun's rays on him, and in his pristine robes, he appeared an angel. In her people's faces she saw fear and awe, and wondered if they thought the same of him.

Katherine took a place across from the bishop. "Your Grace, is aught amiss here?"

"That is what we will soon determine, my lady," Bishop Whittaker said. "We will learn the truth of this child's birth."

Katherine licked her lips. "The truth, Bishop, is that this child came into this world by God's grace, and no other."

"We shall learn that for certain. A trial by fire will determine this."

A low fire burned in a pit encircled by stones. One end of a branch stuck out from the flames. Jane's babe lay on a coverlet on a small table. The bishop looked into Katherine's eyes for a moment, then turned to the fire and removed the stick. Goose bumps sprang on Katherine's arms.

"Has your investigation into this birth revealed something to lead you to this course?" she asked.

The bishop's lips thinned. His lids drooped. "I have learned, my lady, that your services are sought when it is believed a mother and child will not survive a birth. I have also learned all of the women you have attended have lived and that their babes have lived. Not one fatality. Over a course of years. An impressive accounting, to be sure." The bishop's gaze grew more intent on her. "I will test each of the children you have delivered to make sure "tis God's hand at work here."

Gasps and cries came from the crowd. Katherine had walked by several women whom she'd attended during the delivery of their children. "Twas because of her the children would be tested. The bishop clearly had naught the evidence to support a charge against a noblewoman of her high rank, so he would use the children to obtain the evidence he needed against her. A chilling thought, but for the moment, her fear was for the little ones. Her mouth dried. "Your Grace, these children are innocent."

"We shall see."

"If there is to be such a trial," Katherine said, "Lord de Lauren must be present."

"De Lauren's law does not stand before the law of God!" The bishop shouted. "Though de Lauren would deem otherwise, he is not above God. I represent God. My will prevails, not de Lauren's."

She had not meant to suggest that de Lauren's law would supersede God's. Indeed, de Lauren would have no choice but to allow this trial to take place. Were he to forbid it, he would be defying his church. "Twas the bishop's right to hold this trial. Even if he had naught to support doing so.

The bishop turned to Basil. "Bare the child's feet for God's fire. If the babe does not cry out, then we will know it feels no pain from God's touch. If it does, then indeed " 'tis the devil in her burning at the hand of God."

Katherine's heart was racing. Of course, the babe would cry out in pain, and in so doing would be condemned. This child, and others.

"Test me," Katherine said.

The bishop turned to her.

" 'Tis my practices that are suspect. My innocence of wrongdoing will absolve the children I have helped birth. Test me." The bishop would come to her once all of the children failed the trials he would subject them to. Testing her first would spare them. Provided she did not fail. Her failure would condemn them all.

The bishop nodded. His gaze fixed on her. Cold perspiration dampened her skin at the hatred she saw in his eyes. "Hold out your right hand to God, my lady."

She would not cry out. *She would not cry out.*

The bishop brought the flame under her palm, low enough that the fire did not touch her skin. She felt the heat, though, and began to tremble. He raised the stick. Fire licked her skin. She bit the inside of her cheek to contain her scream, and curled the fingers of her other hand so her nails dug into her palms. She would not cry out. She smelled her own flesh burning, and tasted bile. Stars popped in front of her eyes.

She heard footsteps. Moving at a run. A man's shout. The stick was knocked away.

"Marcus! Water!"

'Twas de Lauren. She felt his arm slide around her, strong and sure, drawing her tight against his chest. It felt so good that he was here. She pressed her cheek against his shoulder, burrowing into him.

She knew the flame was no longer on her skin. She could see the stick laying in the dirt. But her hand burned as if it were still afire, and strangely she shivered with cold.

De Lauren's hold on her tightened. He cupped her face in one hand and turned her head so she looked up at him. His eyes seemed to bore into hers.

"Marcus!" De Lauren shouted.

Marcus plopped a bucket at her feet. De Lauren's hand left her face. He crouched over the bucket, pulling her down with him, and plunged her arm to the elbow into the water. Instead of cooling, she felt as if needles stung her.

De Lauren's gaze narrowed on Bishop Whittaker. "Marcus, confine the bishop to his chambers until further notice. Post a guard at the door."

"In your arrogance you set yourself above me, de Lauren. Above God."

Teeth gritted, de Lauren said softly, "Get the bishop from my sight."

Marcus led Bishop Whittaker from the hut. Two young knights shouldered their way through the crowd to offer assistance to de Lauren. "Send everyone on their way," de Lauren said.

A few moments later they were alone outside Jane's hut. Katherine heard the thwack of a woodchopper's ax. The sun was on her back, but she could not get warm.

"You should have come for me, at once," de Lauren said, his tone harsh. His hand remained clamped on her elbow, beneath the water. "Had Marcus not overheard your conversation with Jane, I would not have known what you were about."

"No time," Katherine said. Her teeth chattered. "Had I arrived later, 'twould have been too late for the babe. And in truth, my lord, I would have put you in an untenable position. The bishop was within his rights with this trial. There was naught you could have done."

"I can tell you I would not have permitted him to burn you."

" 'Twas at my suggestion I was tested." She quickly explained the bishop's intention to subject the children she'd helped deliver to trials by fire. "Had you intervened you would have set yourself against the church, and still my practices would remain in doubt."

"Katherine—"

"My lord, if you would take me to task further for this day's event, mayhap you would do so when I can fully appreciate what you have to say. I am having difficulty concentrating on your words just now."

De Lauren exhaled deeply and lifted her hand from the water to peer down at it. Her palm and fingers were blistered red and black. Bits of flesh, from a layer of skin that no longer existed, clung to what remained. Her hand would never be as it had been. She felt her stomach clench over that, but worse, was there nerve damage? She would lose some or all of the use of her hand, if there was. She flexed her fingers to gauge their response. She sucked in her breath at the pain, but her fingers did move.

"How can we treat this best?" de Lauren said, his voice tight.

"First it must be cleansed with soap, and after I have a salve among my medicinals."

"Anson can bring what we need."

" 'Twould be faster were I to retrieve these items myself."

De Lauren's horse was tethered to a tree by the roadside. He lifted her into the saddle, then swung up behind her and spurred his horse to a swift pace across the courtyard. She shivered. De Lauren's arms tightened around her. He held her against his chest, warming her.

They dismounted and moments later entered her bedchamber.

"Where?" de Lauren asked.

She believed he asked after her supplies. "In the satchel, in my trunk."

De Lauren joined her at her bedside table. Katherine pushed the unlit tapers to the table's edge, then retrieved the soap and a small wooden bowl containing the salve from the bag de Lauren held. She set the items on the shiny wood surface of the table.

De Lauren filled her basin with water and returned to the table with it. Katherine dipped the soap into the water. 'Twas her right hand that needed tending. She was awkward using her left. She would have called for Elspeth, but de Lauren took the soap from her. His touch was gentle, yet it felt as if sand were being rubbed into her skin. Her breathing quickened. Sweat beaded on de Lauren's forehead, and his hand stilled.

She knew what it was to cause pain in the name of healing, and had never been able to detach herself from another's hurt. Clearly, 'twas the same for de Lauren. "Pray continue, my lord," she said. " 'Tis necessary."

De Lauren's fingers flexed around the soap, then stilled again. He rubbed a hand down his face and finished the task.

He took the bowl and removed the lid. Dipping two fingers into the salve, he applied the balm to her hand.

"I can summon Elspeth to apply a covering," Katherine said.

But de Lauren had already taken a strip of cloth from among Katherine's supplies.

A few moments later, he glanced up from his work. "Is the wrapping too secure?"

She shook her head. " 'Tis as it should be."

De Lauren carefully released her hand. "I will send your maid to you, now."

"Nicholas, thank you."

De Lauren nodded in response, then left the room.

She did not see de Lauren again until last meal. He sliced portions of pheasant for her. They spoke little and Katherine left immediately after for her chamber.

With Elspeth's help, Katherine bathed then donned a night rail and made for her bed. A dose of poppy would not have been amiss, but the flower muddled the mind. Katherine cared naught for the effect. She gazed out the window at the dark sky . . .

A creak woke her. The room was bathed in soft moonlight. Light reflected off her bathwater in the tub by the unlit hearth. The door between her room and de Lauren's swung slowly inward. De Lauren stood in shadow.

Katherine sat up. "My lord?"

" 'Twas not my intent to wake you," de Lauren said softly. "Find your sleep, Katherine."

He lingered in the doorway for a moment, then left the room.

Had she taken the poppy, Katherine would have considered that she'd imagined de Lauren in her room last night. But she hadn't. If 'twas not his intent to wake her, then why had he entered her chamber?

The question became less pressing as she sat on the edge of her bed and spread salve over the burn. Pain had her perspiring by the time she'd finished. She'd scraped the bottom of the bowl, and would need more today. She didn't relish a trip into the woods, just now, but there was no help for it.

Katherine had Louisa saddled. Marcus met her at the front gates. De Lauren rode up to them and reined in beside Sir Marcus.

"What are you about?" he asked.

"I used up the last of the salve," she said.

"Instruct Anson. He will gather what you need to make more."

"I would prefer to go myself, my lord."

De Lauren frowned. "As you wish then. I will escort you."

Marcus nodded and left them.

"Lead on," de Lauren said.

She rode out through the gates, and turned east, riding onto Stanfield land that was not enclosed by the curtain wall. The moss she needed grew in a distant part of the forest accessible from the land between Stanfield and de Lauren Keeps.

De Lauren fell in by her side. Katherine tucked her injured hand tight to her body, to reduce the jostling. De Lauren peered at her and reduced their pace.

They reached the stretch of land where de Lauren had proposed his town. She tugged on the horse's reins, and the mare came to a stop.

De Lauren glanced over at her and drew his mount to a stop as well.

Katherine scanned the flat, overgrown terrain that joined their lands. "This is where you propose to build your town." Without waiting for his acknowledgment, she went on. "A row of structures offering goods for sale would be built in the center of this parcel of land with routes from the four points leading to it. A carpentry could be situated by that cluster of oak trees. Clear the others east of us, and place a livery there." She squinted in the sunlight at the stream. "A church could be built by that stream."

She realized she'd repeated plans he'd shared with her when he'd first made them five years earlier.

She could see the town laid out as he'd described it, and wanted it for her people. She shook her head at the futility of that desire.

"I've had my fill of the church, of late," de Lauren said.

She glanced at him. His eyes were narrowed on the stream and his lips had tightened. How much did Bishop Whittaker have to do with de Lauren's "fill of the church," she wondered?

"I do not recall Bishop Whittaker being part of your

household, five years ago," she asked softly. "How did he come to be at de Lauren Keep?"

She thought he would not answer. A silence ensued then he said, "In truth, I know not how. 'Twas sometime after I left to fulfill my obligation to the king."

The obligation was an annual one for all of the king's vassals. In peacetime, vassals had the option to pay scutage in lieu of service. De Lauren had been notified to report to the king a few days after their marriage would have taken place, five years ago, but had intended to pay the fine rather than leave her, she remembered. Then there'd been no wedding.

"When I returned from Henry's service," de Lauren said, "the bishop was in residence, and Mother had begun to withdraw."

Katherine could feel de Lauren's pain. "I am sorry, my lord."

De Lauren's hands clenched into fists. "I have wondered what role the bishop played in bringing her malaise about."

"You believe he caused her to go into a decline?"

"Aye." De Lauren grunted. "Whittaker's interest in my lady mother has naught to do with God. 'Tis power he seeks. That is why he attached himself to my house. Years ago, he attempted to use the church to gain control over de Lauren Keep. I did not allow that."

The church was powerful, with men in high positions who fed on the power of their rank. She'd not had firsthand experience with such men. Before now.

"He uses Mother to strike out against me," de Lauren said. "His hold on her is all-consuming. And because of that, I cannot oust him from her life. I must await the day when Mother will see him for what he is and banish him from our midst, herself. The bishop knows his hold on her keeps me tethered." De Lauren faced Katherine. "Did I not fear Mother's grief would be such that she would follow him into the grave, bishop or not, I would have slain him where he stood for his deed yesterday."

His voice was fierce. The muscles in his face pulled taut. She believed he would have done as he said, though not to avenge her. *There are those who would seek to bring me to my knees through you. Be forewarned any such attempt would fail.* De Lauren's words had left an indelible impression on her memory. He'd made his feelings for her clear. Nay, he'd not avenge her, but she knew he would consider an assault to his lady to be an assault to the house of de Lauren. De Lauren would avenge such an attack.

De Lauren rubbed both hands down his face. "I would not sour the day further with talk of Whittaker."

Katherine blinked. Aye, she, too, wanted no more talk of the bishop. She would have liked to forget this talk about him, but could not. According to what she'd just heard from de Lauren and her own observation of the bishop, she believed Whittaker had targeted her to hurt de Lauren. He'd used her people mercilessly yesterday. If given the opportunity, she believed he would again. She was going to have to find a way to protect her people from him.

"Lead on," de Lauren said.

Katherine clucked her tongue at the mare and tapped her heels lightly against its flanks. They rode on for a bit then she said. "We must turn north."

De Lauren did not answer, but drew on the reins and the horse changed direction, into the woods. The branches overhead grew thick here, shading the ground from full sunlight. The forest floor was muddy in places from the recent heavy rains, and the horses kicked up clumps of earth.

Eventually, they came to the clearing she sought. Sun lit the small area. Wild flowers in yellow and white grew in clusters. A stream flowed over rocks and plants.

De Lauren secured his horse to a tree by the stream. The

animal lowered its head to drink. De Lauren did the same with her mount, then lowered her from the saddle.

The moss she sought to make the salve grew by the wet bank. She crouched in the mud with a bowl and a wooden scoop. De Lauren crouched beside her and took the scoop from her, filling the bowl quickly. He left both on the ground, then gained his feet and stood facing the flowing water. A log bobbed above the shallow ripples.

Katherine covered the bowl with its lid, retrieved it and the scoop, and regained her feet. Turning away from de Lauren, she placed the items in the open satchel tied to Louisa's saddle. The horse shifted its feet, and bumped her injured hand. Katherine gasped. She closed her eyes briefly. When she opened them, de Lauren's gaze was on hers. The raw pain in his eyes stopped her breath.

"I cannot stand that you are hurt," he said in a harsh whisper. "The sight of your hand burning will remain with me until I breathe my last."

"I am fine," she said.

"It should not have happened," he said quietly. "You should not have been hurt. This battle was not yours, Kate."

His voice was low and harsh with anger. She could see the muscles in his shoulders bunched tight beneath his green tunic.

Katherine rose to stand beside him, studying his profile. He felt responsible, but 'twas not his fault. "It is over, and the one to be held accountable this day is Bishop Whittaker. I believe your timely arrival saved me from worse," she said.

She'd thought to reassure him, but a shudder went through him.

She reached out and touched his cheek. He grasped her hand in both of his, closed his eyes, and pressed it to his lips.

Katherine heard her heart beating. He opened his eyes. She stared into them. Was there more than guilt there? Tears sprang to her eyes with that hope. She should lower her gaze so he wouldn't see them, but couldn't take her eyes from his, and then it was too late. She felt a tear on her cheek.

He lowered her hand from his lips, and held it tight in one of his. "Do not weep, Kate," he said. He kissed her wet cheek and her chin. "Do not weep." He kissed her lips lightly. His arm slid around her, and mindful of her injured hand between their bodies, slowly drew her to him.

"Nicholas . . ."

He brought his mouth down on hers. She pressed against him. He deepened the kiss, but then drew back. Holding her within the circle of his arms, he said, "Our location is not secure. I will take no chance that we are caught unawares."

No doubt he recalled their last embrace in the king's forest. They were in no danger from the one who'd harmed de Lauren then, but she leaped at the excuse to leave. She wanted this, wanted him and all they would have together, so much, but she could have all or naught. If she misread him . . . Her insides seemed to shrivel with that fear. She had to be sure she'd not seen something in his eyes, felt something in his touch that had not been there.

But if he could love her again . . .

CHAPTER THIRTEEN

De Lauren lifted Katherine onto her mare's back, then mounted his own horse. With the moss she needed to make the healing salve tucked in a bag tied to her saddle, he led her through the forest back to Stanfield.

The growth was dense here, forcing them to ride single file. She was less than half a length behind him, staying close. He could hear the clip-clop of her horse's hooves, yet he glanced over his shoulder, reassuring himself that she was indeed behind him.

She sat erect in the saddle, but she was cradling her injured hand against her waist. Her pain felt like a fist to his gut. Her tears earlier had all but undone him.

He'd been crazed when he'd come upon her with the bishop, yesterday. He could not close his eyes since without seeing her hand in flames. Yet the burning had not been the worst. Had she cried out, the bishop would have accepted that as proof of her guilt, and condemned her as a heretic. Even the king would not be able to intervene. Her life would have been forfeit.

The danger had passed, yet de Lauren broke out in a cold sweat. His hands tightened on the reins, drawing the horse to a stop.

"My lord, is aught amiss?" Katherine asked.

De Lauren released a shaky breath. Without responding, he nudged the horse forward.

★ ★ ★ ★ ★

"Nick, are you listening?"

De Lauren glanced at his brother, seated beside him at the lord's table. Last meal and the entertainment following it had ended. His men now lingered over ale and wine. One thumped a mug against the tabletop and bellowed for a refill from a saucy wench who held a jug above her head, until, with a laugh, the knight yanked her into his lap.

In truth, de Lauren had heard naught Stephen said for several moments now. Not since Katherine left the hall. She'd gone into the kitchen with the cook. And not returned.

De Lauren's shoulders tightened. She was in the kitchen. His unease had no bounds, but as he thought that, he left the table and without a word to Stephen, went in search of her.

De Lauren pushed the kitchen door open. It thudded against the wall, startling a shriek from a skinny girl scrubbing a pot. The cook Katherine had left the hall with dropped a tray. Strawberry tarts plopped onto the floor. De Lauren scanned the room. Only the girl and the cook were inside.

De Lauren faced the cook. "Where is Lady Katherine?"

The cook's eyes widened. "She went out the back way, me lord." Her words came out in a rush as she pointed to the door exiting out to the courtyard. "Didn't tell me where she—"

De Lauren did not hear the last. He was in the courtyard. In the light of the full moon, he saw two men on watch in the tower. Two women strolled over the grounds in the direction of the tenant huts. Katherine was not one of them. Since the bishop had harmed her yesterday, de Lauren had made a practice of knowing her whereabouts at all times. He did not know where she was now and a chill coursed through him. He picked up his pace.

Why in hell did she leave the castle? Where would she have to go at this hour?

Sir Jerley approached from the meadow, and strolled toward the knight's quarters.

"Jerley," de Lauren called out.

The man turned and faced de Lauren. "Aye, my lord?"

"Have you seen Lady Katherine in recent moments?"

"Aye. She was behind the barn. I walked by her." Jerley said.

The air had grown chill but 'twas a bright, clear night. Katherine had left the castle without her cloak and, patting her arms to ward off the chill, now strolled by trees lined up like sentinels. She breathed deep, inhaling the crisp air.

There was no sound coming from the barn. Mayhap, the animals were at rest, she thought with a smile. She should rest as well, but she felt no desire for sleep. Those moments in the woods with de Lauren earlier replayed in her mind. For the first time since her marriage to him she felt a chance to have him remain her husband and to have her son, too.

She stopped on the moist grass and gazed up at the stars. She did not consider herself fanciful, but if she could have one wish . . .

She heard quick steps behind her and turned. De Lauren trampled a patch of weeds and came to a stop in front of her.

She smiled, about to offer a greeting. The expression on his face stopped her.

"I've spoken with you before about your habit of venturing off unescorted," de Lauren said, his voice tight.

Katherine blinked. His face and shoulders were tensed. Clearly, he was angry. Because she'd gone for a walk? "I have not 'ventured off', my lord," she said. "I am merely strolling in the courtyard, as you can see."

He went on as if she'd not spoken. "Since you cannot be trusted to adhere to this rule, Marcus will trail you while within Stanfield as well as without."

His command stunned her. "Surely, you cannot mean this . . . "

"I am not in the habit of saying things I do not mean."

He would have her guarded as if she were a prisoner. That he would do this . . . Obviously, she had misinterpreted him in the woods earlier. She wrapped her arms around herself as tight as she could, holding in a terrible sadness. She would not let him see how he'd devastated her. She walked away from him, deeper into the meadow.

"Do you defy me?" he asked. "You will return with me now to the castle."

"I have done naught to warrant such treatment," she said. The truth of that sparked her own anger. She met his gaze. "And I will not have it."

"You will not have it?" De Lauren closed the distance between them and gripped her shoulders. His voice low and harsh, he said, "You most certainly will have it, my lady. Marcus will follow you like a worshipful pup from morn to eve and then he will escort you to your chamber where you will remain for the night."

"My chamber?" She lifted her chin. "Why not the dungeon, my lord? I believe Stanfield's are quite secure."

"You think I mean to imprison you?" He gave her a little shake. "Do you not comprehend that had you cried out during the bishop's torture, you would shortly be on your way to the king's tower to await execution?" De Lauren's fingers bit into her shoulders beneath the frilly sleeves of her gown, almost down to the bone.

"I could see you as I pushed through the crowd," he said. "Your face had lost all color—your eyes had glazed. Naught has ever frightened me more than seeing you nearing your breaking point and knowing you might reach it before I could get to you."

He stopped speaking for a moment as if he could not go on, yet his eyes were eloquent—trained on her with pain and fear. She stared into them. "I did not believe you would care, my lord."

Two knights sauntered by the barn in the direction of the knight's quarters. Both men inclined their heads to the lord and lady, but neither she nor de Lauren acknowledged the men.

De Lauren's hands lifted from her shoulders and he held her face between his palms. "So much has passed between us. I have tried not to love you, but I do." His eyes seemed to bore into hers. "By all the saint's, I do."

Katherine stared at him and saw the truth of his words in his eyes. Her breath came out in a rush. She wound her arms around his neck in a near–choke hold. "I will always love you," she said.

He clasped her tight against his chest and buried his face in her hair.

Another knight passed by them.

"Come, my lady," he said. "Let us be away."

De Lauren took Katherine's hand in his and led her from the courtyard to her chamber.

A shout came from below, marking the changing of the guards. Somewhere, a dog barked.

De Lauren barely registered it all, intent on the woman before him. She stood at the bed, her calves brushing the mattress. The room was in twilight, but for the bed. Moonlight streamed in through the uncovered window, bathing the bed in soft light.

De Lauren cupped her shoulders and looked at her, just looked at what he held. All he wanted in this life. Still. 'Twas not a realization, but an admission. One he'd spent years trying to deny. For naught. Always in his mind, and in his heart, was Kate. Only Kate.

Slowly, so slowly, he lowered his mouth to hers. "Not one day in five years has passed that I have not thought of you," he murmured. "Not one day I have not wanted you."

He touched her lips lightly with his own, then dragged his mouth across hers in a long caress, savoring the feel of her. The rightness of her.

She whispered his name. Desire speared through him. He slid his hands down to her shoulders, bringing her as close to him as he could with her injured hand between them. 'Twas not near enough. Her frilled sleeves were between him and the skin beneath his hands. His fingers flexed, so badly did he want to feel her.

Eyes on hers, he went down on one knee and clasped the hem of her gown. As he got to his feet, he brought the garment up with him, lifted it over her head then tossed it to the floor. He lowered her chemise. He'd seen her unclothed, yet he went still again, now, awed by her. She was perfection to him.

She went to work on loosening his clothing, her movements awkward with one hand. He helped her and a moment later, they stood skin to skin. He slid his arms around her. His muscles tightened at the feel of her body against his. He sought her lips again. She pressed herself against him, kissing him just as deeply.

Gently, he lowered her onto the lavender coverlet. He kissed his way along her jawline and down her throat. He paused at her pulse point, skimming his lips across that spot and felt her pulse jump. He continued on down her body until they were both trembling.

She gripped his arm. Her fingers whitened, pinching his bicep. He lifted his gaze to her face—to her slightly flushed cheeks, to her eyes half-closed with passion—and moved over her.

Katherine's eyes were closed. She lacked the strength to lift her lids. De Lauren had braced his weight on his arms but his shoulder pressed lightly against her cheek. Warm and slightly damp. She smiled.

He shifted his weight. Her stomach tightened for an instant, recalling their last time together. But this time would not be like that. Nay, he'd not leave her now.

She opened her eyes, and found him watching her. He brought his face down to hers and kissed her long and deep. When he moved away from her, he took her with him, sliding his arm around her, and holding her against his side.

She lay with her head on his chest, listening to his heart beat. It was only now beginning to slow, as was her own. Faith, to be with him like this. She'd been granted a second chance. She closed her eyes briefly, overcome by gratitude.

The tawny cat that had recently begun sleeping in her room meowed loudly.

She needed to see de Lauren again. She turned onto her stomach, and braced her palms on his chest. His black hair was tousled from her fingers. A day's growth of beard darkened his jaw. He'd never looked more handsome to her.

"I thought you'd slept," he said. Her hair was a jumble around them both. She felt de Lauren sift his fingers through it.

She hesitated, but nay, she'd not hold back now. "I've been thinking. To be here with you, like this—I feel I have been granted a miracle."

He smoothed hair back from her face. "Aye. How many times over the years I have thought of you with me, like this," he said.

'Twas the same for her, but she did not say it and risk him asking of William. She did not want to raise the subject of her first marriage. She would tell de Lauren all, but not yet. Not in this perfect moment.

Five years she'd had no contact with him. Faith, how she longed to know about him. "How has de Lauren Keep fared since last I saw it?"

"All is well."

"Tell me, does Old Bram still keep birds?"

De Lauren's eyes grew tender on her. "Aye. And Maude is still running him out of her kitchen with her broom when he seeks out scraps to feed them."

Katherine laughed, remembering both the bossy Maude and her husband, sweet Old Bram, fondly.

"You will see them for yourself when we go there. I will take you for a brief stay in a few weeks time." He lifted her uninjured hand where it lay on his chest and rubbed his thumb over the ring he'd placed there. He kissed it. " 'Tis time the people of de Lauren met their lady."

Something lodged in her throat. She had to clear it to say, "I would like that very much, my lord."

He stacked his hands behind his head and said, "I was thinking mayhap we could go for a brief stay next month. I am giving you advance notice to prepare for a two- or three-day visit, since I acknowledge that you will require, what, six or seven trunks of clothing?"

No doubt he referred to the trips she'd been obliged to make to court during their betrothal. He was teasing her and it thrilled her.

She glimpsed her gown on the floor where he'd tossed it after relinquishing her of it, and could not resist some teasing of her own.

She held her chin on the edge of her hand. "I could travel less burdened if we did not bring my lady's maid. You could fill in for Elspeth. With the ease in which you relieved me of my garments a short while ago, I conclude you are quite accomplished at undressing a lady." Now that she was sure of him, his past dalliances with other women meant naught to her.

He laughed. "Not as practiced as you seem to think. I spent some time at court, trying to forget you." De Lauren's teeth flashed in a wicked grin. "Certain ladies of the court were most obliging."

Katherine raised an eyebrow. "I can well imagine."

De Lauren's expression sobered. "Lord Wardley of Fountainhurst pressed for a marriage with his daughter Lady Caroline."

Katherine was acquainted with Caroline, knew her to be as gracious as she was lovely.

"But I could not put you from my mind," de Lauren said. "I had a responsibility to my holding but I could not marry her. I told Caroline that truth and that she deserved better than to have a husband who was in love with another woman.

"Then, a few weeks ago, my guardsman told me a peasant woman claiming to be Lady Katherine of Stanfield was at my gates." De Lauren's eyes grew fierce. "I have lived these five years without you. The king's army will not take you from me."

Her eyes filled with tears. She pressed her face to his throat and felt his arms enclose her in a tight embrace. "Nor you from me," she said.

After a moment, he whispered into her ear, "And now, my lady, enough talk." He bit softly on her lobe. "If you are agreeable, I would know your delights again."

At some point during the night, they'd moved to the lord's bed. 'Twas from de Lauren's bed Katherine watched the sun rise to a golden line across the horizon. She'd slept little, yet had never wakened so refreshed. She pushed hair back from her face, and sat up against the headboard, drawing the tan coverlet up with her.

De Lauren stood at the washstand, shaving. A linen wiping cloth was tied around his hips, another was draped across his shoulders. The top of her head now reflected in his looking glass, mounted on the wooden stand.

He turned to her. "Good morn."

Indeed it was. "Good morn to you."

She could hear nearby birds twittering. Below stairs, someone dropped something that made a loud clang.

"What have you planned for this day?" he asked.

She intended to seek out Frances, the woman Timothy the shepherd proposed to marry. Katherine had planned to speak with de Lauren about reinstating the monthly court that she'd halted when William was lord. Eventually, she would tell de Lauren about William's rule, and about her marriage to him. She'd not intended either discussion for this morn, however, but now he'd asked her about this day. She told him about Timothy and Frances.

"I will confirm her agreement to the marriage," Katherine said.

De Lauren dipped his blade in the basin, then drew it down his face. "And if this Frances does not wish to wed, you will deny the shepherd's request," de Lauren said.

"Just so," Katherine said. She was watching his reflection and saw him raise one brow. She shifted position. "That is to say, my lord, I will speak with you about denying Timothy's request."

"Indeed will you?"

De Lauren laughed, then cursed as a line of blood appeared on his cheek. "I will certainly look forward to hearing your argument, should it become necessary."

He knew her too well indeed. "I will look forward to presenting it to you," she said, returning his smile. "Should it become necessary."

De Lauren tossed the blade in the basin, splashing water over the sides. He was wiping his face with the cloth when a sharp knock sounded at the outer door. De Lauren lowered the cloth. "Hold Stephen," he called out.

Too late. The door swung inward and 'twas, indeed, Stephen who entered. No doubt Stephen was the only one de Lauren allowed to enter his chamber without waiting for leave to do so, Katherine thought. By the look on de Lauren's face now, she believed that was about to change.

"Nick!" Stephen said. "Why aren't you ready to ride?"

Stephen's eyes met hers and he came to a stop in the center of the room. His face reddened and he averted his gaze from her at once.

"I did not think you would not be alone, my lord," Stephen bowed quickly. His lips thinned briefly, then he said. "Forgive me, my lady."

He left the room. The door swung closed behind him.

Katherine's own cheeks had heated, though she knew the coverlet had bared naught to Stephen. Now her face felt cold as snow. He'd looked upon her with more venom than usual. She was his brother's lawful wife, yet he'd regarded her as if she were naught but a whore. In time, she hoped, she could make peace with him.

De Lauren sat beside her. He reached out and stroked the underside of her chin with his thumb. "I will make certain that does not happen again," he said.

"I do not believe Stephen will enter without your leave to do so, in future, my lord. 'Tis of no import."

Another knock sounded on the door, and Anson called out requesting entrance.

De Lauren shouted. "Nay!"

He was scowling so deeply the skin above his brows had puckered. Katherine smiled. She smoothed his forehead with her fingertip. "Our people are clamoring for your attention, my lord."

"Aye," he said.

But he took her in his arms and gently lowered her to the mattress.

CHAPTER FOURTEEN

Katherine snuggled closer to de Lauren, rubbing her cheek against his chest. His arms tightened around her. 'Twas well past dawn, now. Sunlight streamed in through the uncovered window. A clatter rose up through the floorboards. Her people were about their duties.

'Twas de Lauren's doing that she was not, she thought with a smile.

De Lauren's lips brushed the top of her head. "As much as I would like to spend the day, thus, with you, I cannot."

Katherine turned in de Lauren's arms and rested her chin on his chest so she could look up at him. "And what pressing matter takes you from my bed?" she asked. More than idle curiosity, she yearned to know all that was going on in his life.

He reached out and took a strand of her hair between his fingers. "Stephen awaits me to ride patrol this morn."

Aye. Despite the tension in the air when Stephen had charged into the lord's chambers earlier, she did recall that he'd mentioned going riding.

De Lauren eased his arm from around her. He sat up and reached for his breeches. She watched him dress, watched him cover his hard muscled body and become every inch the lord of the manor.

De Lauren returned to the bed and braced his large hands on either side of her pillow. "Regarding the woman the candle maker would take to wife?" He leaned in close and kissed her deeply, then said with a smile. "Do let me know what I decide on that matter."

Katherine wound her arms around his neck and tugged him toward her for another kiss. "You will certainly be among the first to know."

The sun had set when de Lauren rode through Stanfield's gates for the second time that day. A steady rain was falling. De Lauren nodded to the guardsmen and steered his mount into the courtyard.

His routine patrol with Stephen had been waylaid when they'd come across neighboring Lord Colomby's teenage daughter, alone, at the de Lauren–Stanfield perimeter. The girl had decided to make her way to court, she revealed to Stephen. While at court a fortnight ago, she confided she'd fallen in love.

De Lauren doubted that mightily. As she spoke her gaze was riveted on his brother.

De Lauren cared naught to become embroiled in her matter of the heart and paid no attention to her running dialogue with Stephen on the subject. He simply wanted to see the girl safely home.

Escorting her to Colomby Keep, however, took him and Stephen a half day's ride out of their way, and once they were there, the grateful parents bestowed hospitality on them befitting the king. The day had waned by the time de Lauren declined yet another invitation to spend the night and he and Stephen took their leave.

Anson was in the courtyard to relieve de Lauren of his mount. As expected, de Lauren's tower watch had spotted them before they reached the gate. He tossed his horse's reins to Anson now, and dismounted.

"Good eve, my lord," Anson said.

Another lad ran forward and caught the reins Stephen released.

De Lauren pushed damp hair back from his face and took the drying cloth Anson held out to him. "See that my mount has a good rubdown, Anson," de Lauren said.

He'd pushed the animal hard, riding back from Colomby Keep as if the devil were on his trail. He'd been impatient to return to Stanfield. To return to Katherine.

He found her in the great hall. Servants milled about carrying the remains from last meal back to the kitchens. There was a buzz in the air from a hundred conversations.

Katherine was waving away a platter when he came up to her at the lord's table.

She smiled and her eyes brightened as if a light had gone on.

"My lord, you are returned," she said.

"Aye." Her welcome warmed him.

He bent, and kissed her. She'd bathed recently. He could smell roses on her. He felt her fingers in the hair at his nape. He wanted to hold her tight against him, but his clothing was wet. He straightened away from her and passed the cloth he held across his brow.

"You endured the worst of the rain." Katherine stood beside him and took the wiping cloth he held. She dabbed at his temples. "Will you change clothing now or shall I have your meal served?" she asked.

"I have eaten." De Lauren filled a goblet with wine and drank.

"Oh?"

"I will tell you of it once I'm dry." He kissed her again. "I won't be long."

When he returned, the tables had been cleared and people sat facing the west wall where a table had been set up for the evening's entertainment.

De Lauren slipped into the chair beside Katherine's. She

glanced at him as he rested his arm along her chair's back.

"Now tell me of your day," she said.

He told her of his visit to Colomby Keep.

"The girl was most fortunate you and Stephen happened along," she said softly.

As de Lauren was about to agree, he noticed that his mother was not in the hall. "Did my mother come down to last meal?"

Katherine shook her head slowly. "Nay, she did not."

De Lauren called out to Anson. When the boy reached him he said, "See if my mother is in her bedchamber."

"Aye, my lord."

De Lauren turned to Katherine to resume their conversation and was hailed from the foot of the dais.

He glanced at the man who'd called out to him. The frequent blinker from the troupe of performers.

"By your leave, we will begin the evening's entertainment, my lord," the man called out.

De Lauren nodded.

The entertainer left the floor with a kind of hop-skip movement. His boots made an odd sucking sound as if they were wet. It sounded as if he, too, had been caught in the downpour.

The youngest man in the troupe, the one with wild curling hair, climbed onto a table, bowed, then strummed the lute he held.

"With your permission, milord," the man called out. "I have wrote a song in honor of your lady."

De Lauren inclined his head.

"Fair is the lady of de Lauren. With hair like spun gold and an angel's smile. Oh, this night how fortune has shone upon me. It brought me to her beauty."

The man's voice was a clear strong tenor that filled the hall. De Lauren crossed his arms and glanced at Katherine. She squirmed in her seat. He knew from other such occasions that she cared naught to be a subject for a troubadour. 'Twas commonplace, though, for an entertainer to pay tribute to the lady of the keep or, as she had once been at de Lauren holding, the affianced lady to the lord.

He'd teased her about her modesty in this regard in the past and couldn't resist doing so again now. He leaned over to her and said with a smile, "I will end his song when his words ring false."

Katherine raised an eyebrow, but her stern expression was belied by her twitching lips as she fought back a smile. "I believe, my lord, that I shall request a song regaling your victories in battle for tomorrow's entertainment. What say you?"

De Lauren laughed. Her eyes were alight with humor, her cheeks, flushed. Her hair was unbound. It fell in golden waves down her shoulders and back and rippled around her face. 'Twas her face and form that had initially caught his attention, yet had that been all to her, he would not have sought her hand five years ago. Many beautiful women graced the king's court. Nay, 'twas what he'd found beneath her lovely exterior that had held him enthralled, and one of those qualities was her wit.

Lord Michael had remarked on her sharp mind on several occasions, de Lauren recalled, until he'd asked Katherine's father outright about his intent. The old lord had not denied he had one, but revealed that those conversations had been a test that had de Lauren not passed, would have ended the betrothal. Lord Michael had wanted to ascertain that the man who would be Katherine's husband would not force her to be less than she was to soothe his pride or, worse, to avoid his anger.

De Lauren could not recall the words he'd used that had won Lord Michael's favor, only that he'd spoken truth. He'd have her no other way, and he'd have no other.

That hadn't changed.

The troubadour strummed a final, closing note, then bowed

with a flourish and leaped down from the table. The frequent blinker replaced the troubadour on the tabletop then lowered a hand to the woman in their group. She joined him and they launched into a comedic routine of a husband and wife at market.

Livvy shouted out, "Hey, you been following me and my 'arry around!"

Laughter followed that comment.

De Lauren heard footsteps behind him and glanced over his shoulder. Anson bent and said softly, "My lord, I knocked at your lady mother's door, like you told me, but received no reply."

"See to your meal, Anson."

De Lauren stood. Katherine glanced up at him. He bent and placed his lips at her ear. "There is something I must see to."

"Shall I come with you?"

"Nay. Enjoy the show." He kissed her lightly.

De Lauren left the hall and climbed the steps to the second floor of the keep. The bedchamber his mother was using was on this floor. He knocked. No answer came from within.

"Mother," he called out and opened the door. Candlelight showed embroideries of flowers mounted on the walls and a collection of miniature figurines on a pedestal table. A mis-shaped piece of clay sat in the center of the circle of others. It was supposed to be a cat. He'd fashioned it for her when he was in his seventh year, and learned she liked small statues. It had been part of her treasured collection ever since.

"Ah, Mother," he said aloud, rubbing his hands down his face. "I fear I know where to find you."

As he'd suspected, she was in Stanfield's chapel, kneeling on the cold stone floor, her hands clasped in prayer. She was ever thus, it seemed, at de Lauren Keep. De Lauren had come to hate that chapel, so much so that he'd instructed the resident priest at the keep to wed him to Katherine in the solar.

De Lauren stood at the door, now, observing her in profile. Candle flames flickered off a marble crucifix on the altar. The room smelled faintly of wax. Mother wore her uniform black kirtle and headdress that concealed her hair. 'Twas one step up from a sackcloth. One very small step. It made him angry to see her like this, and it made him feel helpless.

Her eyes were closed, but his bootsteps drummed on the wooden floor and she opened them as he neared.

"I missed you at last meal," de Lauren said, slipping into the pew beside her.

She crossed herself then clutched the bench in front of her. He reached down and grasped her arm to help her to her feet. Sweet Jesu, she felt so frail, he gentled his hold.

"I will dine anon," she said.

De Lauren doubted that mightily.

"My son, I had planned to seek you out as well this night," she said. ·

So long since she'd done that. So long since they'd spent any time together. De Lauren bowed his head. "I am honored. Mayhap you wish to ride across these new lands of ours?" She was not overly fond of horses, but on occasion he'd known her to request escort from himself or Stephen for a ride on de Lauren land.

She clasped her hands. "Nay, my lord, but I do have a request. If you would but grant it."

Softly de Lauren said, "What would you have of me, Mother?"

" 'Tis my wish to go into seclusion."

De Lauren stared at her. "What?"

"I have pondered the confinement of His Grace, Bishop Whittaker, and I wish to be similarly isolated."

De Lauren felt his face heat. "Your wish, Mother, or the bishop's? Has he communicated with you? Is your request his attempt to force me to restore his freedom?" She said naught,

189

but flinched at his tone. The anger drained out of him, and again he felt helpless. "Mother, why can you not see what he has done to you?"

" 'is not what the bishop does to me, my son. 'Tis what I bring onto myself."

"What Mother?" De Lauren's voice echoed in the chapel. "I will ask yet again, what do you that you must forfeit your life in atonement?"

Her gaze lowered. "Please, Nicholas."

He had to strain to hear her.

"Free me from my obligations as a lady of your house," she said. "Allow me to spend my days in prayer."

De Lauren raised an eyebrow. "You wish my permission to withdraw from your family." He gritted his teeth. "Permission denied."

Katherine was inside de Lauren's chamber with Elspeth when he entered his room. The maid was laying out clothes for the night.

His features were pulled taut, Katherine saw. His muscles tensed. Without a word, he went to the window and stood gripping a stone that jutted out from the wall.

Studying him, she said, "I have no further need of you this night, Elspeth. Find your rest."

When they were alone Katherine said, "You were gone for some time, my lord."

"Aye."

Katherine wanted to ask what was distressing him and offer what comfort she could, but did not want to pry. In the past, she'd known him to be a man who kept his own counsel but he'd never shut her out of his life. Five years ago, she would have pressed on and known she would not be intruding.

She didn't press him now. They'd only just found each other

again. She was still feeling her way and was afraid to overstep.

"I was with Mother," he said.

It was an opening, she thought, and took it gladly. "Lady Margaret did not come to last meal. She is well?"

De Lauren grunted. "As well as she has been since the bishop came into her life."

"He is confined now. He can do her no harm."

De Lauren rubbed both hands down his face. "He exerts his influence over her from his confinement, it seems."

Katherine listened while he told her about Lady Margaret's request to go into isolation. "Despite my prodding," de Lauren said, "she will say naught of this hold he has on her."

Katherine felt his pain. She went to him and slid her arm around his waist. She rested her head against his tensed back. "I am sorry, Nicholas."

"Aye," he said. "Enough of Whittaker." De Lauren turned from the window and took her into his arms. "I have missed you this day, my lady."

She'd missed him, as well, had found herself listening for his return, ears pricked as acutely as Anson's hound, no doubt, to the sound of hoofbeats. "And I you," she said.

He kissed the curve of her shoulder but when he inserted his fingers beneath the collar of her gown and began to ease the garment down her body, Katherine placed her hands atop his, staying him.

She smiled and lowered his hands to his sides, then pressed her palms flat against his chest. "This night, my lord," she said, backing him toward the bed. "I would take you where I will."

Eyes closed, de Lauren reached across the bed for Katherine. He smiled as he slid his hand across the cool linens. He'd been in a foul mood upon returning to his chamber earlier, but his lady certainly knew how to chase his demons away.

She'd said she would take him where she would. And she certainly had. Sweet Christ she'd astounded him. Had him panting like an untried youth. Even in memory, the experience sparkled. He believed he would see if he could wake her, and entice her into having her way with him again.

De Lauren extended his arm all the way to the other end of the bed. His hand came away empty. He opened his eyes. The sky beyond the window was black, lit only by a scant quarter moon and the occasional star. He squinted in the shadowed room, then scowled, realizing he was, indeed, alone.

He kicked off the coverlet that had bunched around his legs and left the bed. He opened the connecting door to the lady's chamber. The room was unoccupied but for a tawny cat, snoring on a rope rug by the bed.

The window was across from where he stood in the center of the room. He could see a little more of the courtyard from in here than in the lord's chambers. A light was on in the lord's crypt. Katherine? Surely she would not go there in the middle of the night. But who else, then?

De Lauren went into his chamber and dressed quickly. Out in the courtyard he called out to the burly Trevor, patrolling the grounds.

"Who goes in the crypt?" de Lauren asked.

"Lady Katherine," Trevor said in his barrel-deep voice.

The door to the crypt was wedged open with a rock. A lit taper, in an alcove in the stone, gave off scant light. From the doorway de Lauren could see Katherine from the back, kneeling before her father's effigy.

She glanced over her shoulder at him, turning her head to the light. Her eyes glistened.

He entered the tomb. The air here was chill and smelled of damp. He crouched beside her and reached out, brushing his thumb against one wet cheek. "Kate?" he asked softly. "What has brought you here at this time of night?"

" 'Tis four years this night, that Father died. He took his last breath as the moon rose. I come here at each moonrise on this date."

"July tenth," de Lauren murmured. "Aye."

Her blonde brows rose in surprise. That he knew the significance of this day? He'd learned Katherine's father had died of a lung ailment. De Lauren had not heard of Lord Michael's death until two months after the fact, and then had been saddened by it.

De Lauren took her uninjured hand in his and brought it to his lips. Her skin was freezing. " 'Tis cold in here," he said rubbing his fingers across her palm to warm her. "Will you accompany me into the castle?"

She nodded. He drew her to her feet. With his arm around her, he escorted her into the castle and through the dim corridors to his bedchamber.

Inside, she brushed by him. "I fear I am not fit company at the moment, my lord. Pray find your rest."

Katherine went to the adjoining door and entered the lady's chamber. She crossed the room to the uncovered window and stood facing the dark courtyard.

From the doorway, de Lauren watched her. She looked so hurt and so alone. He could not stand it. He felt helpless in the face of her grief, but he would be damned before he'd leave her to bear it alone.

Her arms were around herself. He took the coverlet from the bed, draped it across her tensed shoulders, then turned her to face him.

"I care not if you are unable to entertain me," he said. "I will remain."

She looked up at him for a moment, then nodded.

A likeness of her father hung above the mantle. The old lord had large, blunt features. The portrait had been fashioned in Lord Michael's younger days, when de Lauren had first known him.

"Did your father ever mention how he and I met?" de Lauren asked.

Katherine shook her head slowly. "Only that 'twas shortly after your own father's passing. He stopped by de Lauren Keep to offer his condolences."

De Lauren nodded. " 'Twas a fortnight later. I was sixteen and had just inherited responsibility for my mother, my brother, for our holding and its people. I was determined to step in for my father and doubted that I would ever be able to. I feared my inexperience would lead to harm for my people and that King Henry would appoint an overlord to oversee the keep for the next two years until I reached my majority."

Katherine's eyes lifted to him, and he lowered his gaze from the portrait to her. "Lord Michael and my father had had a falling out in their youth, my mother told me following the sympathy call. A trivial disagreement that both had stubbornly refused to concede. They were civil to each other when duty warranted it, but that disagreement is responsible for the fact that though we were neighbors, you and I never met as children.

"On that visit, along with his sympathy, your father offered counsel. I very much needed that counsel, but I was suspicious of his motives. I considered that he might intend to usurp my authority and appeal to the king himself for guardianship of de Lauren holding. The matter of our lands bordering each other was ever significant. I thought the king might very well use the opportunity of my father's death to ally de Lauren and Stanfield under your father's command. Once lost, 'twould take a battle to wrest my holding from him. I told Lord Michael to leave."

De Lauren smiled and rubbed his forefinger back and forth

beneath his chin. "He did, but he came back. Each fortnight for a few months. Thereafter, occasionally, and with the pretense of joining me for a goblet of wine. His visits ceased altogether when we both knew I could stand on my own. We lost touch after that, though I'd not forgotten him or what he'd done for me. Then," De Lauren slowed his words and looked into Katherine's eyes. "One summer day I happened upon a maiden plucking leaves in yon woods and escorted her home to her father. 'Twas but shortly after, that maiden claimed my heart." He winked.

She smiled. "Thank you for telling me that lovely story."

"I have others. Your father and I spent a good deal of time together. Would you care to hear another?"

Katherine's smile widened. "Aye, very much."

Two identical overlarge chairs were placed side by side by the unlit hearth. He took Katherine by her uninjured hand and led her to them.

De Lauren could hear rain pattering against the stone. Katherine's head was pillowed on his shoulder. While recalling a comical incident with a stubborn horse, de Lauren had drawn her from her chair, into his lap. He eased his arm out from under her, then gained his feet and lifted her out of the chair.

In the lord's chamber, he set her on the bed. The sky had lightened to a slate grey. Dawn was anon and she'd finally found sleep. How had she spent each previous anniversary of her father's death? She'd burrowed in her chamber to tend to her hurt herself. Done so with an ease that suggested to him it was routine. Where had Norris been on these nights?

A light tapping on the bedchamber door drew de Lauren's attention. Satisfied that Katherine slept comfortably, he went to answer it.

"My lord," Anson said softly, "a messenger has arrived. He

waits by the doors."

"I will speak with him in the solar," de Lauren said.

A young lad stood by the wall inside the solar when de Lauren arrived. He held a wiping cloth to his face and lowered it at de Lauren's entrance. The boy bowed.

"You bear a message for me, lad," de Lauren said.

The boy stood erect. Water dripped from the fringe of hair across the lad's forehead and he blinked repeatedly. "I come from the king's court," he said. "Sir Hugh bade me deliver this to you, Lord de Lauren."

He held out the missive. De Lauren unrolled it. The slanted script was unmistakably Hugh's.

No one to dance attendance on. Would move on to next destination?

They'd found no weak link in Ranulf's allies. So be it. A full battle then it would be.

To the messenger, de Lauren said. "My squire will find you a meal and a bed. On the morrow, you may return with my reply."

The door closed behind Anson and the messenger. De Lauren tapped Hugh's message against his thigh. Hugh and Victor sought his permission to proceed to the town the monk had claimed as his birthplace. De Lauren's reply would be one word: *Go.*

His men would learn if the monk was who he claimed or if he served Ranulf and that was why Katherine had brought him to Stanfield. Her desire to be rid of Brother Ian had been palpable, though. If the monk was not Ranulf's man, then what was she hiding about him?

De Lauren thought of Katherine, asleep in his bed, and glanced out the window at the pink sky. He loved her more than breath, but he could not trust her.

CHAPTER FIFTEEN

Sunlight struck Katherine's face. She opened one eye. For the second day in a row, and the second time in her life that she could remember, she'd slept past dawn.

She couldn't recall coming to bed. No doubt 'twas de Lauren who'd brought her here. Last night he'd made her pain over Father's death bearable, and reminded her that he was a man to share the good and the bad with.

Faith, how she loved him. And he loved her. They'd found their way back to each other. She felt awed by the miracle they'd been given, and so grateful.

She shifted from her pillow to his. It was cool against her cheek and folded in two so it would be firmer, the way he liked. She smiled. She no longer needed to keep the truth of her first marriage or the existence of her son from him.

Tonight. When they were alone tonight, she would tell de Lauren all. She hugged the pillow. And in the morn, she would have her babe in her arms.

Two hours later, Katherine left the hut of Wilfred the hunter. She'd been inside with Wilfred's wife, observing their young son. Each summer, when the weather warmed, the boy's breathing grew labored. Katherine had tried an assortment of treatments over the years, with minimal success. During this last winter, she'd decided to add water lily to the herb blend she usually made up for him, and to start medicating him then, before the illness struck.

This was the first July, in the lad's six years, that he was breathing comfortably. The bright day just got brighter, Katherine thought.

She saw de Lauren in the training field, in the open area beyond the huts. He was addressing a group of his men. Their eyes met. He said something to Anson, who stood by his side. The boy ran over to her with de Lauren's request to join him.

She was happy to comply. She hadn't spent time with him all morning and she'd missed him. She realized she felt like a love-struck adolescent. It felt wonderful.

She lifted her skirts and picked her way over the muddy ground. She wasn't wearing boots, but slippers and despite her dainty steps, the shoes sunk. Water seeped in to wet her feet. She curled her toes but there was no avoiding the dampness.

By the look of the men, they'd been training for some time. They were dirt-stained and sweat-stained. Some were bent over, panting.

De Lauren was again speaking to the group. Shielding her eyes from the sun, she hung back, waiting for him to finish. His voice sounded hoarse. No doubt from telling her stories all night.

She waited until he'd dismissed his knights, then made her way to him. He reached out and lifted her chin, scratching her lightly with his gauntlet. He narrowed his eyes on her face and asked, "How are you this morn?"

She believed he was concerned because of last night. "Better. Wonderful."

"I'm glad."

"You, however, do not sound well at all. Your voice is hoarse, my lord. Does your throat pain you?"

"Nay," he said.

His gaze traveled up and down her body. " 'Tis not my throat that ails me." His arm went around her and he brought her close enough to leave no doubt as to what part of him was in distress.

Katherine smiled. "I will prepare a treatment of nettles that will comfort your throat." She rose on tiptoe, bringing her face closer to his and wound her arms around his neck. She kissed him lightly. "Any other discomfort will have to wait for the moment."

De Lauren groaned and returned her smile. "You can be a cruel woman, Kate."

She laughed.

He winked at her. "Truly, my throat is fine."

Katherine bit her lip, no longer amused. "Indulge me, Nicholas. I have seen throat illness left untended. The infection that resulted was untreatable."

De Lauren looked into her eyes. "Prepare what you will, then."

He kissed her, then set out to where two knights were engaged in hand-to-hand combat.

She needed to mix his medicine. She had the herbs she needed, but she sighed. 'Twas impossible to put pestle to mortar with one hand. She needed Elspeth.

The maid was nowhere to be found inside the castle, Katherine learned an hour later. Faith, where had Elspeth gone? It seemed lately Katherine was always in the position of having to find the girl.

Her maid kept company with Donny, Katherine recalled. But, hadn't Elspeth said recently that she was now spending time with one of the entertainers at Stanfield? The curly haired troubadour. Derrick or Davey or Devon. That was it. Haldrake housed the entertainers. He would be able to tell her where to look for the troubadour.

Katherine found Haldrake, quill and parchment in hand, in

the granary. He was a startling splash of yellow against the grey stone wall behind him. She posed the question about the entertainers to him.

"I've housed the troupe in one of the empty huts," Haldrake said.

Normally the entertainers would sleep in the hall with the rest of the castle staff, but since Ranulf's attack, accommodations were abundant at Stanfield. She put aside her sadness over that, and her anger against Ranulf, and focused on Haldrake.

"I've set them to their practice where they are least likely to disturb," Haldrake went on. "In the field behind the kitchens, my lady."

Katherine winced. Her feet were just beginning to dry.

"Thank you, Haldrake."

"My lady, will you be available to tour the storage sheds this day?"

'Twas a monthly tour she'd neglected of late. She nodded. "Aye. At midday?"

Haldrake bowed and extended his arm in sweeping flourish. "Until midday," he said.

'Twas a glorious day for a walk. Katherine nodded to two women toting baskets of laundry. A boy clasping a leash knotted around the thick neck of Anson's dog stumbled in her path. Mindful of her last encounter with the pup, Katherine dashed out of its way.

The ripe scent of manure struck her as she strolled across the field. And as ripe, was a string of shouted curses coming from where Elspeth stood with Donny and the troubadour.

Katherine made her way to them. No one glanced at her. They seemed oblivious to her presence.

"Can't you see, Elspeth, this whoreson means to have you and then be gone! He ain't going to marry you!"

This was shouted by the stocky Donny. He faced Elspeth.

His face was mottled in anger, and he was pointing to the entertainer who stood with his arms crossed at his chest, a pace behind Elspeth.

"Our relationship is none of your affair," Elspeth shouted back.

"Aye, and an affair is all you'll be having. Likely he'll plant a babe in your belly, and be off!" Donny said.

Donny looked up at Devon. He took a step forward and poked his thick index finger into Devon's chest.

"Hold," Katherine called out, hoping to prevent this from becoming uglier, but her shout was lost as Donny pounced on the entertainer, fist raised. The blow never landed. Devon blocked it with his open hand and seized Donny's fist in his slimmer hand. The stocky Donny surely outweighed the wiry Devon by fifty pounds, yet Devon held Donny's fist at bay. Devon smirked at Donny and smashed his own fist in Donny's face. Blood spurted from Donny's nose.

Devon continued to pound several blows with both fists, in rapid succession. Donny landed in a heap at Devon's feet. The troubadour was no haphazard brawler, but fought with uncommon skill, Katherine realized. Donny had not marked him.

The entertainer drew back his leg to kick the fallen man.

"Enough!" Katherine shouted, then louder. "Enough!"

At her shout, Devon glanced at her. She met his gaze. Donny's arms came up. He grabbed Devon's leg and flipped the entertainer onto his back. Donny straddled the other man, drew back his fist and struck Devon in the mouth.

Elspeth, braids fluttering, pounded Donny's shoulders. "Get off him, you brute! Get off 'im I say!"

Donny complied. His face was a mess. Blood trickled from a mass of cuts. Only one thin line of blood flowed from the corner of Devon's mouth. It seemed to Katherine that Elspeth's sympathies lay with the wrong man.

Devon gained his feet and dusted off his breeches. Donny knelt in the straw, panting. His two swollen eyes widened slightly on her. He winced, shot to his feet, and executed a bow. Blood from his nose dripped onto his shoes.

"Lady Katherine," Donny said. "Begging your pardon, I didn't see ye standin' there."

"Clearly," Katherine said.

Devon, too, executed a bow.

"Sorry, I am, me lady that you saw all this," Donny said.

"Do I need to call for a guard?" she asked.

Donny shook his head. "Nay, me lady."

Devon bowed. "Nay."

"Donny, I'm sure you are needed in the stables," Katherine said.

The groom nodded and took his leave.

Katherine glanced at Elspeth, who stood chewing her lower lip. "Accompany me."

Katherine turned away, leaving the girl to follow, and headed back to the keep. She heard footsteps behind her, then Elspeth was at her side.

"Sorry, I am, me lady 'bout all that," Elspeth said. "Devon and me's going to come see you about getting married and Donny, he just don't want to get that into his head."

"When would you like to wed?" Katherine asked.

Elspeth stammered. "Oh, he ain't said the words yet, but he will. I know he will. He's out of his head about me, he is."

Katherine hoped Elspeth was right about the entertainer's feelings for her. She didn't want to see the girl hurt.

Katherine turned the topic. "We need to speak about your duties at Stanfield. Once again, I found myself in need of you and in the position of having to search you out."

Elspeth's cheeks reddened. "I didn't mean for you to come lookin' for me, lady," Elspeth said. "I just meant to go and watch Devon practice for a few minutes, then get back to me chores. He has such a lovely voice. But then Donny showed up and, well, you know the rest. 'Twon't happen again, I promise," she whispered.

Katherine nodded.

They entered the castle.

"I'll finish folding them clothes, now," Elspeth said from beneath her lashes.

"I need your help with something else first, Elspeth," Katherine said. "I need to prepare a medicine for Lord de Lauren."

"His lordship is ailing?"

Elspeth's eyes had gone as round as a full moon. The girl looked as if she believed de Lauren to be at death's door. "Calm yourself, Elspeth. He is not about to expire. 'Tis merely a sore throat that he suffers from. Together, we will remedy that."

Inside her chamber, Katherine pointed out the prickly nettles from her supplies.

"We need to ground these spines into a fine powder," Katherine said.

She stood over Elspeth, hovering over the poor girl, Katherine realized, while Elspeth went about the task. 'Twas frustration hounding her, and she turned away from her maid. She cared naught to watch Elspeth do what she wanted to do herself. She was possessive over her medicines, and this one, meant for de Lauren, more so.

"I believe that will do," Katherine said, a moment later. "We need a cupful of boiled water."

Elspeth nodded. "I'll fetch it and be right back."

The girl dashed out of the room. While Elspeth was gone, Katherine scooped the powder into a green glass vial. She could not see through the thick glass and the powder vanished inside it.

She'd just finished scooping when Elspeth returned. Katherine added the water to the vial.

"We're done, Elspeth." Katherine narrowed her eyes on the ribbon of steam rising from the medicine.

"I'll be about me chores then." Elspeth executed a quick, awkward curtsy and left the chamber.

Haldrake arrived at the open door, a moment later. A stack of parchment was tucked beneath his arm.

Katherine had forgotten her appointment with the steward. "Is it midday already, Haldrake?"

"Aye, my lady. Is this still a convenient time for us to tour the storage sheds?"

"Certainly. A moment, though."

She needed the liquid cool for de Lauren to drink. Katherine placed the vial on the table beneath the open window.

"Let us be about the tour, shall we?" she said.

After training with his men, de Lauren had spent the rest of the day closeted in the solar with Stephen. He'd relayed Hugh's message that no weak link had been found among Ranulf's allies then said, "A full-scale battle it will be." Stephen had agreed.

They'd taken last meal in the solar, continuing their discussion. Wedges of pie and cheese and hunks of meat illustrated their attack strategy. De Lauren glanced at the food assembled on his table and nodded. He was well pleased with the progress for this first meeting on the subject. Stephen had left the solar a few moments earlier. De Lauren did the same, now. Last meal would still be underway. He should find Katherine there.

She was not at the lord's table, but seated in one of the large chairs de Lauren remembered Lord Michael had favored. She'd changed her gown. Earlier, de Lauren had noticed her with Haldrake, inspecting the supply sheds. She'd been wearing green. Now, she was a vision in crimson.

Marcus sat in the chair opposite hers, bent over the chess board. The young knight's face was scrunched in concentration. His fingers were bent over a rook. De Lauren made his way to them as Katherine said, "I believe that is checkmate, sir."

Marcus groaned.

The knight slumped in the chair and shook his head at de Lauren. "My lord, I am lost. Your lady has beaten me."

"It would appear she has, indeed," de Lauren said. He'd been tired upon entering the hall, but now felt rejuvenated.

"Good eve, my lord," Katherine said.

De Lauren bowed his head. "My lady. Might I try my skill?"

Katherine smoothed her skirts and gave him a saucy smile. "Certainly, if that is your wish."

De Lauren grinned at the smile she gave him. She was an accomplished player, and well she knew it.

He braced the chess board and its pieces across one open hand, then clasped her fingers with his other.

"Nicholas, what are you about?" she asked.

"I would play in private," he said.

Katherine laughed, and he led her from the hall up to his chamber.

Inside the room, he set the board on the small table by the unlit hearth. He moved the chairs so they were positioned opposite each other at the table, then waited for Katherine to be seated. He met her gaze across the tabletop. Her eyes sparkled tonight, with a joy that radiated from her.

"Nicholas?"

He returned his attention to the entertainment he'd planned. He reclined in the remaining chair, and extended one booted foot beneath the table.

The coverlet was pulled back from the window, showing the sky dark with clouds. The air blowing into the room smelled of the expected rain.

"What stakes shall we set?" De Lauren said as he placed the pieces.

Katherine glanced up from the board. "Stakes, my lord?"

"Aye, what will you wager on your skill?"

A slow smile spread across her face. He watched it, captivated.

"What would you have me wager, my lord?" she said.

He rubbed his forefinger beneath his chin as if contemplating the question. "For each capture I make," he said, "you will surrender an article of clothing."

Katherine's head went back and she laughed. She glanced down her body then raised her skirt thigh-high. De Lauren's gaze went to that thigh.

"Other than a shift, I wear only my gown and slippers," she said.

De Lauren's mouth went dry.

"My lord?"

With an effort, de Lauren raised his gaze from her leg. "Then if you wish to remain clothed, my lady," he said, "you'd best be on your guard."

"Hold a moment," she said.

She left the chair and went into the lady's chamber. She returned with a vial containing some noxious smelling liquid. He frowned at the odor, which carried to him from the doorway.

"If you thought to distract me into forgetting to give you your medicine, fie on you, Nicholas."

"Can that brew possibly taste worse than it smells?"

"I have anticipated you, and I will sweeten it with wine."

Katherine retrieved his goblet and wine flagon from the table and carried them to him. She emptied the vial into his cup then tilted the flagon over it. De Lauren covered her hand with his and held the jug over the goblet until it was filled to the brim.

"Drink up, my lord," she said.

She replaced the jug where she'd gotten it, and dropped the

vial into her pocket. De Lauren left the goblet where she'd placed it by the chessboard.

Katherine resumed her seat. The cat who slept by the lady's bed entered the chamber through the connecting door Katherine had left open. The feline jumped into Katherine's lap. Absently she stroked its tawny fur.

A few moments into the game, de Lauren made his first capture. He sat back in his chair, manipulating the pawn he'd claimed between his fingers. "I believe you are indebted to me," he said.

She extended her leg. His eyes narrowed as she slowly slid the gown up her calf. With her thumb and forefinger, Katherine flicked off her slipper.

De Lauren laughed, a thick husky sound that had naught to do with his ailing throat.

Katherine claimed his rook. De Lauren smiled and removed his tunic. The sooner they were unclothed the faster they would move onto the real sport he'd intended.

The game progressed. Chin cupped in her hand, eyes narrowed, Katherine leaned forward and studied de Lauren's latest move. Her mound of conquered chessmen topped his. It was clear she would win this game.

"A fine attempt, my lord, but alas in vain." She smiled wide and moved her queen. "Checkmate. Another round?"

"Aye," de Lauren said, rising from the chair. "But chess is not the game I would play now. Come, my lady. You have brought me to my knees at the chessboard. Pray use the same skill in our bed."

As he drew Katherine to her feet, the cat leaped from her lap and prowled the table's edge.

De Lauren made short work of her gown. She stood before him in her shift. He didn't think he would ever become accustomed to seeing her thus.

He gripped her waist and lifted her high above him. Her uninjured hand went to his shoulders and held tight. Sliding her against him, he lowered her a fraction and kissed her stomach, covered by the slippery fabric of the shift. Then, her breasts. Her lips. With their mouths joined, he carried her to the bed and set her on it.

Her hair fanned out on the coverlet, exposing her throat. He ran his tongue along the side of her neck. She tilted her head back, stretching the column of her throat and giving him greater access. He took it and she grabbed a fistful of the bedclothes.

In the haze sweeping over his brain, he heard retching. Louder. De Lauren raised his head and glanced over his shoulder. The cat lay writhing on the table. The animal swished its tail, knocking the goblet on its side. The few remaining drops spilled onto the chess board.

The cat shrieked, then went still.

CHAPTER SIXTEEN

Katherine left the bed and went to de Lauren. He stood over the still cat. "Is it dead?"

"Aye," de Lauren said.

"But how!"

Katherine looked to the wine goblet. "The wine!" She dug her fingers into de Lauren's forearms. "My lord, your wine!" Katherine felt the strength go out of her legs. The one lying dead now could have been de Lauren.

"Aye, the wine," de Lauren said quietly. "Obviously poisoned."

Katherine looked up into his eyes. "There can be no doubt that the poison was meant for you." She spoke quickly. "The drink came from your jug and all at Stanfield know I cannot abide grapes. Who would do this? Someone on my staff?" Had one of her people observed her earlier unhappiness in her marriage and sought to save her by ridding her of her unwanted husband? Or could one of de Lauren's own want him dead?

"We will see what Anson has to say about this night's work," de Lauren said.

He dressed. Katherine did the same, retrieving her gown from the floor where de Lauren had left it. De Lauren retrieved the goblet on the rug beside the cat, then opened the chamber door.

The boy slept outside de Lauren's room. At de Lauren's call, Anson staggered to his feet, rubbing his eyes. De Lauren picked up the wine jug from the table. "Do you know this to be mine?"

The jug had come from de Lauren Keep, one of de Lauren's personal items that Anson was responsible for and handled routinely. He would certainly recognize it, Katherine knew.

"Aye, lord."

While the boy looked on, de Lauren poured from the jug into the goblet. He handed the cup to Anson. "Drink."

The boy took the cup and put it to his lips. De Lauren knocked the goblet from Anson's hand. It bounced off the stone wall and struck the floor with a clatter.

The boy would not have drank wine he'd poisoned. 'Twas not Anson, then, Katherine thought.

Anson blinked. "My lord?"

"When did you last refill this jug?" De Lauren asked.

"Yesterday afternoon, my lord. Is this the last of it? I'll fetch more now."

"Where did you get this wine, Anson?"

"From the supply cellar, my lord, like always."

"Was the jug out of your hands between the time you filled it, then replaced it here?"

"Nay, my lord, never."

"You are certain?"

Anson nodded and said solemnly. "Aye, my lord."

De Lauren inclined his head to the door. "Go."

When they were alone again, Katherine said, "Let us rouse the household."

Katherine woke Haldrake in his small chamber behind the kitchens with instructions to assemble the staff. Elspeth cleaned both the lord and lady's chambers. She had unquestionable access to de Lauren's room. Katherine did not want to think Elspeth, indeed any one from Stanfield, could harm de Lauren, but if someone on her staff was responsible . . . Katherine pressed her lips together briefly, then said to Haldrake, "Lord de Lauren and I will speak with Elspeth first. Escort her to the solar."

Katherine lit candles, then paced the solar awaiting Haldrake to arrive with the maid. Arms crossed at his chest, de Lauren leaned against the wall. Every few seconds, Katherine glanced his way, reassuring herself that he was safe.

A knock sounded. Katherine called out. "Enter."

Haldrake opened the door slowly. "Our people are gathered in the great hall, my lady, and Elspeth is here."

"Send her in," Katherine said.

Elspeth entered the solar. Haldrake closed the door behind himself. Katherine turned on the girl. "When were you last in Lord de Lauren's bedchamber?"

" 'Twas this afternoon, me lady, when I done me cleaning."

"What did you do in there?"

Elspeth shrugged. "Changed the bed linens. Dusted. Swept the floor . . . " Elspeth's lower lip trembled. "I touched his lordship's armor. I'm sorry, I am, if I left me prints on it. I ain't never touched the like before and I—I—"

"What of Lord de Lauren's wine jug. Did you touch that?"

"I wiped the table it sits on."

"The jug, Elspeth?"

"Nay, lady."

"While cleaning the table, did you spill the contents of the jug and replenish the wine yourself?"

Elspeth shook her head. Mink brown curls bobbed around her face. "Nay. Nay, Lady Katherine."

Katherine pounced on the girl, seizing her hard by the elbows. "If you lie, girl, you will stay entombed in the dungeons until you are dead!"

Tears filled Elspeth's huge brown eyes. She whimpered. "I picked up the jug to wipe under it. Please. Please." Elspeth's voice rose to a shriek. "I but wiped the table under the jug, I swear it. I swear it!"

Elspeth was crying so hard now Katherine could scarcely understand her. Not Elspeth. Katherine was certain the girl told the truth. Who then? Katherine released Elspeth. The girl sagged to the floor as if she were deflated, and lay at Katherine's feet, sobbing. "Leave us," Katherine said.

The girl crawled out the door. De Lauren pushed off the wall. An instant later, Katherine felt him smooth her hair back from her cheek. "We will find the one responsible," he said. "All will be well."

She looked up into his eyes. *All will be well, Kate.* He'd said the same to her the afternoon he'd been struck by the arrow. She'd leaned over him an instant before two knights from their hunting party lifted him off the ground. With her tears falling onto his face, de Lauren had said. "All will be well, Kate." He'd winked at her—an attempt to reassure her that had cost him, she'd seen—and then told her, "We have an appointment with Stanfield's priest I do not intend to miss."

Tears stung her eyes now. Katherine slid her arms around his waist. His arms came around her, tight and strong.

The solar door opened. Stephen strolled into the room. "Why is everyone awake at this hour?"

De Lauren turned with Katherine in his arms and gave his brother a succinct summary of the night's events.

"We must find the bastard at once!" Stephen slammed his fist on the table top.

"I am of the same mind," de Lauren said. "And we shall."

"What is being done to that end?" Stephen asked.

"Katherine is questioning the staff," de Lauren said.

Katherine looked up at de Lauren. "We needs determine who entered the lord's chamber after Anson had been there to refill the wine jug. Haldrake knows where each of Stanfield's people should be at their duties at given times. He keeps a record of such. We can use it to determine if someone was not where he should have been at any time after Anson replenished your wine, my lord."

Stephen nodded. "There are very few tasks that are not accomplished in the company of others. If someone left his post for a time, 'tis possible his absence was missed by another, and that the time away cannot be accounted for."

"I will ask Haldrake to fetch his records," Katherine said. She lifted her skirt with her uninjured hand and took a step away from de Lauren.

The vial slid from her pocket. It struck the floor and broke into pieces. A leaf drifted onto her slipper. Katherine recognized that leaf and sucked in her breath.

De Lauren's gaze lowered to her foot. He stared at it as if mesmerized, then bent slowly and picked up the leaf. From his crouched position, he looked up at Katherine. She saw disbelief in his widened eyes and hurt that stopped her breath. "I believe I recognize this leaf," he said softly. " 'Tis hemlock."

She'd identified plants for him on their various outings, the deadly hemlock plant among them. 'Twas no mistaking the venous, fan-like leaves.

"Aye, 'tis hemlock," she said. And the leaf had been in the vial.

"You!" Stephen shouted.

Her eyes on de Lauren, Katherine whispered, "Never."

"Leave us, Stephen," de Lauren said.

"Nick—"

"Out!" De Lauren shouted. He crushed the leaf in his fist.

The door closed behind Stephen. De Lauren rose from his crouch. Katherine looked up at him and shook her head slowly. "I did not do this. I do not know how the hemlock came to be in the medicine. Faith, if you had partaken of it. . . ." She shuddered.

Katherine clasped de Lauren's forearms. "Heed me. We must find who did this!"

He broke her hold on him and pushed her back from him. "You would do well to keep a distance from me at the moment, my lady," he said.

Katherine stumbled back, striking her hip against the corner of the table. She could hear de Lauren's harsh breathing. In this moment she feared he was capable of doing worse than pushing her. But she could not wait for his temper to cool. The one who wanted to kill him remained at large.

She regained her balance, and stood clutching the table's edge.

"Listen to me," she said. "Nicholas, you must hear me out. It means your life. I am not the one who sought your death." An awful thought struck her.

"I have heard enough—"

"Nay you have not. 'Tis time I told you about my marriage to William."

"You bring his name up to me, now?"

"I hated William." She heard her desperation in her voice. "But I love you, and that was why I married him."

His voice low and harsh, he said. "You must think me mad."

She ignored that. "Five years ago, one month before our wedding, William came to me and proposed marriage. Had he been sincere in seeking my hand out of deep feelings for me, I would have set him down gently. As it was, I remembered William had been in service to my father until a year earlier. I knew him to be avaricious, out for his own gain no matter what the cost. That was why Father had dismissed him. I sent William on his way.

"He told me that if I did not marry him, he would see you dead. I told him if he did not cease such talk, he would be dead."

I will give you a gift this day, Sir William. I will gift you with your life. For if I tell de Lauren of your attempt to force me to your will, this day, he will kill you.

"He said killing him would not save your life."

I am no longer without power or influence to be cast aside at the whims of the Stanfields. I have formed a strong alliance with one who will not allow the houses of de Lauren and Stanfield to join. If I am killed, know that de Lauren will not long survive me.

"Our marriage was but one month away. I dismissed his threat as ineffectual. The way I thought of him." Tears filled Katherine's eyes, blurring Nicholas' face. "The next day we left for King Henry's court. And the day following we went on a hunt in the king's forest." She closed her eyes, recalling the horror.

"You believed 'twas a stray arrow that felled you." She looked at de Lauren. "But William came to me with the truth. The arrow belonged to the ever-intoxicated Lord Bantam, aye, but 'twas stolen from him, and used to fell you. Not to kill, William assured me. But to warn me that if I did not marry him and grant him Stanfield, the next time you would be killed."

Katherine choked, then swallowed. "I knew then William could do as he said. I went to my father with William's proposal."

De Lauren's hands clenched into fists. "You would have me believe you married Norris to save my life?"

" 'Tis the truth."

"You would not recognize the truth if it leaped before you. Here is the truth, my lady, as given to me by your father when I stormed Stanfield with your note clutched in one fist and my sword in the other. Your father blocked my path to you, and God help me, I would have struck him down had I not seen pain in his eyes that mirrored my own.

"Katherine erred in her feelings for you, he told me. She felt honor-bound to do her duty by her title and lands and marry well. But she is in love with William Norris. Because of his land-less state she had vowed to put her feelings aside and make a match with de Lauren Keep, but she has found that she cannot go through with the wedding."

All the reasons she'd given her father, Katherine remembered.

"Landless. Penniless. Norris came to you with nothing. But himself. I could not compete with that."

"You must believe me—"

"Enough."

"Nicholas—"

"A pity for you, your attempt to bring about my demise failed. You will have no other opportunity. You will leave this room for one in Stanfield's tower."

She could not be imprisoned in the tower. With de Lauren's assassin at large. With no way to see her son. "You are making a mistake. Please, my lord, do not do this."

'Twas within his power to imprison her in the tower for the rest of her life. None would gainsay him. Not even the king. Tears blurred her vision. "Nicholas." Her voice quavered. "Do not lock me away."

De Lauren stared into her eyes. He closed his own eyes briefly then clenched his jaw and opened the door. "Guard!"

An instant later, a man she did not recognize charged into the room.

"Escort Lady Katherine to the tower," de Lauren said.

The guard approached Katherine. She stood her ground.

"If she will not walk, carry her," de Lauren said.

The guard reached out to her. She held up her shaking hands. "I will walk," her voice, thick with tears, came out hoarse. "I will walk," she repeated.

All too soon, she reached the tower. The heavy metal door clanged shut behind the guard. Katherine covered her face with her hands and wept.

"Lord, I yield!"

De Lauren blinked at the young knight laying on his back in the mud that now covered the training field. A slow drizzle fell for the third consecutive day. There was not a dry spot of land in all of Stanfield.

The knight's face was ghost white, his eyes bulging with fear. De Lauren stood over him, sword raised above his chest, in · position to deliver the death blow. He lowered his sword and shouted, "Next!"

The knight scrambled to his feet and dashed across the training field, away from de Lauren. When no one took the young soldier's place, de Lauren turned and faced the assembly behind him. His men stood in a line to take a turn sparring with their lord. It was one of the training methods de Lauren used, so he could gauge his men's skills himself.

Jerley, next in line, made no move toward de Lauren. "Jerley!" de Lauren said.

Jerley's prominent Adam's apple bobbed. Step lagging, he shuffled over to de Lauren and raised his sword waist-high.

De Lauren dispatched him with two solid blows. "You disgust me, Jerley. Next!"

Sword clutched tight in his fist, de Lauren looked about him for another adversary. There were no more men in the line. De Lauren had faced them all. His men stood in a wide circle, panting, perspiring, some doubled over.

"With you sorry lot, I may as well open the gates to our enemies!" De Lauren shouted. "Again! I will see if I can make men from you maids."

The sun was a thin red line on the horizon when de Lauren turned his back on his knights and strode from the training field. Anson ran forward. De Lauren tossed his sword to the lad and took the linen cloth Anson held out, without breaking pace. He wiped his face wet with sweat and rain, then draped the cloth across his shoulders.

As he neared the castle, his gaze rose to the tower where Katherine had spent the last two nights. There was no window, yet he peered at the stone as if he could see into the room. The thought of Katherine in there was eating away at him. Sweet Christ! He must be out of his mind. She'd wanted him dead. *She'd wanted him dead.* De Lauren gritted his teeth and lowered his gaze.

He took the castle steps two at a time. Two maids scuttled out of his path as he entered the great hall. Stanfield's people went about their tasks, preparing for last meal, quickly and quietly. No laughter. Indeed, no conversation. De Lauren heard his own bootsteps as he made his way out of the hall, and into the corridor. By now all at Stanfield knew of Katherine's exile to the tower, and her people mourned her fate.

Marcus paced outside the solar. He stopped when de Lauren reached him. "My lord, I need to speak with you." Marcus said.

The young knight passed his hand across his lips. Indeed, Marcus still wore his chain mail. The links and his breeches and boots were dusty. His fine brown hair stood on end as if he'd just removed his helm. He'd been on patrol, since dawn, and appeared to have come directly here when his shift ended.

De Lauren opened the door to the solar. "Inside," he said, and preceded Marcus into the room.

Marcus had scarcely closed the door, when he broke into speech. "My lord, I have made a grievous error. I have been remiss in my duty to you, and, may God forgive me, my lapse almost cost you your life."

De Lauren narrowed his eyes on Marcus. "Speak."

Marcus nodded. "A few days ago, I escorted Lady Katherine into the woods. We shared ale from a skin she brought. Shortly after, my vision blurred and my eyelids grew heavy. That is the last I recall until I heard Lady Katherine calling to me. I opened my eyes and saw her face above mine." Marcus shook his head. "I believe I lost consciousness. Lady Katherine claimed I fell ill. I recall but one other time when I felt as I did that day, and that time I had been drugged by a whore and her companion, and my purse stolen. I suspected the ale in Lady Katherine's skin had been tampered with, but your lady had suffered no ill-effects, so I dismissed my suspicion." Marcus' sharp green gaze lifted to de Lauren's. "But, my lord, when I assisted Lady Katherine into the saddle, I felt the mare's coat, wet with perspiration. Clearly, the horse had been ridden hard and very recently. About to untie the reins, I saw they were merely looped over the branch, not twice-knotted as is my habit. The mare was where I'd secured her, aye, but clearly, she'd been untied and ridden.

"Lady Katherine had not returned here for help, since we remained alone. I wondered where she'd gone. And I wondered if she'd not wanted me to accompany her, and placed something in my ale so I could not." Marcus rubbed the back of his neck. "I did not want to give credence to the thought that Lady Katherine had drugged me. I chose to accept her explanation that I'd merely taken ill, and said naught of it to anyone. Moments ago, upon my return to the castle, I learned of her attempt on your life. I should have voiced my suspicions when they arose, my lord. I have no excuse."

"Nay, you have none." De Lauren felt a muscle throb in his cheek. "Collect your belongings. Return to de Lauren Keep at once where you will await my decision on your future as one of my knights."

Marcus opened his mouth, but said nothing. His face looked dazed, as if de Lauren had struck him. Marcus swallowed, then bowed low. "Aye, my lord."

He made his way to his chamber. Anson followed and poured wine into de Lauren's goblet as de Lauren slipped off his dirt- and sweat-stained tunic and put on clean garments.

"I will see to your meal, my lord," Anson said.

De Lauren nodded, though he had no taste for anything but the wine. Anson collected the soiled garments, and left the room.

Dark, low-hanging clouds made the sky a slate grey. De Lauren slumped in the armchair across from the window, watching them, and raised the goblet to his lips. He downed the wine, then reached for the jug Anson had placed on the small round table.

A knock invaded the silence.

"Go away," de Lauren called out.

The door opened. Stephen entered the room.

De Lauren glanced at Stephen, then back out the window. "Are you hard of hearing, this evening, brother? I said 'Go away.'"

"You are drunk," Stephen said.

"Nay, but I am working on it," de Lauren said. "I would do so in solitude."

Stephen perched on the edge of the bed and clasped his hands between his knees. His voice low, he said, "I saw Marcus in the knight's quarters. Packing his belongings, at your command, he told me. He would not say what had prompted you to dismiss him."

De Lauren took a mouthful of wine and did not reply.

"Jerley suffered a broken arm as a result of today's training," Stephen went on, as quietly. "Smythe, a sword wound to his shoulder. Woods has swelling and bruising in the area of his ribs.

"I await your word, Nick, and I will ride to the king and inform him of what has transpired here. Given Katherine's crime, I am certain he will accommodate her in his own tower. She need not remain here to torment you. You will be rid of her."

Aye, he could rid himself of Katherine by branding her an attempted murderess. Henry would be merciless with one who would take the life of one of his vassals, thereby weakening the throne.

Again, de Lauren did not reply.

"I see no reason to delay—"

"Enough!"

Stephen sat in silence for a moment, then slowly gained his feet and left the room. De Lauren flung his goblet at the wall.

CHAPTER SEVENTEEN

Ranulf waited in Gerard Montrose's solar. This room faced east to catch the sunrise. The sun had risen hours earlier, yet the day was grey and candlelight provided the only illumination in the room. 'Twas July, and Montrose had called for a fire to be lit. Ranulf wiped sweat from the back of his neck. The room felt hot as an oven.

Montrose sat by the fire, a thick coverlet spread across his lap. He'd deteriorated further in the time since Ranulf had come here seeking Katherine three weeks earlier. Montrose's skin was as pale as parchment and stretched thin over protruding bones in his face and hands. Doubtful Montrose would live to enjoy Michaelmas. Mayhap, Ranulf thought, he would install Ellis here, as his vassal, when Montrose departed this earth, and King Henry gave him the holding to oversee.

Where the devil was Ellis?

Ranulf had arranged to meet with Ellis at Montrose Keep. De Lauren hadn't relaxed his guard for miles around Stanfield, and Ranulf had no wish to reside in Stanfield's dungeon. Montrose Keep was the closest he dared get to Stanfield.

A knock on the solar door drew Ranulf's attention.

"Enter," Montrose said.

'Twas little more than a whisper. A squeaky whisper that grated on Ranulf's nerves and could not be heard on the other side of the door. He released a harsh, impatient breath then shouted. "Come."

The door opened and a guard entered. "My lord, a man at the gates is here to see Lord Ranulf. He's given his name as Sir Ellis."

"What say you, Ranulf?" Montrose asked.

Ranulf had told Montrose naught of why he'd come here. The less said of his plans for de Lauren, the better. King Henry would not look kindly on discovering that Ranulf had ordered the murder of one of the Crown's vassals.

Ranulf ignored Montrose and said to the guard, "Admit Ellis to my chamber."

Montrose leaned forward in the armchair. "Speak with Sir Ellis in here, Ranulf. I will leave you to your privacy. I have gone too long without seeing my lady Grace and I will use this time to seek her out."

The guard left. Montrose slowly gained his feet. Leaning heavily on a cane, he shuffled out of the room.

A few moments later, Ranulf admitted Ellis into the room.

"Well?" Ranulf said.

Ellis closed the solar door. He removed the cloak he wore over threadbare breeches and tunic in a dirt brown, and flung the cloak onto the chair Montrose had vacated.

"A problem, my lord," Ellis said.

Failure. Ranulf inhaled deeply and slowly, straightening his shoulders as he did so.

Ellis held up his hands, palms out. "I followed through with our plan to use poison. Rather than spoil de Lauren's wine however, I made use of a golden opportunity to taint medicine our dedicated healer, Lady Katherine, prepared for him. Apparently, though, a cat ingested that medicine—I know naught the details of how this came to be." Ellis raked hair back from his temples. "The cat died in de Lauren's presence. 'Twas no chance for me to learn the plan went awry and remove the cat's carcass before de Lauren found it." Ellis sighed. "I did as you bid me, and set the evidence for the poisoning so Lady Katherine would be blamed for it. I did so, though, before I knew de Lauren yet lived. She is, as we speak, a guest in Stanfield's tower. As long as she remains exiled, I cannot make another attempt on de Lauren's life or he will know she is not the one seeking his death."

Ranulf's grip on the goblet shook. "You have taken a simple plan and complicated it. Nay, we cannot make another attempt while Katherine resides in the tower."

Ranulf needed her guilt in the matter of de Lauren's death to be irrefutable, so he could then refute it and coerce her into marriage. Would she choose death, or marriage to him, if he would produce an assassin to take her place on the executioner's block? Katherine was a survivor. Ranulf believed she would choose to live.

Damn Ellis for this failure! Ranulf had waited long enough to make Stanfield and Stanfield's lady his. As to making Katherine his, he would wait to bed her. He would know for certain that a babe she carried was his offspring and not that whoreson de Lauren's.

"This plan will go to naught if de Lauren decides to make Katherine's residence in the tower permanent," Ranulf said.

"About that my lord, I believe all is not lost. I have learned that Lady Katherine has been keeping a secret. She has a son."

"What?"

"Aye. The boy is in the care of Sir Guy du Monde, commander of Stanfield's guard. I followed her from Stanfield on one of her forays into the woods and discovered she had secreted her son in a cabin south of Stanfield. De Lauren knows naught of him. I overheard Lady Katherine tell Sir Guy that. She believes, however, that de Lauren is close to learning of the boy's existence and she fears that result." Ellis pursed his lips. "Sir Guy has since moved the child. I know naught where at the moment. If it is your wish, however, I will find out."

"A son," Ranulf said. The existence of a child changed everything. It no longer mattered if de Lauren were killed while Katherine was in the tower, because Ranulf would not need the threat of her execution to coerce her into marriage. Katherine would beg to marry him if her doing so meant her son's life.

Ranulf tapped his forefinger against his bottom lip. "Aye, Ellis, do determine where Guy has taken Katherine's son."

How long had she been locked in the tower? Katherine rubbed her forehead. There were no windows to mark the dawn and the setting sun. Had she been in here three days? Four? 'Twas one or the other, she was certain, but she didn't know which and that very fact terrified her. Already, her days had blended until she knew naught when one ended and another began.

If de Lauren deemed she should die in this room, she would surely be mad long before that happened.

And while she slowly went mad, de Lauren's assassin was free to make another attempt to kill him.

She heard wood scrape against wood and knew the bar that secured the door was being lifted. Another meal?

Her stomach balked at the thought of food. The last tray, piled high with partridge, was on the table, untouched. Despite his anger and hurt at what he believed was her latest betrayal, de Lauren had not ordered rations of bread and water for her. All of her meals were what she knew to be the best of Stanfield's fare.

The door to the tower room opened, causing a slight breeze. The flame, from the slim taper in a dish on the table, flickered but did not extinguish.

Stephen stood in the doorway, backlit by the torches in the stairwell. Each time a guard delivered a meal, she asked to see

Stephen. So many requests and he had not come to her. But he was here now.

"Stephen . . . " She spoke his name in a hush.

"You have incredible gall," he said. He did not venture farther into the room. "For the life of me, I cannot fathom why you would call for me. Know that the only reason I am here is to prevent you from sending a similar summons to my brother."

Katherine's heart beat harder at mention of de Lauren. "How is he?"

"That you would ask me that." Stephen exhaled a quick, impatient breath. "Contemplating handing you over to our king to face his justice. At first light, I hope, that is what he will do."

Stephen's words chilled her.

"Until then, I will deal with you," Stephen said. "Now, why have you sent for me?"

Katherine pressed her hands together in front of her. "You are the one person I trust with Nicholas' life. You must hear me. I am not the one who wants him dead."

"Is this why you asked for me? To hear more pleas of your innocence." Stephen started back out the door.

"The true assassin remains at large, free to make another attempt," she called out. "You must find him. Before it is too late."

"Too late?" Stephen turned quickly, and took a quick step toward her. "My brother will be safe as long as he keeps his distance from you."

He clenched his fist, but turned away from her, out the door. The door slammed behind him.

"Come back!" She ran to the door, reaching it as it closed in her face. "You must come back!" She struck the wood with the flat of her hand. The sound of footsteps faded and she knew he could no longer hear her.

She pressed her forehead to the door and murmured, "Come

back, before it is too late."

De Lauren upended his wine jug. Naught poured out. He knocked the empty jug off the table, then stalked to the door of the solar and flung it open. The door thudded against the wall.

"Anson!" De Lauren shouted the boy's name though Anson was a mere arm's length away. "More wine."

The boy arrived with another jug almost at once. De Lauren refilled his goblet. He lifted it to his lips, then glimpsed Haldrake in the open doorway, but did not invite him into the chamber.

"I have come to speak with you about Lady Katherine, my lord. Specifically, sir, her exile to the tower room."

De Lauren eyed the older man above the rim of the cup. "You have forgotten your place, Steward."

Haldrake's naturally pale face paled further. " 'Twas not my lady who tampered with the medicine." Haldrake squared his shoulders and lifted his chin. " 'Twas I, my lord."

"Be gone."

Haldrake swallowed and cleared his throat. " 'Tis the truth, my lord. 'Tis I who should suffer your wrath, and not my lady."

De Lauren's grip on the goblet tightened and he lowered it from his lips. He crossed the room to the doorway, and with the hand that wasn't holding the cup, seized Haldrake by the shirt front. "Tell me why you would do this."

Haldrake cleared his throat. "I made my way into Lady Katherine's chamber and tainted the medicament in the—"

De Lauren shook Haldrake. "Not how, but why. Tell me why you would seek my death and I will take you at your word. Tell me why."

To de Lauren's own ears, it sounded like a plea.

Haldrake's bushy grey eyebrows rose. His mouth opened, but he said nothing. Clearly, he had no answer. De Lauren's presence at Stanfield protected the keep and its people from Ranulf and other enemies. Haldrake had no motive to seek his death, and they both knew it.

De Lauren unclenched his fist and let his arm fall to his side.

"Be about your duties," he said quietly, "and do not try my patience further with falsehoods."

Haldrake's eyes watered as he left the solar. De Lauren lifted the cup to his lips. There he held it, but did not drink. He'd wanted to accept Haldrake's confession. So desperately did he want Katherine with him, he'd almost accepted Haldrake's false confession and condemned an innocent man. He'd condemned Marcus. Condemned the knight whose only crime was loyalty to his lady. It was Marcus' duty to take Katherine at her word. He'd performed that duty, and been punished for it.

De Lauren exhaled deeply. He would right that wrong and reinstate his knight. As soon as he could take time away from Stanfield, he would ride to de Lauren Keep and speak with Marcus.

A door thudded to a close above stairs. The door to the tower room? De Lauren's gaze darted to the ceiling and remained fixed there as if he could see through the stone. See Katherine . . .

If Katherine had her way, he'd be three days dead. And he loved her still.

De Lauren rubbed the heel of one hand to his eye, then hurled his goblet into the hearth.

She was his enemy. She'd taught him that bitter lesson five years ago, though she now denied that betrayal. And repeated it.

He'd not forget again.

The tower door opened with a whoosh. The taper on the table had burned out moments ago, leaving Katherine in total darkness. Light flickered into the room from the torches in the stairwell. De Lauren entered.

Katherine was seated on the narrow pallet, arms around herself against a draft blowing in from the north wall at her back. She pressed one hand to the stone and slowly gained her feet.

"Nicholas . . . " she said in a breathy whisper. "Nicholas, you are well." She closed her eyes. "Thank God."

"You would do better to pray for your own continued health," he said.

Gone was the anger he'd shown following the poisoning. A coldness had replaced it unlike she'd ever seen from him before, and it frightened her more than any anger could.

"I've come to a decision about your incarceration," he said.

Katherine curled her fingers, clutching the stone. Stephen had said he'd encouraged de Lauren to send her to the king . . .

"My lord, if you mean to send me to Henry—"

"You will remain at Stanfield," de Lauren said. "And henceforth you will act as my food taster."

She was back in the lady's chamber. After de Lauren made his announcement, he'd instructed Sir Cavendish to return her to her room.

The taciturn Cavendish stood outside the chamber while Elspeth assisted Katherine at her bath. After three days in the same gown, Katherine relished being clean again.

A sharp rap on the door was followed by Sir Cavendish's command. "The maid is to leave, my lady, as soon as she's seen to you."

Katherine nodded to the teary-eyed Elspeth and the girl left the room.

A breeze was blowing in through the window. Katherine stood in front of it and took deep breaths. The air was cold on her damp skin, but cold air was better than the stale air of the tower.

De Lauren had appointed her his food taster. She knew he didn't believe she was in any danger from the poisoner, because she was the poisoner. Whoever had added hemlock to de Lauren's medicine had set her up to be blamed credibly by using her skill with herbs.

Would de Lauren's killer taint food she would now be tasting, and risk losing her as his scapegoat? Mayhap, if the assassin decided that de Lauren's death was worth that cost.

A knock on the door drew her attention.

"Come in," she said. Her voice sounded so thin.

Anson entered the room. "You are to come with me, my lady," he said. "Lord de Lauren has commanded it."

Katherine nodded. "Lead on, Anson."

Sir Cavendish trailed behind Katherine as she followed Anson below stairs and into the great hall. Her people huddled by the walls, faces drawn and solemn. She heard weeping. Their fear was palpable. Doubtless her incarceration had both confused and frightened them. They'd only just regained their stability after Ranulf's attack, and her imprisonment had rocked them.

De Lauren was seated at the lord's table. Anson and Cavendish escorted her to the dais, then left her at the foot of the stairs to take the last steps to de Lauren, on her own. Her feet felt heavy. She lifted them with effort and climbed the stairs.

She felt every eye in the hall on her. Her people would be reassured at seeing her, and unharmed. She felt grateful to de Lauren for giving them that reassurance.

He'd allowed her to bathe and change clothes, rather than humiliate her before her people. She was grateful for that, as well.

She reached the lord's table and took her place to de Lauren's right. Stephen sat to de Lauren's left and his eyes bulged at the sight of her. Katherine looked quickly away from him.

A serving girl deposited a tray piled high with pheasant and partridge and sweet pies. De Lauren's favorite.

Without looking at Katherine he sliced a pie and speared a small chunk on the end of his eating knife. He held it out to her. So her duty as his food taster would begin. And he would eat after her, believing himself safe in doing so. Her stomach knotted with fear for them both.

De Lauren selected choice tidbits of pheasant and partridge and presented them to her, as well. He handed her his goblet to drink from. She winced. If his wine were not poisoned, then the wine itself would make her ill. But the goblet contained water. Katherine took a sip, then set it on the table.

She'd eaten little while in the tower, but had no appetite. She chewed slowly, fearing each bite would be more than her stomach could hold, and poisoned or not, would come back up.

But before long, de Lauren lowered his eating knife. He'd consumed little, as well, she'd noticed.

"Nicholas—" she said.

He inclined his head and an instant later Sir Cavendish came to her.

She was being dismissed. She fought back a wave of frustration. Clearly, though, naught would be gained by pressing him further this night. She looked down at her hands in the lap of her blue gown. "I am quite capable of finding my way to my room on my own, my lord."

De Lauren looked at her, his eyes cold. "Do not mistake me, my lady, Cavendish is not your escort, but your jailer. He will return you to your room and he will remain outside your door throughout the night. In the morn, his replacement will spend his day trailing you. You will be guarded as completely out of the tower as you were within it."

Chapter Eighteen

Katherine knelt at her daughter's grave. She passed her hand over the tufts of grass that had sprung since the ground had been disturbed. She'd been so afraid that de Lauren would keep her imprisoned in the tower and that she'd never again come here to her child.

That had not happened. That had not happened. She'd been repeating that to herself since her release last night, whenever the horror of the last three days resurfaced.

At de Lauren's orders, Sir Cavendish or another knight now trailed her wherever she went. Today, 'twas Sir Cavendish who was her jailer. The large knight, who looked as solid as the castle, stood a distance behind her, giving her privacy with her child.

Sir Cavendish was a man of few words, unlike Sir Marcus. She'd wondered why Cavendish rather than Marcus had been assigned to her. She'd asked Sir Cavendish about Marcus and been told the young knight was no longer at Stanfield.

That was not the only change she'd noticed at the keep. Gone was the laughter that she'd heard from her people while they went about their chores. Around her now, she saw tense, unsmiling faces.

Her imprisonment in the tower had left them shaken, she believed. If de Lauren had wanted to assert his authority, he could have done no better than to have imprisoned their lady. If the lady of the keep could be sent to the tower, no doubt her people feared for themselves.

Katherine knew de Lauren had not sent her to the tower to flex his muscles to Stanfield's people. He believed her guilty of trying to kill him. She felt as if something heavy landed on her chest with that thought. She could not blame him. The evidence against her was damning, and he believed one more betrayal to add to her list.

He did not believe what she'd told him about her marriage to William. And because de Lauren did not believe her, he remained vulnerable.

She had to find the one who'd tried to kill him. In the solar, before de Lauren had discovered the hemlock in her vial, she'd told him of her plan to consult Haldrake's duty schedule for the castle staff.

Katherine pressed a kiss to the small cross marking her daughter's grave, then gained her feet. With Sir Cavendish at her heels, she set out to see Haldrake.

Two days in the tower room had renewed Katherine's appreciation for large, open spaces. The ground was soft and wet from three nights of rain. She could see worms squirming in the dirt. The pungent smell of them was in the air, but after the stifling tower, their odor was a welcome one.

Haldrake's room, behind the kitchens, doubled as his work room and housed the records he maintained for the keep. As usual when Haldrake was not abed, his door was open. He was bent over papers when Katherine arrived at his door. Sir Cavendish took up a position outside the chamber and Katherine entered the room.

Haldrake rushed to her side and in an uncustomary breach of protocol, clasped her uninjured hand in both of his. "My lady." He squeezed her fingers. "You are well?"

"Very."

He nodded, and for a moment appeared unable to speak.

After the last few days of naught but hostile faces around her, Katherine felt herself in much the same condition.

She cleared her throat. "I need your help, Haldrake."

He bowed. "I am ever at your service."

"Someone within Stanfield has tried to kill Lord de Lauren. I have to find him before he can make another attempt."

"What can I do?" Haldrake asked.

"You keep a record of assigned duties. The vial that contained the poisoned medicine meant for Lord de Lauren was in my chamber. I need to find out who could have had access to it."

"Let us have a look."

Haldrake went to a stack of parchment on his writing table. Katherine smiled, seeing the corners of the pages were perfectly aligned. He looked through them a moment, then withdrew one sheet.

Katherine bent over Haldrake's desk and reached out to the candle, bringing the light close to the page. Haldrake's record could not be completely accurate. One neglecting his post or leaving early, or two people deciding to change duties for the day, would not necessarily be reported to Haldrake. Still, if she knew where everyone was supposed to be, she had something to confirm or deny.

"Any changes of late?" she asked as she skimmed Haldrake's notes. She compared the duty schedule for the day in question with days before it. If someone had recently requested another post, she wanted to know the reason for that request.

"I removed drawing of well water from the girl Sarah's list of chores. She came to me with the tidings that she is with child." Haldrake cleared his throat discreetly behind his fist. "She has miscarried on two previous occasions. I have noted that Chloe has assumed that task."

Katherine nodded. The change and reasons for it were noted in Haldrake's precise script.

Of particular interest were the chores that placed people near her chamber. She would confirm those first.

With the promise to return the duty schedule, Katherine left Haldrake. The only people who would not have to account to Haldrake for their time were children, soldiers, and those not associated with Stanfield. She would need help in placing de Lauren's men. She didn't know who would be willing to help her with that. Doubtless the men would not seek to help the lady they believed had tried to kill their lord.

She moved on to Stanfield's visitors. She didn't trust Bishop Whittaker. She didn't know if he would go so far as to kill de Lauren to further his own ends, but it was a moot point, anyway. The bishop was under guard. Ian, the seminarian, was still visiting Stanfield. She needed to look into his whereabouts. And she needed to place the entertainers for that day.

With the ever-present Sir Cavendish, she narrowed her focus to those who worked near her chambers. Let him know what she was about, she thought. Let him report her investigation to his lord. It mattered naught if de Lauren knew what she was doing.

Katherine spent the rest of the day verifying that her people had been at their assigned posts. The situation demanded that she work quickly, but as she did she feared she would overlook something in the rush and that oversight would ultimately cost de Lauren his life.

Her own salvation was tied to his. She had to prove her innocence to him. All was lost if she could not.

She saw de Lauren only at mealtimes. While she worked through Haldrake's list, de Lauren spent his time closeted in the solar with Stephen.

The door was again closed, she saw now as she passed by it. In two days of investigation, she'd found no one who'd been where he shouldn't be. But someone had been out of place, and she would find him.

A curious twist to the attempt, she thought again, was the poisoner's effort to implicate her. By placing the hemlock in her vial, the finger of blame had been pointed at her. Whoever wanted de Lauren dead had left no doubt that he also wanted her blamed for the crime.

No doubt since she'd pocketed the vial, she'd helped bring about that end. It appeared that she'd removed the proof of what she'd done. Mayhap had she left the vial in plain sight, she could have used that to introduce some doubt of her blame in de Lauren's mind. If only . . . She shook her head. No point torturing herself with "what ifs." What was done could not be undone.

Katherine turned a corner and reached her destination, the kitchen. She could account for a great many of the castle staff by speaking with Livvy. It took many people to feed Stanfield's population.

Livvy was inside, overseeing preparations for last meal. "Me lady," Livvy said with a sniff. "So glad I be to see you out the tower and back amongst us."

"Thank you, Livvy. I need to speak with you," Katherine said. "Let us talk outside." She led Livvy to a table. The aromatic smells from the kitchen wafted through the open door and the sun was bright and warm. Sir Cavendish took up a position in the shade of the castle.

"I have a list of all of the people who worked in the kitchens on the day the attempt was made on Lord de Lauren's life," Katherine said. "I need you to confirm that these people were, in fact, here."

Livvy squared her shoulders, and her ample bosom jutted out. "Ye can count on me, Lady Katherine."

Katherine withdrew Haldrake's schedule from her pocket and recited several names.

"Aye, they was all here, though Glenda left before her time was up."

"Glenda?"

"I had the girls cleaning up after second meal—watching them I was—'specially that Glenda, lazy tramp. Got her mind on the lads and not on scrubbing pots let me tell you." Livvy nodded. "That young hunter, Kyle, come in fluttering over her. I sent him on his way, telling him not to distract the girl from her work. She tell me bold as brass that her days in the kitchens was almost over. How's she was going to get herself a light job—mayhap something like upstairs bedchamber maid. That Sir Stephen would soon see to that. She's been spending her nights with Sir Stephen lately, you know," Livvy said with a nod. "I told her that until that fine day come, she had pots to scrub. But Sir Stephen came for her and she went off with him."

Katherine nodded. That accounted for Glenda.

Livvy clasped her hands at her ample waist and scrunched up her face. "I remember Anson popped into me kitchen that afternoon. The boy has a fondness for pie and he brung in that pup he took in?"

Katherine felt her patience stretching at the snake-like trail Livvy was taking to answer the question, but Katherine knew if she interrupted the cook or redirected her, Livvy would start the recitation from the beginning. Katherine took a couple of deep, calming breaths.

"Well didn't that dog cause a fuss?" Livvy went on. "It come in and knocked over a small table where's I had turnips waiting for last meal. I took after it meself with me broom, but that dog took off under that there low table and there was no ways I could get under it to get the dog. I yelled for Anson to get his animal out o' me kitchen." Livvy clucked her tongue. "The boy did, though not before the animal tore a strip from Elspeth's gown."

"What time was Elspeth here?"

"Had to be going on two o'clock, 'cause I'd just put the apple pies in to bake. She come in to ask to borrow some ear bobs from Beatrix, the big girl what carries in the water. Told Beatrix she was meeting her young man—you know that entertainer fellow—for something special."

Two o'clock. Katherine wondered if that meeting was why her laundry had not been done that day. She was going to have to speak with Elspeth again about her duties.

" 'T'aint right if you ask me, her carrying on with that fellow when Donny's expecting to marry her." The corners of Livvy's mouth turned down. "Sure that entertainer, he's a fine one to look at, but in real life, how far will that get you?" Livvy nodded briskly. "Not far I can tell you." Livvy sniffed. "I left the kitchen for a few minutes after I put me pies on to bake. Went in to the hall to see what was taking the girls so long to clean up after second meal. Had me dander up over it, let me tell you, I walked right into Brother Ian coming down the stairs."

Katherine frowned. "Brother Ian?"

"Aye. He stepped off the stairs, on his way down, you see. I had me mind on them girls lazing about instead of doing what needed doing. Poor Brother Ian." Livvy looked sheepish. "I walked into him so hard, I knocked him on his backside, I did. I expect he's still feeling that fall. Was there aught more you needed to know, lady?"

Katherine shook her head slowly. "My thanks, Livvy."

Katherine rose from the table. She left Livvy and headed for the chapel.

Father Juttan was kneeling before the altar when Katherine opened the door to the chapel. The smells of candle wax and wine were pungent in the air. Katherine crossed herself, genuflected, then sat in one of the backless benches to wait until the priest had finished his prayers. It was a short wait. Father Juttan joined her at the bench.

"Hello, my lady," Father Juttan said. "I prayed you would be returned to us."

"Thank you, Father."

"I have visited people who have been similarly confined. If you have need of God's comfort, I am available to pray with you."

Katherine had known Father Juttan since childhood. He'd comforted her when she'd lost Mother and more recently Father. And she'd sent him away when he'd come to her after William's death.

"My thanks Father," Katherine said. "But that is not why I've come. I need to speak with Brother Ian. Can you tell me where I might find him?"

The priest smiled, lifting the sagging skin around his face. "Indeed I may and it is my delight to do so. He's returned to follow God's path. As we speak, he is en route to rejoin the good brothers of the monastery outside his hometown of Guildford."

Katherine narrowed her eyes. "When did he leave?"

"Four days ago."

Someone poisoned de Lauren's medicine four days ago.

"At what time did he leave?"

"As to that, I'm uncertain," Father Juttan said. "He did not tell me his plans, nor did he seek me out to say his fare-thee-well. I found a brief letter from him thanking me for my counsel and telling me he was leaving."

"Did it not strike you as odd that he would not say his good-bye in person?"

"Not particularly. Brother Ian is a man of few words. In his time with me, he spoke little. I would have welcomed an opportunity to wish him well, but I do not question his choice in this matter."

"Do you still have Brother Ian's letter?" Katherine asked.

Father Juttan nodded. "I'll fetch it."

The letter was indeed brief—two hastily scrawled lines—that told her no more than Father Juttan had.

He smiled as Katherine returned the letter to him. "He's traveled a long journey," Father Juttan said, "but by God's grace has found his way back to the church."

Katherine wondered if it had been a desire to return to the church that had prompted Ian to leave Stanfield or if, after having added hemlock to de Lauren's medicine, Ian believed his foul deed done and no longer needed to stay on. The timing of his leave-taking was exceptional.

She had no true proof of the man's guilt. A hasty leave-taking on the day of the murder attempt could be naught more than coincidence. But she had to know for sure.

Four days since Ian left. Faith, he could be anywhere by now. Katherine got to her feet. Ian had to be found. But for that, she needed help.

Katherine went in search of de Lauren. If the absent Brother Ian was responsible for the murder attempt, then de Lauren was safe. Brother Ian's timely exit from Stanfield served one other purpose. It raised the possibility that she was not the poisoner.

Katherine sought de Lauren in the solar where she'd known he'd been spending a great deal of time lately. The door was open and the room was empty.

She went next to the training field, and found him there. He was not engaged in any exercises, but stood facing Stephen and another knight who were engaged in swordplay. Her throat tightened when she spotted de Lauren. Faith, how she missed him.

She fought back that hurt and concentrated on the reason she'd sought him out.

It looked to Katherine that a training session had just ended. Only Stephen and his opponent stood with swords raised, while other knights were making their way from the field.

De Lauren was intent on the mock battle. Katherine stepped in front of him. She was not tall enough to obstruct his view of Stephen and the other knight. He continued to watch them over her head.

"My lord, I must speak with you."

De Lauren ignored her, but his lips firmed and she knew he'd heard her. She turned away from him and headed to where Stephen stood. His sword was raised. She seized the hand that held it. His opponent's sword sliced through Stephen's blue tunic, above the gauntlet that covered his forearm. Stephen inhaled sharply. He lowered his sword and turned on her.

De Lauren's hand landed on her shoulder. He spun her toward him. "Have you lost all reason? You are truly blessed Stephen did not run you through with his sword."

She ignored that and said to him, "Brother Ian left Stanfield abruptly on the day your medicine was poisoned. Earlier, he'd been seen leaving the castle's second story. 'Tis possible he added the hemlock to the vial. We must find him and learn the truth."

De Lauren's gaze lifted from hers. "Prepare to resume, Stephen."

He'd dismissed her out of hand. "Nicholas, have you not comprehended what I've just told you?" Katherine said.

His eyes met hers again, and his seemed to glitter with anger. "First you bring the good brother into our midst. Then you argue to have him removed. Now you want him back? Tell me, my lady, what is your association with him?"

Katherine felt the knot in her stomach tighten. "I discovered Ian as I said I did. Injured on the road."

"Aye, but which road?" de Lauren said. "Not the one you named, remember?"

She made no reply to that. "Please, time passes and we have already lost four days."

De Lauren leaned over her. He gritted his teeth. "I will hear no more."

De Lauren walked away. She could hear her heart pounding. Again, she reached out to Stephen and seized his hand.

"Desist," Stephen said. "Or I will not be responsible for the consequences."

Katherine did not release him. Instead she tightened her grip. "Can you dismiss what we've learned about Ian? Can you take that chance and risk another attempt on Nicholas' life?"

Stephen's mouth tightened. "Nay, I would not risk my brother's life. I would have you locked in the tower until you are dead."

CHAPTER NINETEEN

De Lauren stared at the parchment on his writing table. He and Stephen had spent the last few days outlining their strategy for the attack on Ranulf. Plans were almost finalized and de Lauren had set a date to march on Warbrook Keep—one week from today.

A knock sounded on the door.

"Enter," de Lauren called out.

Cavendish stood in the doorway. "My lord, you wished to know when Lady Katherine would leave Stanfield? She plans to gather herbs in the forest."

"When?"

"I left her in her chamber with her maid to change clothing. I will collect her once I have saddled her mare."

"Be about it," de Lauren said. "And Cavendish? Send in my squire."

"You wanted me, my lord?" the boy said an instant later.

"Anson, ready my mount."

De Lauren had not forbidden her to gather herbs. Katherine retrieved her satchel from her chamber and with Sir Cavendish by her side, rode out of Stanfield.

The horses' hooves plodded over the damp earth. Low-hanging clouds promised more rain and there was a chill in the air that her cloak could not stave off.

"There, up ahead, lady, is a clearing. Is it the one you seek?"

She had no set destination. This spot would serve.

"Aye, Sir Cavendish," she said. "Let us dismount here."

A few minutes later, Sir Cavendish lowered her from her horse. While he tied the reins to a tree, Katherine poured the refreshment she'd brought. A tart lemon drink that she'd learned was Sir Cavendish's favorite. The drink was a little more potent today due to the liberal helping of poppy she'd added to it.

She was going to see Sir Guy. At their last meeting, when he'd told her he would be moving her son to another location, he'd told her he would return to the cabin each Tuesday and await her there until sunset. He would be there this day. She needed to learn where he'd lodged her son and she needed his help to find Ian.

As she had with Sir Marcus, Katherine turned to Sir Cavendish now, and offered him a drink.

She was leaping at shadows. Katherine came to that conclusion when she glanced over her shoulder for the fourth time in as many minutes, and saw nothing but leaves swaying in a slight breeze and two squirrels carrying twigs. Her time in the tower had taxed her nerves.

She'd left Sir Cavendish asleep beneath a tree. A light rain began. Thick leaves sheltered this part of the woods, but for the drops that filtered through the branches overhead. She would not have the shelter for long. The road she sought came into view. Katherine raised the hood on her cloak.

An hour later, she rode into the clearing and reined in. The cabin door opened. Sir Guy came out to meet her. He lowered her from her horse and secured the reins to a post by the door.

"Let us talk out of the rain, my lady," he said.

Inside the cabin, rain tapped on the wooden roof. The window was open, making the room chill and damp.

Katherine removed her hood and looked to Sir Guy. "Tell me of my son," she said.

"He is safe. We are residing in the town of Kerwick, ten miles south of here. We have told the tale that I am a merchant, that the child is mine, and my wife died in childbirth."

She released a slow deep breath. "How long will you remain in Kerwick?"

Deep creases formed on Sir Guy's forehead. "The people there have no cause to suspect we are not what we claim. Still, I would not linger long. If someone has learned of the boy, that someone will make inquiries and eventually make his way to Kerwick."

Katherine agreed. Her son remained vulnerable.

"How go plans to return to Stanfield?" Sir Guy asked.

No doubt Sir Guy hoped she'd made progress there and could soon return Michael. "De Lauren is ever more suspicious of me." Katherine updated Sir Guy on her own precarious situation with de Lauren and her investigation to find de Lauren's would-be assassin.

"I like not that you are alone in this situation," Sir Guy said. "Tread carefully, my lady. You may also be in danger from this assassin."

"I am ever on my guard," she said. She paced the cabin's dirt floor. "I need your help to find a man named Ian, Sir Guy."

"The one you treated at Stanfield?"

Katherine went on to tell Sir Guy her suspicions about Ian. "If Ian is responsible for the poisoning, then de Lauren is safe now that Ian has left Stanfield. Until Ian learns that de Lauren did not die. 'Tis my hope that you can find able men to help you." She reached into the pocket of her cloak. "I have brought some of my jewelry to be used to buy the help you need. Promise whatever further payment you must."

She placed the small velvet pouch in Sir Guy's scarred palm.

"I will do what I can," he said. "A few names come to mind of men I can enlist. I have known them to act with discretion. Of course, I will remain with young Lord Michael."

Katherine nodded. "My thanks, as always, Sir Guy."

Sir Guy bowed his head.

"I had best be away," Katherine said.

Sir Guy frowned. "I hear—"

The cabin door opened. Sir Guy drew his sword and whirled toward it, putting himself between the door and Katherine.

Katherine met de Lauren's gaze across the room and her stomach dropped.

"So, this is where you come, my lady, to replenish your herbs," de Lauren said. "Pray tell me what herb grows in this cabin?"

Katherine had not the saliva to speak. She swallowed. "My lord—"

" 'Tis not far from here that Brother Ian claimed he'd met you. I confess when Sir Cavendish came to me this morn, and told me he'd be escorting you into the woods, I did wonder if you would venture in this direction."

Sir Cavendish went to see de Lauren. Katherine had not considered that de Lauren would trail the man he'd set to trail her.

"I thought you might come here to meet with the good brother," de Lauren went on. "I could think of no other reason for you to return to these parts, since my men searched these cabins and found them to be abandoned."

De Lauren must have searched the area after Sir Guy had moved Michael, or else he would have found her child himself. Cold sweat broke out Katherine's spine. "You followed me from Stanfield," she said softly.

" 'Twas not easy. You traveled a circuitous path. I was hard pressed, indeed, to keep you in my sight."

She had not been leaping at shadows, at all. She'd led de Lauren here. She closed her eyes.

"I've wondered about your fate, Guy."

Katherine opened her eyes. "Sir Guy has been making his way home since the battle that claimed William's life," Katherine said.

De Lauren crossed his arms and looked to her. "Not so, my lady. Guy was spotted at Stanfield on the day of Ranulf's attack."

Katherine straightened her shoulders. "You are well informed."

"Guy was seen leaving the keep in the company of Old Middy. Escorting the woman to safety, Guy? If so, the keep has long been secure, yet you have chosen to stay in this cabin. What have you been doing?"

Sir Guy said naught.

De Lauren focused on Katherine and his voice went cold. " 'Twas exceptional fortune for Ranulf that he was not at his holding when I marched on it, my lady spy. No doubt word of that attack is but one of the messages Guy has relayed to Ranulf from you."

Katherine could not deny the accusation without supplying another reason for Guy remaining at the cabin. She was out of lies.

"There will be no more messages," de Lauren said. "Guy will be accompanying us back to Stanfield."

With Sir Guy at Stanfield, who would safeguard Michael? "Sir Guy," Katherine said slowly. "Leave."

"I think not," de Lauren said.

Guy raised his sword.

Katherine was about to shout "nay," but she saw that despite the threat from Sir Guy, de Lauren had not drawn his own sword. He stood as he had been, with his arms crossed.

De Lauren bared his teeth in a cruel smile. "If you force me to bloody my sword, Guy, Katherine will also occupy a cell in Stanfield's dungeon, do not doubt me."

Sir Guy tossed his sword to the floor.

At Stanfield, Katherine listened while de Lauren ordered Sir Guy imprisoned in Stanfield's dungeon. A woozy Sir Cavendish returned from the woods. De Lauren dismissed him from his duties for the remainder of the day and assigned another knight, Sir Rupert, to guard her.

De Lauren loomed over her in the courtyard and said, "I trust Guy's screams this night will not disturb your rest."

De Lauren nodded to the doughy Rupert. "Escort my lady to her bedchamber."

De Lauren left the courtyard, then, and she was alone with the knight, in the shadow of the castle.

Inside her room, Katherine walked to the window, then back to the closed door. She had not removed her cloak and it swirled around her ankles. De Lauren's parting words haunted her.

She would repay Sir Guy's loyalty with pain and abandonment. She could not tell de Lauren the truth of her son and spare Sir Guy de Lauren's vengeance. De Lauren was so angry and hurt. Would he kill Guy? Katherine closed her eyes tightly.

What of her son? Without Sir Guy who would safeguard him until she could bring him home?

She needed to find Ian. She'd tried to get de Lauren to listen to her claim of another assassin. And Stephen, as well. Neither one had believed that the danger came from another source.

She had one more person at Stanfield to whom she could appeal.

Lady Margaret was on her knees in a darkened corner of the chapel, a darker smudge in her unrelieved black gown and headdress, Katherine saw from the chapel doorway. Again, Katherine was struck by the physical change in the great lady since she'd last seen her. In this moment, though, there was another significant change that disturbed her more—Lady Margaret's changed feelings toward her.

Katherine was hoping to enlist Lady Margaret's aid with de Lauren. A formidable task. No doubt Lady Margaret, too, believed Katherine had tried to murder Nicholas.

Katherine stood on the threshold. She found she had to will herself to the task of approaching Lady Margaret. Katherine had cared a great deal for de Lauren's mother. She still did. She had no wish to see herself reflected in Lady Margaret's eyes.

Lady Margaret was kneeling before a statue of the sacred heart of Jesus. Katherine joined her at the bench.

"Forgive my intrusion, my lady," Katherine said. "I must speak with you about Nicholas."

Lady Margaret blinked. "Katherine?"

Lady Margaret's tone was soft but held no warmth. Katherine pressed on. "I have come to appeal to you to ask Nicholas to find Ian, the seminarian who had been here, at Stanfield, until four days ago. I believe it is possible that he is the one responsible for the attempt on Nicholas' life."

Lady Margaret frowned. "I do not understand." Her gaze lifted to where Sir Rupert stood by the door. "You remain guarded. Surely if this Ian is responsible as you claim, Nicholas would not have you under guard."

"He does not believe me, my lady. And because he does not, he remains at risk. I beg you to consider my claim. Not for my sake, but for his. If this Ian wants Nicholas dead, he will eventually learn his first attempt failed and will make another. Please do not dismiss me out of hand and risk Nicholas' life. We both love him."

Lady Margaret shook her head slowly. "Your history does not

bear out your claim of love for my son."

Nay, it did not. "My lady, there is much you do not know." 'Twas time de Lauren's mother, too, learned the reason she'd married William.

Katherine told Lady Margaret of the plot against Nicholas, five years ago. After she finished, Lady Margaret shook her head. "Nay, 'twas Lord Bantam who fired that arrow."

"My lady. 'Twas Bantam's arrow that pierced Nicholas, but he was not the one responsible."

" 'Twas Bantam."

"Bantam was merely a pawn, as I told you—"

"Aye he was a pawn!" Lady Margaret shouted, "but not in the plot you've described. Bantam was my pawn. 'Tis because of me my son almost died!"

Tears filled Lady Margaret's eyes.

Katherine went cold. What did de Lauren's mother know of that foul deed? "What are you saying?"

Lady Margaret's shoulders shook with the force of her tears. Katherine hardened her heart to the other woman's torment. She had to know what Lady Margaret knew.

"My lady, what are you saying?" Katherine asked again.

Lady Margaret pressed her trembling fists to her brow. Through her tears, she said, "Five years ago, I became well acquainted with Guy when he escorted you to de Lauren Keep to visit my son. We fell in love. Guy and I spoke of marriage. I did not want to detract from your wedding to Nicholas. We agreed to keep silent and wait.

"On our last visit to court, I'd complained to Guy that we'd had no opportunity this stay to be alone together. Then the king called a hunt. I planned that we could slip away and be by ourselves while the hunt was under way. Lord Bantam invited himself to join Guy and I for the afternoon. I set out to remove him from our midst. I knew Bantam had a weakness for strong spirits. That morning, I brought along enough strong drink for him to drown in and, as I'd hoped, he lost interest in accompanying us." Lady Margaret lowered her hands, exposing her tear-ravaged face and clasped her hands in a bloodless grip. "Shortly after I led Guy to a spot I'd selected for our tryst, Bantam shot a stray arrow into Nicholas. Because of my lust for Guy, my son was almost killed."

Katherine stared at her mother-by-marriage, taking in what she'd heard. She believed she'd just learned the sin Lady Margaret had spent the last five years atoning for. Katherine shuddered, thinking how the cruel, self-serving bishop had used Lady Margaret's guilt to further his own ends.

Lady Margaret and Sir Guy did not wed. Clearly, their relationship had ended as a result of the events of that day. But Lady Margaret's lips had quivered when she'd spoken his name, and Katherine believed the lady still cared for Sir Guy. If Katherine could prove her innocence in this latest attempt on de Lauren's life, Guy would be found innocent as well, and released from the dungeon. Mayhap, then, Lady Margaret and Sir Guy could have a second chance.

Katherine could not free Sir Guy, yet, but she could free his lady.

Katherine sank to her knees in front of the great lady. "Hear me, my lady. 'Twas not Bantam who harmed Nicholas." Katherine curled her fingers over Lady's Margaret's cold hands. "You had no hand in his coming to harm."

Lady Margaret shook her head slowly. "All and sundry know 'twas Bantam who wounded Nicholas."

Katherine shook her head slowly. "Nay, my lady. Lord Bantam was set up to be blamed, as I've explained. You are innocent."

"No one knows of this plot. You did not come forward."

"I have told you, I could not. My marriage to William and

my silence about that conspiracy guaranteed Nicholas' life."
Katherine looked into Lady Margaret's eyes. "Now again, my
lady, there is another who seeks Nicholas' death. Help me to
save him."

"I have only your word that another assassin exists and you
have much to gain with this tale." Lady Margaret hugged
herself. "I wish I could consult with Bishop Whittaker . . . "

Katherine exhaled and said quietly, "My lady, whether or not
you believe me guilty of attempting to poison Nicholas, now,
you can believe me when I say you had no part in what happened to Nicholas five years ago."

Katherine gained her feet and slowly left the chapel. She
could expect no help from Lady Margaret, either, in the search
for Ian. She was going to have to find him, herself.

CHAPTER TWENTY

Katherine entered the stables and glanced around, peering into the shadows. No one was about, but then few would be as second meal was under way. With a glance at Sir Rupert, leaning against an oak, she let the door close behind her.

A peg in the corner held two shirts and three pairs of breeches. She chose the largest shirt and the smallest breeches and stuffed them into the satchel she carried. She needed a hat and found one laying by a bucket. She added that to her satchel.

She was going to leave Stanfield and this time she'd not dress as a woman. She had a long distance to cover. Best for her safety that she travel as a lad. Best that when de Lauren called up a search no one he encountered could claim they'd seen a woman matching her description. She lifted her hand to her hair. She would cut it short as a boy's, then make her escape through Stanfield's passages.

Without Sir Guy, there was no one to safeguard her son. She would secure him, then set out to find Ian.

In his letter to Father Juttan, Ian claimed he was going to the monastery near Guildford. The monastery was not much of a lead, if as she suspected, Brother Ian was no "brother" at all. Yet it was all she had. Along the way, she would stop at villages and ask if anyone matching his description had been seen there. Kerwick was the nearest town. She would begin her inquiries there when she went to get Michael.

Katherine walked briskly across the dirt and straw floor. Her mare snuffled as she passed it. She reached out and patted its nose. "Be at ease, my fine lady. We needs be quiet for this day's work." How Katherine wished she could take Louisa. But she could not secrete a horse in the woods as Sir Guy had for her trip to de Lauren Keep. Not while under guard from Sir Rupert, or one of the other knights assigned to her.

Nay, when she exited the secret passages for this trip, she would travel on foot until she reached Kerwick, and could purchase an inconspicuous mount from there.

The old mare in the stall near Louisa's tossed its head. Bells tinkled. Katherine narrowed her eyes at the sound, then gazed at the string of bells around the horse's neck. There was no mistaking this horse. She belonged to Ian. But why would Ian have left Stanfield without his mount? Even were he not who he claimed, and used his affection for the mare as part of his disguise, he would not set out on foot. Had he taken a swifter beast?

Katherine glanced around the stable. Some of the stalls were empty. But then they would be. De Lauren's men would be riding the beasts while on patrol and about their other duties. Katherine tapped her forefinger to her lower lip. Donny would know if any of the horses had gone missing.

Katherine found the groom in the great hall. People were intent on second meal. A stew, by the look and smell of what was in the trenchers on the tables she passed.

Donny was sopping up gravy with a heel of bread, at a table by the north wall. Katherine made her way to him. He was alone at one end of the table. Laughter rose from three men seated at the other end.

The groom stood when she reached him, and swiped the back of his beefy hand across his glistening and bruised lips. Four days later, the cuts on his face were beginning to scab and the bruises had turned a dull yellow.

"Me lady, have you need of me?" he asked.

"To answer a question, merely," Katherine said. "Are any horses missing from the stable?" Katherine asked.

Donny rounded a corner of the table. "I just left them to take me meal. They was all there."

"Not in the last moments," Katherine said quickly, "but in the last days."

Donny shook his head. "Nay, lady."

"How is it that Brother Ian's horse is still at Stanfield when he is not?"

Donny shook his head. "Can't rightly say, lady. I heard tell he'd left but he never come for his horse." Donny shrugged. "Are you wanting me to get rid of it?"

"Nay." Katherine bit down on her lip for a moment. "Brother Ian did not arrange with you to care for his mount in his absence?"

Donny shook his head. "Nay." He pressed his lips together. "I never seen him again after he said he would talk with Elspeth for me—you know about her and that entertainer." Donny's lips curled in a sneer, for an instant. "Brother Ian being, you know a man of God, I figured maybe she'd listen to 'im."

"Ian offered to speak with Elspeth on your behalf? When was this?"

Donny removed his cap and scratched his bald scalp. "Brother Ian come upon me in the stables to check on his horse, that day what that troubadour and me went at it." Donny lowered his eyes then peeked up at her through his lashes. "You seen us, remember lady?"

Katherine recalled the incident.

"When did he speak with Elspeth?"

Donny's lips tensed. "Well, that's the thing of it—he didn't. Brother Ian come upon me a little while after that entertainer and me was done. I was alone, mucking out the stalls. Brother

255

Ian come in for his daily visit with Clara. He brung her a tart from his meal.

"Anyways, he seen that I was fretting. We got to talking, and he offered to talk with 'em. With Elspeth and the entertainer. I told him not to waste words with the likes of that one, but I was hoping he could say something to her like 'twas me and not that bas—beggin' your pardon lady—that entertainer she should be with. Brother Ian talked to the entertainer, but Elspeth said he never come to her to chat." Donny's lips pressed together. "He left without talkin' to her."

"How do you known Ian spoke with the entertainer?"

"I seen them going into that hut where that troupe is bedding down. Brother Ian went in there with that Devon."

"When was that?" 'Twas possible Devon may have been the last person to have seen Ian at Stanfield. Katherine hoped Ian may have given some clue to his destination.

"I was on me way to last meal when I seen 'em."

Devon was not in the hall partaking of second meal. From there, Katherine made her way to the meadow where he practiced his skills. The three other people who made up the troupe were about their business, but not Devon. She posed the question of Devon's whereabouts to them, but none could tell her where he was. Katherine went next to the hut Haldrake had told her the entertainers were currently occupying.

'Twas Sir Rupert guarding her again this day. He leaned against one of the trees by this trio of huts. Katherine put her jailer out of her mind and knocked on the scarred door. No answer. She opened it, and looked in from the doorway. No one was about. Three small trunks took up a small space on the dirt floor. Two wooden cups, a jug, a handful of balls lay about the place, but no Devon.

She had hoped to speak with him without delay, and had to

stifle a sigh of frustration. No help for it, she would have to speak with him later. At the very least, she knew where to find him following last meal.

She closed the door and turned around to leave. Devon was coming up the road, strolling toward the hut.

His lean cheeks were ruddy and his brown locks tousled. He was chewing a blade of grass. He removed it when he reached her, and bowed low.

"Me lady? I am honored. Welcome to me humble abode."

"I need to speak with you, Devon," Katherine said.

"Is there somethin' special you were wanting for this night's performance?" He swept past her into the hut.

Katherine stepped over a pair of breeches by the door and followed him inside. She left the door open. "I have not come here about the entertainment," Katherine said. "Did you speak with Brother Ian a few days ago, before he left Stanfield?"

"Brother Ian's gone somewheres?" Devon asked.

So much for asking Devon if Ian had mentioned anything of his travel plans. "Ian left Stanfield four days ago," Katherine said. "Did you speak with him on that day?"

Devon frowned.

"I do not mean to pry into your conversation," Katherine said. "I merely wish to establish if you'd spoken with him on that day, and if you know where he went after you spoke."

She was hoping to find someone who'd seen Ian leave Stanfield and had observed which direction he'd gone in. It would eliminate the monastery as his destination, if he had not headed south toward Guildford.

Devon crossed his arms and leaned back against the wall. He crossed one ankle over the other and frowned. "I'd be right happy to help you, me lady. But truth is I didn't have no chat with him on that day or any other, that I can recall. We didn't have a lot to say to each other. Him being a monk, you know?"

Donny had seemed so certain. "Are you quite sure you did not speak with Ian then?"

"Aye, lady, I be sure."

Katherine nodded. Apparently, Donny had been mistaken, which meant Donny was her last link to the monk. She would ask the guards who were on watch four days ago, if they'd noted Brother Ian leaving the keep. She held out little hope that they had. The guards were focused on those wanting to get into Stanfield, and not those wanting out. "My thanks," she said. "I'll leave you to your business."

"I've got something special worked up for tonight's show," Devon said. "Sure to be a pleaser."

Katherine gave him a small smile. "I shall look forward to it." She moved her foot. Something clung to her heel. She shook her foot to dislodge a neck chain, thread thin and with a tiny cross dangling from it. It reminded her of her own as it had the first time she'd seen it on Brother Ian, the day she'd encountered him in the woods. The cross was pewter and bent at the tip, removing any doubt in her mind that this item did belong to Ian. Several links were stained with dried blood.

Ian had been inside this hut. She rounded on Devon and felt a prick in her side. He'd taken the few steps that separated them without making a sound.

"Do not call out to your guard, my lady," Devon said. " 'Tis my blade that you are feeling. It is deadly sharp and if you inhale deeply 'twill slide through your skin as easily as would a hot knife through butter."

"I will not call to Sir Rupert," she said slowly, her gaze on Devon's.

He smiled showing bright, aligned teeth. "Nay, you will not, though I am now going to return the blade to my boot. For if you do, you will never again see your son."

"My son?"

"You have paled, my lady. Do not swoon. Remember, if Sir Rupert feels compelled to intervene, your son will be lost to you, I vow it."

Katherine was not in danger of fainting, but had to restrain herself from going for Devon's throat. She nodded to him. He slid the dagger into his boot and stepped back from her.

"Who are you?" she asked.

Gone was Devon's rough speech, replaced by the accent of a nobleman. She recalled his exceptional skill in his fight with Donny. "Obviously you are not a troubadour."

He bowed low. "Ellis of Warbrook, my lady. At your service."

Warbrook. "You are Ranulf's man."

Again, Ellis bowed.

" 'Twas you who attempted to kill de Lauren, not Ian?"

Ellis rubbed his forefinger across his lower lip. "Guilty. The good brother was merely in the wrong place at the wrong time and had to be eliminated."

Katherine exhaled a shaky breath, "You killed him. Why?"

Ellis leaned back against the wall, arms crossed at his chest, one ankle crossed over the other in the same position he'd been in before Katherine had found Ian's cross. "Allow me to entertain you with a story, my Lady Katherine. It will enthrall you, I warrant it.

"I'd learned from Elspeth about the medicine you and she prepared for de Lauren," Ellis said. "As well as keeping me entertained at night, she has proven invaluable with her information about your activities, my lady. Unbeknownst to her, the silly chit." Ellis' smile widened. "Unfortunately for Ian, he arrived at your bedchamber door as I opened it to leave. He'd come in search of Elspeth. I glanced quickly over my shoulder, and told him that Elspeth was inside, unclothed, in the lady's bed and would be distressed to be discovered by him. The poor man had the grace to flush. I asked him not to mention this tryst to anyone. Not for myself," Ellis splayed his hand at his chest. "Should the lord or lady learn of this, I would only be turned out, but Elspeth, who was one of Stanfield's people, would surely be beaten."

"Ian readily agreed to keep silent. He wished a word with me, he said. 'Twas a meeting of the minds, since at that point, I certainly planned to see him again.

"Ian informed me he would come to my hut later in the day. And he did. But he didn't leave here alive. I can show you where he's buried, if you like."

She would have liked to cut his beating heart from his body. "You are so smug, assured that I will not expose you, but I need proof that my son yet lives."

"I assure you he does."

"The word of a murderer?" Katherine sneered. "Forgive me if I need more. I want to see him."

"Impossible."

"If you do not take me to my child, I will believe he is dead." The words threatened to choke her. "After I have told this tale, how long do you think de Lauren will let you live?"

"My lady," Ellis sang softly, batting his lashes, mocking her. "Recently freed from the tower, yet still under guard. You are little more than a prisoner, yourself. You wield no power here and will not be taken seriously."

" 'Tis likely Father Juttan will also recognize the monk's bloodied neckchain. Brother Ian's horse is still in our stables though he is no longer at Stanfield. These will spark questions."

Ellis pouted. "An oversight, the horse."

"De Lauren will seek answers."

Ellis frowned. "You are under constant guard. Were I so inclined, how do you propose to flee Stanfield, unobserved?"

He was less certain of his position. Katherine felt weak-kneed from relief, but pressed her advantage. "After tonight's performance, ride one of the horses that pull the entertainers' cart, out of the keep. Ride into the trees beyond the gates and await me there. I will join you shortly after."

"And how will you get past the guard? By magic?"

"I will meet you, be assured of it."

Ellis raised an eyebrow, then nodded.

Katherine blew out her torch, then emerged from Stanfield's passages, into the thick growth that concealed them. The density of the trees and bushes here, and the clouds that dimmed the light of a half moon, made her surroundings almost as dark as it would have been in the passages without the flame.

Ellis was where she'd told him to be. Her eyes adjusted to the near darkness and she saw him atop the horse, and made her way to him. She'd donned a black gown, and cloak with a hood to conceal her bright hair. She knew she blended in with the night.

She stepped out from the trees in front of him. Ellis gave a little start and then his eyes narrowed and a smile slowly curved his lips.

"You are here?" He nodded. "My compliments, my lady. A pity that we are not on the same side of things."

Katherine ignored that. "We must share the mount."

She tensed. She'd considered that Ellis may search her person for a weapon. She'd concealed a dagger in what she hoped was the least likely place he'd check—her half-boot.

But the brash knight did not dismount to search her.

Instead, Ellis reached down and held out his hand. Katherine grasped it with her gloved hand and he pulled her up behind him. With great reluctance she placed her hands at his waist.

"We shall have to ride like the wind to return here before we are both missed," Ellis said, over his shoulder. "There is still the matter of de Lauren's demise."

She longed to retrieve the dagger and sink the blade into him now, but could not do so. Not before he'd shown her her child.

Ellis applied his riding crop to the horse's flanks and the beast charged forward. Carrying two people taxed the horse's strength, but Ellis kept the animal moving with steady use of the crop.

He stopped once at a stream and allowed the horse a brief drink and a briefer rest, and then they were off again.

Thunder rumbled in the distance. They stayed within the trees, avoiding other keeps and their night patrols and reached Ranulf's holding as a midnight fog shrouded the air.

Ellis rode up to the keep's gates.

"Who goes there?" A thick-voiced guard called down.

" 'Tis Ellis, Hervert. Let me in."

The gates opened and Ellis directed the horse into the courtyard. Two knights patrolled the grounds. Each led a large black dog on a leash. The beasts snapped and snarled and rose onto their hind legs, as Ellis reined in. 'Twas only the firm grip of the knights who held them, that kept the dogs from pouncing.

Katherine rubbed her suddenly dry throat. Warbrook Keep was a forbidding place. Only guards were about. No servants strolled the grounds or leaned against the castle, taking in the night air.

Ellis dismounted, then reached up to Katherine. She dismounted unaided.

"And who's this you've got with you, Ellis?" One of the guards asked. His small eyes darted over her with obvious interest. He reached out and his hand neared her face.

Katherine narrowed her eyes in a frosty look. The man licked his lips and his hand lowered.

Ellis laughed. "This one's not for the likes of you, Browning," Ellis said. "But I haven't forgotten my promise. I'll pick out a tasty morsel for you next time I venture into town."

Katherine pushed the disturbing thought of the fate that awaited some unfortunate girl and said to Ellis. "The night wanes. Where is my son?"

Ellis' smile faded. He turned away from the men and set out for the castle. Katherine followed him.

Inside, he led her to a room off the great hall with a writing table and several carved oak chairs. The room was dark and chill. Ellis did not light tapers, but left the door open to the torchlight filtering in from the hall.

He left her alone in the room that Katherine believed was the solar. Alone, with the door open and unguarded. Doubtless, he had no fear she would leave this spot. She would stand here until the crack of doom to see her child.

She did not have so long to wait. Arms crossed, she was pacing between the table and door when she heard footsteps approaching. She stopped walking and lowered her arms. Ranulf entered the room. A lad, bearing two thick lit tapers, dashed out from behind the Warbrook lord. The boy went to one wall and stood there, ramrod-straight. Rather than setting the tapers in dishes, he raised his arms and held the candles aloft. It looked like a practiced routine to Katherine.

"Lady Katherine, come to call," Ranulf said.

She turned away from the boy and looked up at Ranulf. He towered over her. Light reflected off his golden hair, and illuminated his face. Broad forehead, prominent cheek bones, square jaw. His features were large and masculine, undeniably handsome. Katherine found him repulsive.

"Where is my son?" she asked.

He took a step closer. Katherine held her ground though her legs felt as though they were sinking in mire. She craned her neck and looked into his pale blue eyes. "Where is my son?" she repeated.

One side of Ranulf's mouth curved in a winsome smile. "Safe. With the two women."

She believed he referred to Middy and the nurse. "I want to see him."

Ranulf laughed. "You have spirit, Katherine. Even when you have been bested, you do not give ground. How I will enjoy you when we are wed!"

"All of this to wed me?" she said.

"Stanfield Keep is worth much. Men would die for it. And have." Ranulf gave her a devilish grin. "Like your William."

She did not care to hear William referred to as "hers" but said, "William died in battle."

"Aye. How fortuitous for me that his death came a mere fortnight after my own lady wife's demise, freeing us both for remarriage? I will remind you my lady, that I am a man who makes his own luck."

"You killed William? And your own lady?"

Ranulf's jaw tightened. "As to my lady, her death should have come much earlier. But William," some of the tension eased in Ranulf's jaw. "He lived exactly long enough."

"What are you saying?" Katherine asked softly.

"I sent William to marry you since I was married at the time, and unable to wed you myself. I wanted control of Stanfield. I gained that through William. He became my puppet."

"You sent William." She stopped speaking for an instant, taking in the enormity of it all. Her heartbeat picked up its pace. "You were the one who wanted de Lauren dead?"

"Not dead, then. Merely not married to you and allied to Stanfield. You really did save his life, Katherine, by marrying William. De Lauren would have been dead low these five years, had you not."

Katherine felt goosebumps spring on her skin, despite her warm clothing.

"He has managed, however, to claim Stanfield, after all. I must be rid of him now."

Katherine felt her temper flare. "And being the lesser man, you fear meeting de Lauren in battle and must resort to treachery to eliminate him."

Ranulf closed the distance between them and raised his arm to strike, but held back. "Nay. A mark would raise questions. There will be time after we are wed to bring you to heel. I shall undertake that task with all vigilance."

"I want to see my son."

"You give no orders to me. You will do precisely as I say or I will present your son to you as I left your daughter at Stanfield. Surely you have not forgotten the sight of her small body minus its head?"

Ranulf had decapitated her daughter. Katherine felt the wind knocked out of her as if he'd delivered the blow he'd threatened. Tears flooded her eyes before she could stop them.

"Tears become you, my lady," he said.

She hardly heard him. She had not seen her daughter upon her return to Stanfield, because de Lauren had ordered the child buried. Katherine had believed he'd acted to hurt her. Clearly he'd come upon the girl in that condition and had acted to spare her. Her babe . . . Sweet Mary . . .

Katherine passed her trembling hand across her wet cheeks.

"Heed me, my lady. Heed me well. In a few moments, Ellis will escort you back to Stanfield. I pass his assignment to kill de Lauren onto you. I will allow you three days in which to accomplish this task. I care naught in which manner you send him to hell, but kill him you will."

"You will not have Stanfield when I am imprisoned for murder," Katherine said. "Ellis has already arranged it so I am suspect. Should de Lauren perish, I will surely be blamed."

"Ellis arranged your guilt at my command. Aye, you will be

blamed for de Lauren's death, but if you agree to wed me, granting me Stanfield, I will produce an assassin to clear your good name before Henry claims your head. I had originally thought the promise of your life would induce you to agree, but now, ah, now, your son's life as well depends on your cooperation."

"I do not believe that you have not already killed him," Katherine said.

Ranulf snapped his fingers. A man entered the solar, cradling the babe against his chest. Clearly, Ranulf had intended to show the boy to her all along. No doubt he knew how seeing him would affect her.

Katherine ran to the boy. Again, she felt tears in her eyes. She blinked them back so not to obstruct her view of her son. So beautiful. He slept in the man's log thick arms.

She reached out to take her son. The knight stepped back, and turned away.

"Nay!"

But he walked on and left the room.

Ranulf ran his finger tip across her lips. She fought back the urge to bite him.

"Three days is little time," she said. "De Lauren is a cautious man and he suspects me. He keeps his distance from me."

"From what Ellis has told me, I do not believe that has always been the case. You are lovely," Ranulf's gaze warmed. "Such beauty can rob a man of his wits. He will let down his guard for a prize such as you, I do not doubt it.

"Ellis will escort you back to Stanfield, now. Three days, my lady. Ellis must return to me with news of de Lauren's death in three days. Your son will not live one day longer."

Ranulf gave Ellis another horse for the ride back to Stanfield. Fear for her son had Katherine's stomach churning like a storm-tossed sea. She vomited into a bush, then gained the saddle of the packhorse she'd previously shared with Ellis. She rode by his side out of Warbrook's gates.

The sky was no longer the inky black of deep night. Dawn was a short time away.

Ellis set a breakneck pace, despite a thick fog. To prevent suspicion they had to be back at Stanfield before they were missed. Doubtful she'd been missed, thus far. De Lauren, she recalled, was no longer sleeping in his bedchamber. Had not since her return from the tower. He would not have sought her out last night and discovered her gone.

Three days. If she didn't kill de Lauren in three days, Ranulf would kill her son.

Sweet Mary, how could she do it? Even to save her son, how could she kill Nicholas?

She could not.

She only had three days. She had to act against Ranulf now. The element of surprise would aid her. The only way to remove Ranulf's threat was to take back her son.

Katherine followed Ellis deeper into the woods. The path narrowed. In a short time, they would be forced to ride in single file. Katherine bent and curled her fingers around the dagger in her boot. Slowly she withdrew it.

The path narrowed further. Her mount's flanks brushed the stallion Ellis rode. Ellis was a mere arm's length from her now. She turned in the saddle and plunged her dagger into his neck.

His eyes widened. He jerked in the saddle. Blood burbled in his mouth and he toppled to the ground.

He was still. The dagger was imbedded to the hilt. She remembered his words to her in the hut. Her blade, too, was sharp, and had, indeed, pierced his skin as a hot knife would have butter.

She dismounted. Ellis wore nothing to connect him to the

house of Ranulf, since he was masquerading as an entertainer. She squinted into the gloom. She couldn't have Ellis' body found and alert Ranulf. Would Ranulf's patrol extend this far? Nay, she didn't think so. They were a considerable distance from the keep.

Ellis's clothing would not be credible on her, yet she needed a disguise to sneak back into Warbrook Keep. She removed her cloak. The linen of her kirtle was too fine to be servant garb. She used her dagger and cut off the fine gold braid around the hem, collar, and bell-wide cuffs. She removed the heavy gold belt encircling her waist. It bore the Stanfield insignia in the heavy buckle. It could not be found. Where to leave it? With her knife, she dug a hole and buried the belt. Someday, someone would dig up quite a find. De Lauren's ring. She could not be found with it. But she couldn't bring herself to discard it. She removed it from her finger and wedged it into her bodice.

She cut the fine fabric of her gown, then seized the two ends and tore. The rip made the gown look like a cast-off. She rubbed dirt in the soft material, pulled the pins from her hair, and rubbed dirt there as well as she had for her trip to de Lauren Keep.

Her half-boots looked too good. She scuffed the toes and scraped the sides against a large rock. She was ready.

The sky had lightened to a pewter grey now. Katherine mounted her horse. She would need Ellis' horse for Middy and the nurse. She tied the horses' reins to her own mount and steered both beasts back to Ranulf's holding.

CHAPTER TWENTY-ONE

De Lauren stood on the parapets, watching day approach. Last night's fog had lifted, and the sun now peeked over the horizon. He'd spent the better part of the night at this wall, looking out at the fog-shrouded land.

A short distance away, his men were moving about. Day watchmen replacing those who'd stood guard from these battlements throughout the night. Two of his men inclined their heads briefly as they passed him. His presence up here at this time no longer surprised them or brought them to attention. Sleep eluded him, of late, and he'd made a practice of spending his nights in this spot.

From the corner of his eye, de Lauren saw movement in the stairwell, then Sir Hugh stepped onto the battlements. So Hugh was back from the trip to Brother Ian's town. Only just, de Lauren thought, since Hugh still wore his armor. Road dust dulled the links of the chain mail. He carried his helm tucked under his arm. Sir Victor was a pace behind Hugh, and he, too, looked road weary.

Their arrival meant they'd learned if the monk was who he claimed. De Lauren was long past ready to hear what they'd found out.

He greeted his knights then asked, "What news from Guildford?"

"The monk is indeed a monk," Hugh said. "Brother Ian was attached to the monastery outside of Guildford until his involvement with a woman from the town."

That confirmed what Ian had told Father Juttan about himself. "Find your meals and beds," de Lauren said. "You have earned both with this work."

Hugh and Victor left the battlements. Sound carried up from the courtyard. Stanfield's people were beginning their day. De Lauren had matters to see to, as well. He turned away from the wall toward the stairs.

Heavy footfalls on the steps drew de Lauren's attention. An instant later, Sir Cavendish charged onto the battlements.

"My lord," Cavendish said, panting slightly. "Lady de Lauren has left her chamber. I know naught where she's gone."

De Lauren eyed Cavendish and said in a lethal whisper. "How can that be when you secured her in there last night and then remained outside her door until this morn?"

Cavendish drew himself up until he stood straight as a lance. "As to that my lord, I was not outside her chamber last night, but within it. Lady Katherine requested my assistance in moving the tub. When I bent to lift it, she struck me in the head. 'Twas the water pitcher she'd used, I saw when I regained consciousness and found it by my bound feet. She'd also bound my hands and gagged me." Red seeped into Cavendish's cheeks. "I was trussed up like a Michaelmas goose, my lord. Lady Katherine's maid found me this morning, and released me."

"When did you enter her room to perform this service?"

"I escorted her to her chambers, almost immediately after the entertainers performed, and she approached me about the tub shortly thereafter."

Obviously, she'd not gone to such lengths for a midnight stroll. De Lauren believed he could search the keep, but he would not find her here. She'd planned to leave Stanfield and to have the entire night before anyone noticed her absence. Heat surged to his face.

Had he gone to his own chamber last night, he would have noticed Cavendish missing from his post. De Lauren directed some of the anger he was feeling at himself. Unlikely she'd left through the gates. His knights knew she was under guard at all times and would have detained her. Nay, she would have gone out through the passages.

Still, he would ask if one of his guards had allowed her to leave. If that were the case, there would be the devil to pay, but the guard would have noted her direction.

De Lauren roused Sir Warren and Sir Gawain from their beds in the knight's quarters. The men had been on watch at the gates last night. They stood before him, blinking at the sunlight streaming in from the door de Lauren had left open. He asked about Katherine.

Gawain rubbed his unshaved cheek, making a rasping sound. "Nay, my lord," he said. "Lady Katherine did not ride out last night."

The passages then, as he'd suspected. She was obliged to leave without a horse to make exit from there. Traveling on foot significantly reduced the distance Katherine could cover in the course of the night. De Lauren gave Sir Vincent the order to dispatch men to search the woods.

She'd left Stanfield to go where? To Ranulf, her ally? De Lauren believed that was exactly where she was headed and his anger climbed another height.

"Lord de Lauren?"

De Lauren faced Sir Warren. The man's thin hair stood on end.

"What is it Warren?" de Lauren asked.

"I know naught if this signifies, but that troubadour, Devon, rode out last night."

"When was this?" de Lauren asked.

"Early. I'd just come on watch right after hearing the man sing."

And Katherine had struck Cavendish upon returning to her room, after that same performance. Coincidence? Or had she and the entertainer left Stanfield together? There would be no doubt about that or about where she'd gone if the entertainer was Ranulf's man.

De Lauren turned to Anson. "Find Haldrake and determine where he housed the jongleurs."

A short time later, de Lauren, with Stephen at his side, faced the two remaining men and the one woman who made up the entertainment troupe. The trio huddled together in the small hut. First light had long arrived and the troubadour, Devon, had not returned for the dawn rehearsal they'd planned.

"How long has Devon been a member of your troupe?" de Lauren asked.

"This was his first time with us," the woman spoke up. Her voice was a screech that de Lauren had believed feigned for the show, but, clearly, was not. "See our troubadour was killed by a thief in the last town we was in," she went on. "Devon happened to be passing through like we was. He was looking for a job and he joined us. Lucky we was to find 'im. Without a troubadour we don't got much of a show."

"The troubadour was killed and Devon happened along," de Lauren said. 'Twas quite a coincidence. On its own, though, it meant naught. "Where did he perform before meeting you?"

The three entertainers exchanged blank looks, then the woman spoke up again. "We asked him to sing, me lord, and once we heard 'is voice, we didn't ask no questions, just told him to join up with us, straight away."

"Which trunk belongs to the troubadour?" de Lauren asked.

"That small one," the woman said, pointing a stubby finger

at one corner of the room where three trunks had been placed side-by-side.

De Lauren went to the trunk and upended it. He crouched over the pile, and sifted through it. One pair of breeches. Two shirts. A wooden ball. A flute. That was all of it.

De Lauren had not expected to find anything questionable in the trunk—even if the entertainer was not what he claimed to be, doubtful he would leave something to reveal that fact where it could be found. But de Lauren would make certain of that. He upended the trunks that belonged to the other entertainers, satisfying himself that he'd left nothing unchecked. There was naught of any import in the other trunks either.

De Lauren gained his feet. "Did Devon mention that he would be leaving the keep last night?"

Again, the entertainers glanced at each other. They shook their heads. The man with the thick beard spoke up. "Lady de Lauren's maid, Elspeth, she be the one to ask, me lord. Devon's been spending his nights with her."

De Lauren left the hut. Anson stood on the outside of the door. As de Lauren passed him, he said to the boy, "Find Lady Katherine's maid. Bring her to me in the solar."

"The maid wasn't seen leaving with the entertainer," Stephen said, falling into step beside his brother. "She must still be here. Think you the girl can be of any help?"

De Lauren glanced at Stephen. The sun poked through the branches of trees they walked beneath, and for an instant Stephen's face was shadowed.

"Mayhap if this Devon took her into his confidence we will learn something of import," de Lauren said. "If there is something to be learned. We still do not know that this entertainer is not what he claims." What they did know was that Katherine had left.

They climbed the castle steps.

"I think our search party will have to ride all the way to War-brook Keep to find Katherine," Stephen said. His voice was tight with anger. "Think you she plans to return with Ranulf's army? She has had ample time to observe our defenses and to relate her findings to Ranulf."

De Lauren wanted to pommel something and would relish seeing Ranulf riding up to Stanfield's gates just now. "We have yet to determine if Katherine went to Ranulf," de Lauren said. "Let us see what Sir Guy knows of her escape."

De Lauren led Stephen down the stairs to the dungeons. Somewhere, water dripped onto stone. Torches cast flickering shadows on the walls.

De Lauren reached the cell that held Sir Guy. The guard raised the bar that secured the door. De Lauren ducked his head beneath the low door frame and stepped inside. Stephen followed.

A nub of candle dripped wax onto its metal holder. The taper's light reached only as far as the end of the small table it sat on. Guy was in shadow, prowling the tiny floor space.

"Bring a torch," de Lauren said to the guard.

There was no room for another man inside the cell. The guard stayed by the door, holding the torch aloft.

Guy squinted against the light. He was unshaven. His brown hair streaked with grey, unkempt. He was dirty, but unharmed. Despite what he'd told Katherine, de Lauren had not ordered her commander tortured. Guy had not acted on his own in Katherine's deception, but on her orders.

"Now that you are imprisoned, Guy, and Katherine's attempt to kill me failed, she has left Stanfield," de Lauren said.

Guy went still. His surprise was unmistakable, and unwelcome. Clearly Guy knew nothing of Katherine's escape. De Lauren hoped he'd fare better when he asked about the troubadour. Before he could, Guy spoke up.

"Lady Katherine had no hand in the poisoning."

Stephen scoffed at Guy's defense of Katherine. De Lauren ignored his brother's outburst. "That is her claim," de Lauren said.

Guy resumed pacing. " 'Tis the truth. The real assassin has cast blame on her."

De Lauren crossed his arms. "The real assassin being the monk?"

"Aye," Guy said. "Lady Katherine was suspicious of him."

De Lauren felt another burst of anger. "Do not play the fool with me, Guy. I have learned the monk is who he claimed, and no assassin."

"We had hoped otherwise."

"No doubt you hoped I would believe otherwise, until Katherine could make good her escape last night," de Lauren said. "It appears she made away with a troubadour performing in Stanfield's hall. Tell me Guy, is this troubadour Ranulf's man?"

Again Guy stopped walking. "She has left Stanfield? With a man you think may be from Warbrook Keep?"

"We're finished here, Stephen," de Lauren said, turning to the exit. It was obvious Guy did not know of Katherine's escape plans or if a knight of Ranulf's had infiltrated the keep.

"She would not willingly go to Ranulf," Guy said.

De Lauren faced Guy, again. "She knocked my guard unconscious. Bound and gagged him, then made her way out through the passages. Aye, it appears she was unwilling," de Lauren said.

"She would not willingly go to Ranulf."

Not willingly. 'Twas the second time Guy had used those words. De Lauren's gut tightened. He narrowed his eyes on Guy and said softly. "What pressure could be exerted on her to force her to go to Ranulf?"

Guy did not reply.

"You claim she would not go to Ranulf willingly," de Lauren said. "Tell me, then, what is his hold on her?"

Guy shook his head. "I will say no more."

De Lauren grunted. "Obviously that is because there is no more *to* say. If you had the means to support your claim, it defies logic that you would withhold it from me."

He gritted his teeth, angry with himself for giving Guy's statement any consideration.

He left the cell. Stephen followed him out of the dungeon and to the solar. Anson and Katherine's maid stood in the corridor, by the closed solar door. The girl's eyes were huge in her white face.

Inside the room, Anson went to the window and drew back the coverlet. Sunlight gleamed off the polished writing table.

De Lauren turned to the girl. "Were you with the entertainer—Devon—last night?"

"Nay, me lord."

"When did you last see him?"

"Not since he was singing in the great hall." The girl bit her lip. "I made sure I finished me chores I did I—" Tears welled in her eyes.

De Lauren softened his tone. "I am not taking you to task," he said. "I need you to answer some questions for me. That is all."

The pulse in her throat was beating visibly. She nodded.

"Did you arrange to meet with the troubadour today?"

She gathered the folds of her gown in both fists. "Nothing so formal as a meetin', me lord. Dev and me just find each other when we can during the day." She peeked up at de Lauren from beneath her lashes. "Beggin' your pardon me lord, but is Dev in trouble with you?"

"That remains to be seen," de Lauren said. "Tell me, do you

know where this Devon performed before joining this troupe?"

The girl tugged hard on her bottom lip. Tears fell onto her cheeks. "I don't know if 'twas before he joined up with these people but he was all the way in London."

De Lauren was hoping to find a lord in the vicinity who would remember the troubadour performing in his hall. "You are certain he said London?"

"Aye. I know for sure 'cause when I asked him where he got the etching of the falcon that be on his back, he told me he got it done in London."

A falcon. De Lauren eyed the girl. "You know this etching to be a falcon and not some other bird?"

"I ain't never seen a falcon up close, but that's what Dev called it. It be on his left shoulder blade." The girl sniffed. "It ain't the whole bird, though, just the head."

De Lauren heard Stephen swear softly.

De Lauren inclined his head toward the door. "Go."

Elspeth curtsied and dashed out of the room.

"No doubt now that the troubadour is Ranulf's man," Stephen said when they were alone.

The falcon head was the Warbrook crest.

And both Katherine and Ranulf's man had left Stanfield last night.

"Make ready, Stephen," de Lauren said. "We ride for Warbrook Keep."

Servants and soldiers strode across Ranulf's courtyard when Katherine arrived at Warbrook Keep. She'd left her mount, and the one Ellis had ridden, tied to two trees a distance from the castle. She could not risk the animals being found and arouse curiosity about them.

She kept to the trees until the sky lightened and Warbrook's gates were opened for the day. She waited and watched. Eventually, knights and men at arms rode out for the first patrol of the day. Servants carrying small baskets for berries set out for the forest. Katherine left the trees and made her way through the gates. She'd left her cloak and gloves draped across the saddle and dressed in servant's garb as she was, she blended in with Warbrook's people. The guards on watch at the gates paid her no mind.

Inside the courtyard, there was an eerie quiet. No laughter. Little conversation, and that in hushed tones. The people walked with eyes downcast, their movements furtive, as if they feared drawing attention to themselves. Knowing what she did about Ranulf, Katherine was not surprised. Her stomach tightened thinking of her son here.

But he was alive. Ranulf had not harmed her child and would not until he'd received proof that she had killed de Lauren.

Katherine picked up a bucket by the well, half-filled it, and crossed the courtyard. She needed to find her son and Middy and the nursemaid, and then find a safe place to stay until evening when they could make good their escape.

Where would Ranulf have housed her babe?

Katherine carried the bucket into the keep. People within the castle walls moved as quietly and carefully as those without, she saw. Her own stealthy behavior did not seem out of place here.

She climbed the stairs with the filled bucket, as if she were bearing water to one of the bedchambers. Her grip on the bucket whitened the scarred flesh on her burned hand. Unlikely the skin would heal any better, but she was grateful she'd regained strength. She held the bucket in her left hand and lifted her skirts with her right.

She reached the second level. There was no one in the hall. Chamber doors were closed. She stopped by one and stood listening for movement within. She heard naught. She reached for the iron handle. Perspiration dampened her palms. Someone could be inside, asleep, or at some activity she could not hear from the corridor. She knocked. No response. She opened the door. No one was in the bedchamber.

She went on to the next room. And then the next. A serving woman came out of the second to last chamber on the floor.

"You're new to upstairs chores," the woman said softly, as she closed the chamber door behind herself. It was a statement not a question, and Katherine was glad not to have to respond and risk her accent giving her away.

"You'll have an easy time of it, this, your first day," the woman went on. "There's only that one room what's left." She pointed to the last chamber on the floor. "I've cleaned the rest." She looped a strand of red hair streaked with grey behind her ear. "I'll leave you the last room to do."

Katherine watched the servant cross the hall then descend the stairs until she was out of view. Katherine went into the last chamber and found it vacant as all the others had been. She moved up to the third level. The tower room was on the floor above that one. She forced the thought of her child in the tower, deprived of heat and light, from her mind.

She reached the second level and heard a babe crying. Katherine picked up her pace and followed the sound to the second chamber. She opened the door. Middy glanced up from the babe she was rocking in her arms. The old woman frowned and pressed the child closer to her sunken chest. "What be your business here?"

"I have come for my son, Middy." Katherine's voice cracked.

Middy's mouth opened. She pressed her lips together briefly, then said, "Me lady. 'Tis really you!"

Katherine blinked back tears. "Aye."

The nurse was perched on the end of one of two cots, Katherine saw, as she set down the bucket. The room was no more sparse than any of the other chambers she'd entered. Like the others, there was a small table and washstand and naught more. Ranulf had not seen fit to spend his coin on comforts or decorations for the chambers at Warbrook.

Katherine crossed the room to Middy and took her babe. Tears glistened on his lashes. He'd not been harmed, though, thank God. Michael was plump and perfect.

When she'd entered the chamber, she saw Middy and the nurse had not been abused, either. They were groomed and a tray on the table showed the remains of a morning meal. Katherine had not eaten since last night, and her stomach rumbled. She would consume the baked bread that remained on the tray, but not yet. She could not stop looking at her child.

"How long have you been at Warbrook?" Katherine asked.

Middy frowned, adding another crevice to those that criss-crossed her face. "We was brought here two nights ago."

"From Kerwick?"

"Aye, from Kerwick. We was found out. Sir Guy feared we had been and that was why he moved us. Ranulf's men come to the little house Sir Guy put us in." Middy shook her head. "I fear the worst has happened to him, me lady. He rode out to see you. I'm thinkin' he did reach you since you know we was in Kerwick. But after meeting with you, he didn't come back to us. I asked the guards what brought us about Sir Guy. They would tell me naught."

Katherine would have liked to reassure Middy that he was well, but could not say that for sure, and so she said nothing. "Time passes, Middy. We will wait until last meal has been served. How soon after that are the remains removed?"

"Not 'till morn when a girl brings first meal," Middy said.

"That will aid our escape. I need to find a place to hide until then. I will return for you. Be ready."

Katherine kissed Michael, then placed him in Middy's arms. She took the bread from the tray and slid it into her pocket.

With a last glance at her son, she picked up the bucket and left the room.

Chapter Twenty-two

Katherine walked in the shadows cast by flickering torches on the walls of Warbrook Keep. Last meal was under way. The second floor was deserted. The bulk of the population would be in the common hall. A few moments earlier, a maid delivered a tray to Middy and the wet nurse then made her way back down the stairs. Katherine had delayed going to them until their meal was served. She did not want to risk a maid discovering that the two women and child were gone.

Now they had to hurry to make their escape before the gates to the keep were closed for the night.

Middy and the nurse stood ready when Katherine slipped into their room. She picked up her son, and cradled him in the crook of her right arm. She stuck her uninjured hand in her pocket and curled her fingers around the dagger.

"We go," she said.

She peeked into the corridor again, then nodded to them. The women fell into step behind her. Katherine kept to the shadows, her babe cradled against her chest as she led Middy and the nurse out the way she'd come. Ranulf's holding, like Stanfield, had little-used stairwells, dusty and forgotten, in remote sections of the castle. Katherine had discovered one such set of stairs and headed to it. Treacherous was getting through the hall, to that stairwell.

She held her breath when she set foot on the first step down. At the bottom, again there was danger. Long shadows marking twilight gave some cover, but there were spaces when for a time, they would be open to detection. An observant guard or tower watchman . . .

Katherine shook her head. Thoughts like those would paralyze her if she allowed them. She did not want to further risk her son's life, but they could not remain in the stairwell forever. Inaction posed the greatest risk.

"I have two horses tethered in the woods," Katherine whispered to Middy and the nurse. She did not explain how she came to have an extra mount. "We must hurry. We will have to ride through the night to distance ourselves from Ranulf's searchers," Katherine said.

"Where do we go, lady?" Middy asked.

The hours while she'd waited to retrieve her son, Katherine had considered where she would take him from here. She had to find a place to hide him until she could prove to de Lauren that she was innocent in the attempt to murder him, and put things right between them.

She was afraid to secrete her son and the women in a town, as Sir Guy had. Ranulf would surely send out spies to scout out towns and villages.

She could not count on any allies William had made. Since her father's passing, William had destroyed the alliances her father had built up in favor of lords as disloyal as himself.

"We ride to Scotland," Katherine said to Middy. "You may recall Mother had mentioned in passing that she had distant relatives there." Mother had died when Katherine was twelve and Katherine could not recall anyone from Scotland ever paying a call, yet she would appeal to them for sanctuary for her child.

Scotland, though, was so far away. They had to reach the border, first. Before the men Ranulf would dispatch caught up with them.

"Ranulf knows naught of my Scottish kinsmen, and to most of the English, Scotland is a savage land that holds no appeal," Katherine said. " 'Tis my hope Ranulf will not believe that I would consider Scotland an option, and will only make a token search for my son in that direction."

And once she'd safeguarded her child, she would return to stop Ranulf from killing de Lauren.

Katherine stopped speaking as they exited the keep. From the shadow of the castle, she saw Warbrook's gates were open. The guards were on duty, shooting dice. A man glanced up as they made their way across the courtyard, but three women and a babe did not look threatening, and he returned to the play.

Katherine headed for the forest where she'd hidden the horses. Middy's step was lagging.

" 'Tisn't much further," Katherine said. She clasped the old woman's elbow and propelled her along.

Eventually, they came to the spot where Katherine had left the horses. She handed her son to the nurse then boosted Middy onto the horse she'd shared with Ellis. It was the larger of the two, better to take the weight of the two women. They took turns holding Michael until they'd all mounted. Katherine mounted last and then leaned across the saddle to reclaim her son from Middy. Again, she balanced him gently in the crook of her right arm.

Scotland was west of Warbrook Keep. They were already pointed in that direction. Katherine tugged on the reins and set off.

She kept the horse to a trot. With her babe in her arms and the use of her one awkward hand, she negotiated the narrowly spaced trees with great caution.

She rode in silence, glancing around her and keeping her ears trained for the thud of hoofbeats. Behind her, Middy and the nurse exchanged only the occasional comment. No doubt they were as alert to their surroundings and their situation as she was, Katherine thought.

Just up ahead, their path widened. This section of woods was coming to an end. She could see a road beyond, and beyond that more forest.

She glanced back at Middy and the nurse. "Be prepared to stop at the end of this path. We will check the road to make sure there are no other travelers to see and remember us and if all is clear, we will cross to the other side."

Katherine slowed her horse to a walk. The road loomed ahead. Soon she would reach—

She heard horses nearing, and glanced over her shoulder.

Three riders bent over their saddles, galloped toward them. She hugged her son to her and shouted, "Ride!"

Digging her heels into the horse's flanks, she spurred the beast into a furious gallop. If she were overtaken . . . Again she fought off a fear that threatened to immobilize her. She could not let Ranulf's men catch her. Her son's life depended on it.

"Halt!"

The shout rang out from behind her. Katherine bent over the saddle, mindful of low-hanging branches that would sweep her from the horse. She cleared the trees and was now on the road. She clutched her babe to her. She could hear him crying. That she could not stop to comfort him cut through her like a knife.

This horse Ranulf had given Ellis for the ride back to Stanfield was swift and sure-footed. Katherine recognized a full-blooded stallion when she rode one. Apparently, Ranulf had spared no expense to get them back to Stanfield to kill de Lauren.

But his men rode blood stock as well. One rider separated himself from the group, and rode up alongside her. He reached out for her reins. Katherine snatched her dagger from her pocket and stabbed his hand. He wore no gauntlets. She heard him hiss, and he fell back.

A second knight gained on her other side. The side she held her babe. No way she could stab him. He reached out and grabbed the horse's reins, yanking hard. Her horse whinnied and reared back, kicking up clumps of dirt. Katherine clutched the pommel and the horses's flanks to keep from sliding from the saddle. The horse landed once again on all fours.

"This way, milady," the knight who held her reins said, and turned her mount back toward Warbrook Keep.

The third knight caught up with them, then took up a position at the rear. Katherine was now enclosed by the three men.

Ranulf met them on the path. It had gotten darker in the last few minutes as evening wore on, but she could see him clearly. His face was red. His light eyes, bulging.

"Lady Katherine," he said. "and the young lord of Stanfield."

He did not look surprised to see her, and to see that she held Michael. Katherine realized why when Middy and the wet nurse came into view behind him. No doubt Ranulf had questioned the women and learned that Katherine had returned to Warbrook Keep.

The women were on foot. A knight moved his horse to Middy's heels and nudged her in the back with his mount's nose, urging her on. The wet-nurse held a hand to her bruised cheek. Katherine pressed her lips tightly together at Ranulf's abuse of the woman.

Ranulf's voice boomed in the silence, drawing Katherine's attention from the other women. "Bring the babe to me," he said.

"Nay! Leave him!" Katherine shouted.

She huddled over her child. The knight who was now bleeding from the wound she'd inflicted, rode up behind her. He seized her by the elbows, and held her while another knight pried Michael from her. Once the child was taken from her, she was released.

Ranulf rode to the knight who now held her son and raised his sword over him.

"Ranulf!" His gaze went to her and she pressed her dagger to her heart. "If you slay my son, I will follow him in death. I swear it. Without me, Stanfield will never be yours."

A knight reached out to her. Katherine jerked back, slitting her gown where it covered her heart, and nicking the skin beneath it. The man went still.

Katherine held Ranulf's gaze, not daring to blink. A muscle flexed in his jaw. Some of the redness faded from his cheeks, though, and his tensed shoulders rolled back. He lowered his sword.

Katherine shook her head. "Nay, that is but a temporary appeasement. Your men will overpower me the instant I lower the blade and you will kill my son."

Ranulf inclined his head to the bleeding knight. "Return the babe to his mother."

Katherine kept the blade against her chest and reached for her child. She was trembling. Michael began to mewl. Katherine realized she was squeezing him and eased her hold.

Ranulf leaned forward in the saddle and braced his arm on the pommel. "Twins, Katherine," he said. "Ellis was quite pleased with himself for that discovery. Since you returned here, I conclude you have killed him. Tell me Katherine, did you also kill your daughter to save the heir to Stanfield?"

"You are vile."

Ranulf's gaze hardened. "You would do well to curb your tongue and to endeavor to please me, my lady. After we are wed, mayhap I will give your son to peasants to raise. He will never be Lord of Stanfield, but he will be alive. Displease me, and he will not remain so."

If given the chance, Ranulf would use her son as a hostage to her good behavior. Katherine tightened her hold on her son.

"You are mad," she said softly. "We will not be wed. De Lauren suspects you and I are allied. My absence from the keep will put him on guard. He will not stand open-armed at Stanfield's gates, awaiting you to kill him."

Ranulf's lip curled in a sneer. "Nay, he will not. He will save me the ride to Stanfield and come here to meet his death."

Ranulf sounded so certain. His confidence undermined Katherine's own. Perspiration broke out between her shoulder blades.

Ranulf inclined his head. "And you, my lady, will have delivered him into my hands."

"You expect me to go to Stanfield and bring de Lauren here?" Her attempt at sarcasm failed when her lips trembled.

"You will bring him to me without setting foot from Warbrook. His lady is here. He will come."

"You are wrong. De Lauren holds no tender feelings for me."

"You have taken great care to conceal your son's existence from him. He believes he will retain the holding even if you are dead. Regardless, he will come. Whether he believes you my captive or accomplice, he will come." Ranulf's gaze grew intent on her. "For love of you. To honor his vows to protect you. To reclaim what is his. Or, to mete out his own vengeance on you. The why matters naught to me, but do not doubt he will have his reason. And he will come."

Katherine's mouth dried. She was afraid Ranulf was right. De Lauren would come to Warbrook because of her. Not out of love, she knew, but for revenge for all he believed she'd done to him. She'd come to Warbrook Keep to save him and now, may have lured him to his death.

Dawn was still a time away when de Lauren gave the signal to break camp. Men rolled to their feet, from the ground where they'd bedded down. Squires bustled about serving bread, meat, and ale from provisions packed at Stanfield.

De Lauren had ordered a halt in this wooded area, only after the animals were spent. All haste was not necessary, he knew. A few hours here or there would mean naught in reaching Ranulf, but a white-hot rage was driving him.

In short order the packing was done and Stephen joined de Lauren at his horse. "The men await your signal to mount," Stephen said.

De Lauren climbed into the saddle and raised his sword.

He led his men out of the woods. Sir Victor rode by his side, bearing the de Lauren standard. The flag snapped in the wind. The hooves of five hundred horses pounded the ground, loud as thunder. De Lauren made no attempt at stealth. This would be no surprise attack.

At midday, de Lauren reined in on the road beyond Warbrook. His men drew their mounts to a stop, behind him. The ground trembled to a halt. A silence followed, a moment of calm. The last Ranulf would know, de Lauren vowed.

He focused on the battlements, his gaze narrowed against the sun that shone down on the rooftop like a beacon. Though daytime, the keep's gates were closed. Archers stood behind the crenellated wall, their bows notched. Men staggered beneath the weight of vats no doubt filled with hot oil. Some were taken to the wall to be poured onto his men as they attempted to scale the castle, de Lauren knew. Others would be upended onto the floor to make the stone slick, in case his men breached the battlements.

De Lauren dismounted. Stephen reined in beside him and did the same.

"The keep is showing the effects of your last attack," Stephen said.

"Aye," de Lauren said.

He'd ordered all the wattle-and-daub structures burned. Ranulf had not yet rebuilt them. The land still bore the tracks of de Lauren destriers and was bare of trees and plant life. A virtual wasteland. A half-built addition to the castle still formed a heap where it crumbled when a team of de Lauren's horses pulled it apart. De Lauren hoped he would have an opportunity to show Ranulf the devastation he would wreak this day, before he killed him.

"The keep looks devastated," de Lauren said. "But its defenses are not. Ranulf has reinforced the curtain wall, gates, and castle door that we destroyed. From the men we can see about the place, Ranulf has significantly rebuilt his army.

"Ready our archers, Stephen, to shoot flaming arrows onto the floor and into the vats at your signal," de Lauren said. "The oil will act as an accelerant and the resulting fire that will spread briefly over the stone will provide a distraction. While Ranulf's men beat the flames, our men will scale the walls from the same unguarded position we used last time."

"I care naught for your plan," Stephen said. " 'Tis sheer madness, Nick, to walk into Warbrook Keep alone."

De Lauren kept his gaze on the castle. "Your objections are still duly noted, but we will proceed."

Stephen's breathing grew harsher. "I know you are expecting treachery from him. That he will accept your challenge only to get you inside the holding. Aye, you know he will not meet you on the field of honor and settle your differences at sword-point." Stephen shook his head. "Your challenge will gain you entrance to Warbrook, but Ranulf may have you killed as soon as you are behind his walls."

"Nay, brother. I will kill him."

Stephen's fists clenched. " 'Tis because of Katherine you do this. Despite all she has done, you will not risk her life in a full-scale battle. Can you not see your love for her may well cost you your life?" Stephen gritted his teeth. "What I would not give to have her die this day!"

De Lauren turned and seized the collar of Stephen's hauberk in one fist. "She will not die," de Lauren said. His throat had tightened. He cleared it and repeated, "She will not die." He held Stephen for a moment longer, then released him, abruptly.

"Nick—"

"I am going into Warbrook Keep, Stephen. I will find Katherine and when you breach the keep, I will give her over to you to be taken to safety while I finish this with Ranulf. I need to know I can entrust her to your care."

Stephen released a deep breath. He said quietly. "You have my oath." He turned away, saying, "I will see to the men."

De Lauren looked at his hands, still bunched into fists and slowly uncurled his fingers. She would not die. For all she'd done to conspire with his enemy to kill him, he was bitter and furious. He would never trust her. Would never have the life he'd wanted with her when he returned her to Stanfield. Yet return her he would. Because the thought of her dead made him want to die himself.

Ranulf accepted the challenge, as de Lauren knew he would. When his messenger returned with Ranulf's reply, de Lauren said to Stephen, "Wait until dusk. Give me until then to goad Ranulf into producing Katherine. When the sun sets, proceed as we planned."

Stephen nodded and de Lauren looked to Warbrook's battlements. Despite his agreement to the challenge, Ranulf had not relaxed his defenses, anticipating no doubt that when he killed de Lauren dishonorably, Stephen would attack the keep. Ranulf's archers were at the ready. Men were still bringing oil.

De Lauren's own archers were in line facing the keep. They would not attack the battlements until later, but stood ready to defend their lord now, in case Ranulf had given the order to shoot an arrow into de Lauren when he rode across the open road to Warbrook's gates.

With Ranulf's men occupied defending the keep, de Lauren would take Katherine out through the garderobes, and deliver her to Stephen.

De Lauren turned to his brother. "I will see you inside the keep."

De Lauren mounted his horse and rode to Warbrook's gates. They opened to admit him. Men-at-arms rushed to him. One seized the reins. De Lauren dismounted. A guard relieved him of his sword, then took up a position at his back. Two others went to his sides. They led him into the hall, passed one guardsman who stood on one side of the door. With the three watching him, that made four guards altogether and Ranulf himself to overcome.

The great hall smelled of stale rushes and rotted food. Indeed he could see bones, discarded from previous meals, atop the rush-covered floor. Two dogs were chained to a wall. They growled low in their throat at de Lauren's entrance.

Ranulf was seated at the lord's table in the great hall. The table was uncovered. A deep basket was by his chair. De Lauren could not see what, if anything was inside it.

Katherine sat in a similar chair, though a significant distance from Ranulf. She wore a purple gown de Lauren had never seen on her before. It was too long. It covered her feet and spilled onto the wooden planks by several inches.

De Lauren's tensed muscles relaxed at the sight of her. He did not have to devise a means to get Ranulf to bring her to him.

"Ah, de Lauren," Ranulf called out. "We meet again. I have been telling your lady how I have been looking forward to this reunion." Ranulf crossed his arms and grinned. "She, however, has not missed your attentions, at all. It has been my great pleasure entertaining her these last days, and nights."

De Lauren clenched his jaw. He knew Ranulf was trying to elicit a reaction from him and said naught.

Ranulf lounged in his chair, crossing his arms, and extending his booted foot on the plank floor. "William Norris had complained to me that the lady Katherine was as frigid as the north wind, yet with me she burns hot as fire."

De Lauren eyed Ranulf and his fingers flexed, so badly did he want to wrap them around the man's throat. "You rattle your tongue like the village gossip, Ranulf."

Ranulf laughed. "I believe you weary of my conversation. Let us see if your lady will fare better with her words. Katherine, a word for Lord de Lauren."

Katherine did not reply.

Ranulf arched his blonde brows. "I believe silence ofttimes speaks as well as words. But come my lady," Ranulf said. He kept his gaze on de Lauren. His eyes glittered. "Have you no proper greeting for your lord husband? I will allow you that he remains so, for the next few moments, that is."

"You have long coveted that position," de Lauren said. "You will go to your grave still coveting that which is mine."

" 'Twill not be I who goes to his grave, this day, de Lauren."

"Meet me at sword-point Ranulf." De Lauren went on, goading him. "Come, show me if you have yet learned how to hit your mark."

Ranulf's cheeks reddened. "What, de Lauren? Do you seek another wound by my hand?" Ranulf's fingers flexed on the hilt of the sword he wore at his waist. "Are you so eager for another scar to match the one you no doubt bear above your heart?"

De Lauren narrowed his eyes on Ranulf. "You fired the arrow the day of the hunt?"

"Oh, aye," Ranulf said, his voice low and menacing. "An inch above your heart was my target, I recall, and my aim, of course, was true. A warning only. Be assured, had I wanted you dead, you would have been so. But at that time, it served me to let you live."

"So you could pressure Katherine to marry William Norris and control Stanfield," de Lauren said softly, recalling what she'd told him.

"It no longer serves me to let you live, however," Ranulf said. "You cheated death and my knight, by feeding your poison to a cat, but you will not cheat death again."

Katherine had been telling the truth about her marriage to William, and about a plot to kill him five years ago that had extended to this day. She'd been telling the truth about all . . .

For an instant de Lauren felt as if the stone beneath him had melted, leaving him with naught beneath his feet. Then a hot rush of blood surged through him.

Ranulf was responsible for the anguish they'd both suffered for the last five years. De Lauren honed his gaze on the Warbrook lord. In a deadly whisper, de Lauren said, "You should have killed me then."

De Lauren held Ranulf's gaze and willed the Warbrook lord to come to him.

A babe cried out.

De Lauren blinked, as Ranulf did. Each man took his gaze from the other.

The crying was coming from the basket at Ranulf's feet, de Lauren realized. What was a babe doing there?

Katherine sprang from the chair and started toward Ranulf. She took two steps and then was jerked back. She caught her balance on the chair's arm. Her gown swirled around her feet and de Lauren saw a manacle around her ankle and a length of chain bolted to the stone beneath her chair.

Ranulf had chained her like a dog. De Lauren clenched his fists. There would be payment for that, too, he vowed.

The babe was still crying.

"Be silent!" Ranulf shouted. He looked to Katherine. "I will silence your brat, my lady," he said. He drew back his booted foot and kicked the basket.

Katherine cried out.

"Katherine's brat?" de Lauren said.

The basket slid forward a few feet, close enough now that de Lauren could see the babe inside. The shade of blonde of his hair. The shape of the eyes. The slightly upturned nose. No mistaking the resemblance. The boy was clearly Katherine's son.

His gaze darted to Katherine. Tears were sliding down her cheeks and off her chin. He saw confirmation of the boy's identity in her eyes.

She had a son and she'd kept it from him . . .

Katherine's brat? De Lauren's voice echoed in her mind.

Ranulf had been instructing his messenger when he learned de Lauren was outside the keep. De Lauren had made his way here on his own.

When Katherine had seen him enter the hall, the hair on her nape prickled. Ranulf had relayed de Lauren's challenge to her, but surely that challenge would not take place here at Warbrook? Such events involving high-ranking vassals took place at the king's court, with his sanction and in his presence.

How could de Lauren have requested to meet Ranulf here?

In his own keep, Ranulf would not meet Nicholas on the field of honor. Without the king to gainsay him, Katherine knew Ranulf would simply slay his most powerful adversary.

De Lauren, though, was not meekly waiting for death. He was taunting Ranulf and vowing to kill him. She did not doubt that de Lauren had Stephen or Sir Hugh ready to storm the keep with their army, but when would they do so? What were they waiting for? And why had de Lauren not simply besieged the keep, and remained safely outside until it had been taken?

Those thoughts vanished when Ranulf revealed that she'd not betrayed de Lauren—not recently and not five years earlier. The truth had freed them. She and de Lauren would start anew with no secrets between them. The truth had also freed Lady Margaret, who so desperately needed to know for sure that she'd not harmed her son. De Lauren could now confirm that for her and set his mother free of the guilt that had kept her enslaved to the self-serving bishop. The great lady would send the bishop on his way, now able to resume her life. Able to pursue a second chance at love with Sir Guy.

And what of Katherine's relationship with Lady Margaret? With the truth revealed, Katherine had no doubt that she and her mother-by-marriage would find their way back to the love and trust they'd once felt for each other. The same could be said of her relationship with Stephen. He would learn the truth upon their return to Stanfield, or sooner than that if he led de Lauren's army in this attack., and when he did, all would be put to rights between them.

Katherine's heart raced. If they escaped Ranulf, all would be well.

Michael cried out again. A lone burst of sound, and then she could hear him snuffling and knew he'd fallen asleep.

She looked up from Michael and saw Ranulf watching her child.

"Have you comprehended it, de Lauren?" Ranulf said. His lips curved in a slow smile. "The still-born female was a twin. Katherine birthed twins. She has perpetuated the ultimate deceit on you. Played you for a fool." Ranulf laughed. "Behold the rightful lord of Stanfield."

De Lauren had discomfited Ranulf with his goading, Katherine had observed, but now Ranulf fixed his gaze on de

Lauren, and smirked in unmistakable triumph.

Katherine looked to de Lauren. Rage had darkened his eyes, and the muscles of his face were pulled taut.

She could not stand to see it, and looked away from him. She'd believed that once he knew she was innocent of betraying him, he would love her again. And that out of that love he would overlook the loss of the prize of Stanfield and would raise another man's son as his own.

But by the anger in his eyes she could see how wrong she'd been. His words to her on their wedding day replayed in her mind. *Five years ago the only jewel I sought from Stanfield was you.* Five years ago, but not now. Clearly, he did not love her now as he had then. His reaction to the news of her son removed any hope.

All of her fears for Michael returned. If they escaped Ranulf, what would she do now that de Lauren knew of her child?

Shouts rang out from above stairs. Ranulf half rose in his chair. "Elbert. Wendel. See what this is about."

The guards rushed out of the hall, taking the steps two at a time. De Lauren seized the sword of the guard beside him, who'd glanced to the stairs when the shouting began, and ran it through the man. De Lauren then turned and did the same with the other guard flanking him while that man was still withdrawing his blade.

Ranulf leaped from his chair. He drew his weapon. "Come to me, de Lauren," he shouted as he ran to the center of the hall.

Ranulf had barely raised his blade, when de Lauren was upon him. The clang of swords rang in the hall.

The battle was close. Ranulf parrying de Lauren's every thrust.

Katherine jerked the chain. The two men were moving ever closer to the basket that held Michael. She had to get to him.

Shouts rang out from the courtyard. "To arms! To arms!"

The clang of swords and screams followed.

Katherine believed de Lauren's men had breached the gates.

De Lauren's sword struck Ranulf's a powerful blow that drove Ranulf back. De Lauren continued, raining punishing blows. He had Ranulf on the defensive. The Warbrook lord stumbled back several paces.

They were a scant few feet from her babe now, Katherine saw. She jerked the chain, again, and felt the skin on her ankle tear. She spotted an axe mounted on the wall behind her. 'Twas a decorator piece, encrusted with jewels, but it had a blade. If she could get to it, she could use it to sever the chain. She pulled hard, then again, wincing, as the manacle bit into bone. She rose on tiptoe and reached up. Her ankle bent at an awkward, painful angle. Slightly more pressure and she feared it would snap. Blood flowed onto her slippers. Her fingertips brushed the blade. Katherine whimpered. She could not grasp the handle.

De Lauren brought his sword up for another parry. Instead of meeting de Lauren's thrust, Ranulf raised his sword over the babe. With a roar, Ranulf lunged to deliver the death blow.

This time she could not save her son. Katherine screamed.

De Lauren dropped to the ground and rolled, covering the basket with his body. Ranulf's blade sank into de Lauren's shoulder. Blood gushed from the wound. De Lauren lifted his sword, and impaled Ranulf on it.

Katherine had stopped breathing when Ranulf had aimed his sword over her son. Her breath came out in a rush. Her legs buckled. She sank to her knees on the cold stone.

Ranulf slumped forward, onto de Lauren's wounded shoulder. With a groan, de Lauren flung Ranulf to the ground.

De Lauren gained his feet and came to her.

"Avert your face," he said. She looked away. He brought his sword down on the chain. She felt the jolt all the way up her leg, but the links broke. She still wore the manacle, but she was no longer bound to the floor.

She staggered to her feet and limped to her child. He was wailing, his eyes open and damp with tears. Tears filled her own eyes. She scooped him up into her arms, pressing him to her chest. He quieted, but she did not ease her grip.

The door to the keep slammed open. Stephen charged into the hall, followed by other men wearing de Lauren's colors.

Stephen ran up to his brother. "Your arm?"

De Lauren shook his head. " 'Tis naught."

Stephen nodded.

De Lauren turned away from his brother and addressed his men. "I want the entrances to this hall secured. Vincent, you and Victor take up positions at the stairs. Jerley and Cavendish, to the corridor. Raymond and Gawain guard the front door.

"Stephen, take the remaining men with you and give what assistance may still be needed to secure the upper levels."

Since none of Ranulf's men had come down the stairs, de Lauren's men had the situation well in hand, Katherine thought.

De Lauren went on. "Let it be known that Ranulf is slain. Tell all to lay down their weapons or prepare to join their lord."

De Lauren's men rushed to take up their assigned positions. Bootsteps thudded like a stampede on the stairs. For an instant, the room was a blur of activity, and then the men were gone, and she was alone in the room with de Lauren.

He was breathing hard. His mail was flecked with the blood of the men he'd killed and with his own. His wounded arm hung at his side, his shoulder invisible beneath the red flood.

Katherine set her babe in the basket and raised her hem. She tore several ragged strips from the linen. She went to de Lauren. "You are hurt," she said.

She realized she'd stated the obvious and shook her head. She reached out with a strip of cloth, and dabbed at the blood.

So much of it, she could not see the gash made by Ranulf's sword.

"Your wound needs cleansing." Her hand was trembling. "And bandaging. And . . . " She could not seem to hang on to her thoughts.

"I will survive," de Lauren said.

She looked up at him. "As will my child, because of you," she said softly.

"Did you believe I would let Ranulf kill the boy?"

Tears stung her eyes. "It would have been expedient. Stanfield belongs to my son."

"Aye."

Her lips quivered. "The holding will never be yours."

"Aye."

She shook her head slowly. "Had Ranulf slain my son, you would have all you'd wanted from this marriage."

De Lauren reached out with his uninjured arm and cupped her chin in his hand. He peered down at her. "Had I but wanted Stanfield, I could have forced your father to honor our betrothal agreement five years ago. Henry would have supported my claim. Look at me, Kate. Look into my eyes, and tell me 'tis Stanfield I want."

Katherine stared into his unwavering gaze, then gasped softly. Tears slid past her lashes, and she reached out to him.

De Lauren's hand lowered from her chin. She felt his arm wind around her. He pulled her hard against his chest, and covered her mouth with his.

AUTHOR'S NOTE

The botanical treatments that Katherine prepared throughout this novel were used for the medicinal purposes indicated during the historical time period of this story. That being the case, however, these treatments should not be considered effective in treating such illnesses, nor should they be considered harmless. These botanical preparations should not be administered.

ABOUT THE AUTHOR

Karen Fenech is also the author of the contemporary romantic suspense thriller *Unholy Angels*. She lives with her husband and daughter. Visit Karen's Web site at www.karenfenech.com.